MALARKEY'S IMAGINOMNIBUS 4
Ominous Orbs

A Speculative Fiction Anthology

SULK

Malarkey's Imaginomnibus
Ominous Orbs Copyright © 2024 Ross Young

All stories © the original authors, reprinted with permission. All rights reserved. This book or any portion thereof may not be reproduced in any manner whatsover without written permission of the publisher except for the use of brief quotations for review purposes.

This anthology is a work of fiction any resemblance to places or individuals, alive or dead, is purely coincidental.

Love's a Ball © NT Anderson
The Will-O-Wisp in the Office © Peter James Martin
Firefly Glow © Rose J Fairchild
Felons and Freaks © Jon Ford
Promotion Day © Kayla Hicks
August Shaw and the Orb of Destruction © Alex Minns
The Radiant Star © Anya Pavelle
The Shadow Trials © SJ Covey
Untapped Potential © Melissa Rogers
A Load of Balls © Ross Young
Add to Cart © Halo Scot
Hex, Lies and Blue Balls © Chris Hooley

With thanks to Anthony Wright, editor.

CONTENTS

MALARKEY'S IMAGINOMNIBUS 4
Ominous Orbs

Love's a Ball **NT Anderson**	10
The Will-O-the-Wisp in the Office **Peter James Martin**	27
Firefly Glow **Rose J. Fairchild**	44
Felons and Freaks **Jon Ford**	51
Promotion Day **Kayla Hicks**	69
August Shaw and The Orb of Destruction **Alex Minns**	85
The Radiant Star **Anya Pavelle**	105
The Shadow Trials **SJ Covey**	119
Untapped Potential **Melissa Rose Rogers**	137
A Load of Balls **Ross Young**	155
Add to Cart **Halo Scot**	172
Hex, Lies, and Blue Balls **Chris Hooley**	185
Acknowledgements	204

Welcome to Malarkey's ImaginOmnibus volume 4

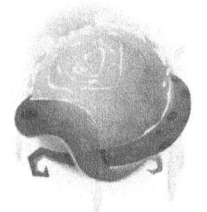

*R*eader, dear reader, welcome once more into the pages of Malarkey's ImaginOmnibus. Tales of twisted delight reside within these pages. To inspire and confound, to instil wonder and fear, joy and disgust, for something different trust in us.

Before you dive in, take caution, take heed, for some of these stories may nightmares breed. Malarkey's is fun, it's strange and bizarre, but everyone has limits and we might push things too far. With that in mind, if you'd be so kind, please accept these warnings, bear them in mind.

Stories may include violence, sex, drugs, foul language, murder, sexual violence, depictions of an adult nature, blood, gore, and groan inducing puns.

Now, one more, please enjoy the delights we have in store. This volume's theme, to conjure up dreams, was ominous orbs, globes of mystery, round creepy objects and the consequences the misuse of them might cause. As you can imagine, things get quite odd, and more than one author gave 'spooky balls' a knowing nod...

Love's a Ball

NT Anderson

The widow reached to open the wood-framed screen door at the back of her house, then changed her mind, letting it slap against the jamb. She walked over to one of the rocking chairs on her porch and slumped into it with a sigh. The knocking sound could be heard in the distance again, and she closed her eyes.

That same sound had been carrying on incessantly the night Mack died. Or the night he was murdered. Opinions varied, but Cora MacDonald believed it was the latter. However, not being one to declare conspiracy theories, she decided to keep that particular point of view to herself.

Urban legends about the forests had plagued Oregon since long before Oregon had a name. Stories of creatures stalking, interfering with, and sometimes harming innocent people were commonplace. Most unaffected locals shrugged it off, knowing that where the forest brought some folks peace, it gave others the creeps. The latter could easily be mind-fucked into believing just about anything about the sound of a squirrel's scurry, the shadow of flapping wings, or even the whisper of a gentle breeze.

So, the inhabitants of the area refrained from contributing to the rumor mill. But now Cora had a story of her own—one that had turned her whole world upside down.

The knocking continued…

Mack MacDonald was nothing if not enterprising. Farming made him a solid living, even providing the extra income he needed when he and his wife had taken in his nephew Bronson during freshman year of high school. That was after the boy became fed up with his mother, who was Mack's alcoholic sister, and his father, who was the token town ne'er do well. Having never had children of their own, Mack and Cora weren't exactly prepared for the expense of a teenager, but the farm didn't let them down.

That didn't stop Mack from looking for other ways to improve his income, though, so when he built a new metal seed barn, he decided to make good use of the old wooden one by converting it to a vacation rental. Once the renovation was complete, he was satisfied with the outcome but felt the one thing missing was a log seating area around the backyard fire pit. That was how he found himself a couple hundred yards into the forest behind the crop fields, working hard with his chainsaw to beat an impending rainstorm.

High above his head, the treetops swayed while the rumble of distant thunder loomed ever closer as the storm drew near. His peripheral vision caught three deer running to safety. The oddly pleasant smell of sawdust and two-stroke from his chainsaw filled the air as he sliced through a log, letting the engine die down after he completed the swipe.

The sky flashed with light, and across the range, Mack heard a tree splinter and fall. It was getting increasingly dangerous out here. He needed to finish up quickly.

He set down his chainsaw, rolled the freshly cut log near the other two, and prepared to complete the fourth and final log. He'd never get them down the mountain before the storm, but as long as they were cut, he could ask his nephew to drive up with him on the four-wheelers the next day to help retrieve them.

The sky rumbled once more, this time closer to Mack's location. His vision strained as the trees blocked whatever bit of light made it through the charcoal clouds overhead.

One foot in the wrong place was all it took.

Love's a Ball

As Mack reached for his chainsaw, his boot slipped on a silky bed of pine needles. Attempting to correct himself mid-fall, he leaned in the direction of the last log, spun around a quarter turn, and landed on his back. There was a split second when Mack thought everything would be okay. Then the back of his neck felt hot, and something trickled across his skin. He couldn't feel his fingers, and his lips were ice cold. Above him, the trees parted, and the clouds dispersed, making way for a bright light that should have been blinding but was, instead, comforting.

Mack wasn't sure what was happening, but he felt calm and peaceful. The light drew him in, but a nearby scurrying distracted him for a moment. Was that something soft against his arm? Through the pounding in his ears, Mack could have sworn he heard a chittering sound. Soft fur pressed against the back of his head. The trickling stopped.

Something tried to help him.

Out of nowhere, Bronson's voice boomed above the storm. "Get away from him, you fucking demons!"

Mack tried to focus when he heard the shouting. A large outline appeared, the scurrying became frantic, there was a dull thud against a log along with more cursing and desperate screeching…and the trickling resumed.

"No, no, no, *no*!"

The peaceful light called to Mack again, and this time, he accepted the invitation.

* * *

Cora set the bottle of wine on the counter and straightened the welcome note that was placed next to it. She hadn't been too sure about the idea of renting out space on their property to strangers when her husband first suggested remodeling the old barn, but she agreed to his plan anyway. Now she had to admit that the extra income was nice. Their farm barely kept her head above water since he'd passed, and this took care of the rest.

Exiting through the kitchen door and making sure the keyless entry was enabled, Cora wandered toward an old pine in the yard and turned to look at her husband's work. He'd done a fine job with the place. The exterior maintained the look of a barn, complete with faded wood siding, but the inside told a whole different story with a small but gourmet country kitchen, a combination sitting-dining room with a picture window that overlooked the backyard, and two large bedrooms boasting king-sized beds, rustic furnishings, and their own en suites.

Outside, Mr. MacDonald had added a concrete patio in front with various standing and hanging pots filled with bright flowers and a brick paver patio in back with more plants, a grill, and a comfortable outdoor seating area. She only wished she had a better solution than unsightly folding chairs for around the firepit.

Cora was just about to get choked up thinking about her dearly departed husband when the cursed drumming sound in the distance brought her back to the moment.

She closed her eyes as the thumping continued. In the thick of the pines surrounding her farm, something was beating on an old, hollow log. She hated this sound more than any other in the world. Sometimes it knocked as if on live, standing trees, and sometimes it was more of a thump on dead wood, but the beat was still the same.

With each strike, the echo sent a chill up her spine. *Something* was trying to communicate with…something.

Rubbing her temples, Cora opened her eyes to see Bronson's faded red pickup truck turning into the driveway that led to her barn-turned-vacation rental. Bronson was her nephew by marriage, a lumberjack by trade, and a generally thoughtful guy who had been looking out for her ever since his uncle had passed, although she could tell he'd been having his own issues to contend with lately.

Despite a challenging start to life, Bronson had always been an easygoing, big-hearted kid, who had grown into an easygoing, big-hearted man, his alarming six-foot-four menacingly muscular build aside.

Cora turned back toward the barn-house. "Hey, sweetheart," she said when she heard the slam of the truck door and the crunch of boots on gravel.

Bronson playfully leaned around his aunt and gave her a kiss on the cheek. "Aunt Cora." He stood next to her, draping an arm across her shoulders. "Admiring the old man's work?"

A long sigh came out like a sad hiss. "Yessss."

He gently squeezed her shoulder. "He's got you covered, you know." Cora turned to see Bronson's eyes looking skyward. "I know you know that, but it's still worth mentioning once in a while." The tall lumberjack glanced down at his aunt. Behind his beard, she saw his lips parted in a sad smile.

Grateful for his presence, she wrapped her arms around her nephew's waist and embraced him as best she could considering their height difference, her head landing on his chest while his seemingly oversized arms engulfed her.

"Thank you, sweetheart," she said before disentangling from him and turning toward his truck with narrowed eyes. "I'm sure your uncle is keeping a close eye on you, too. He loved you as if you were his own." Cora squinted her eyes some more. "Still running around with Melanie Thompson, I see."

"Just wish I had looked out for Uncle Mack the same way," Bronson mumbled with a frown. "And I'm not 'running around' with her. I'm dating her." He waved his hand at Melanie to indicate she should get out of the truck, but she just waved back and resumed looking at her phone.

"Kinda rude not to get out and say hi," Cora remarked. "If y'all are doing more dating than running, that is."

"She's just shy."

Cora snorted. If there was anything that defined the Thompson girl, shy wasn't it. Cora had never really cared, though—until recently. In their rural farming community, most folks kept to themselves, choosing to work hard instead of sticking their nose where it didn't belong. Lately, though, Cora had been hearing that Melanie was going around calling Bronson 'strange.' Bronson's protective aunt didn't like that one bit, although she knew she needed to do something to put a stop to his curious philosophies about creatures in the forest lest he tell anyone else in town.

Cora bit her tongue on the subject of her nephew's love life. "What do you mean you wish you'd looked out for Mack? Bron, if I've told you once, I've told you a thousand—"

"Yeah, I know, Aunt Cora," Bronson interrupted. "What happened wasn't my fault. According to you. But those damn ball-tailed cats come out of nowhere and—"

"Darling, I understand that working in the forests like you do, you probably see and hear a lot of things. Maybe some of it starts to get in your head. But we have guests arriving today, so I really need you to stop talking about boogeyman things. Next you'll be suggesting we have Bigfoot on the mountain, and then they'll be scared enough to cancel their reservation!"

Bronson opened his mouth but appeared to think better of arguing with his aunt.

* * *

The couple walked through the automatic doors of the terminal at Rogue Valley Airport, stopping to survey their surroundings. Beyond the parking lot, in the distance, they could see the mountains that had called them to this locale. A forty-five-minute drive would bring them to the base of Mount McLoughlin, the Oregonian range they would be exploring.

"I'm itching for a good run," Sam said, taking a deep breath of fresh air.

Marisa did the same and noted a hint of salt from the Pacific Ocean to the west mingling with the scent of pine to the east. She turned her attention to a decorative tree between parking aisles E and F. "I'm itching for a good scratch."

Sam looked down at his wife and smiled, reaching his hand around her back to assist. "Soon, babe. Let's get settled first." He glanced at the sky. "I rented a Jeep. Hope they took the ragtop off."

As they waited for the rental car shuttle, Marisa thought about how grateful she was for her husband's willingness to do most of their vacation planning. It was an area in which he had far more experience than she did. In fact, she'd never traveled so much in her life as she had with him over the past few years. Yet, while she appreciated the lovely locales he chose for them to visit, she was hoping this trip would be a much calmer experience compared to their last two adventures.

"Where are we staying?" she asked as the shuttle arrived, slowing to a stop at the curb in front of them.

"A converted barn located on a working farm. Should be a good place for our…shenanigans," he replied with a big smile.

"But, Sam, farms are open spaces, and we prefer the woods."

"I know. It looked really cool, though, with lots of trees in the yard, and the base of the mountain will be a quick run from it." He shrugged. "Something different."

Love's a Ball

Let's hope it is different and we actually get some peace this time, Marisa thought.

* * *

Relaxing with a cold beer for each of them, feet propped on cushioned ottomans, Sam and Marisa took in the view from the back patio of the farmland that extended to the base of the mountain range. While the green of the crop spread far and wide, the leaves on the distant trees were giving up the ghost, turning to bright shades of red, yellow, and orange.

Sam leaned his head back and took a deep breath of the crisp, clean air. "I've always loved Oregon in the fall."

"Didn't you want to go for a run tonight? Check out the area?"

"My head says hell, yeah," Sam said with a sigh. "But my body isn't on board. It's been a long day."

"Agreed." Marisa closed her eyes, soaking up the last bits of sun before it would begin to set. "I feel like I could fall asleep right here."

A mile away, from the towering pines, came a sound that made her eyes snap open again.

Knock…knock…KNOCK!

Now it was Marisa's turn to sigh. "But that's not going to happen because—"

"Do not even try to pin this on me."

"—we can't go anywhere without—"

"Nope. I'm not taking the hit for this, babe."

"—you getting us into *some* kind of mess—"

"Fine. Just ignore it. It has nothing to do with us anyway."

"—with *your friends* in the area!" Marisa stood up and stomped her foot.

"*My* friends?" Sam stood and squared off with his wife.

Marisa opened her arms wide. "You have to admit that whenever we travel, things get—"

Knock…knock…KNOCK!

"—weird. I never had this problem until I met you."

Sam looked over his wife's head toward the sound coming from the mountains, then he returned his gaze to her and smiled. "That's because you didn't go anywhere until you met me. Come on. We'll sleep later."

She shook her head but took the hand he offered, and the two began jogging in the direction of whatever the forest held in store for them.

* * *

Two months prior, Cora found herself in the middle of a lightning storm, just about fifty yards into the forest, surrounded by police and the coroner, heartbroken, and attempting to comfort a grief-stricken Bronson when he arrived twenty minutes after her. She listened in stunned silence as the coroner described the head injury Mack had sustained. She slowly shook her head no when the police asked if she knew why he'd been out there.

Bronson remained silent until the questions were finished and all that was left was for the emergency services personnel to lift Mack's lifeless body onto a stretcher.

He tugged gently on his aunt's arm and walked her behind a tree, away from the scene. "This is all my fault." Tears began to stream down Bronson's face as soon as the words left his mouth.

"What? Oh, honey, that's nonsense," Cora consoled.

Bronson wiped his nose on his flannel sleeve. "I couldn't stop them."

"Stop who? You were here?"

Bronson nodded. "I tried to kill it, but I missed. It was too late anyway."

"Kill what? But you didn't get here until after I did."

"I chased it. Got a distance away before I circled back."

"Chased *what*? Bron, for goodness' sake, please tell me what's going on here."

With a big sniff, Bronson told his aunt the details he hadn't wanted to share with the police for fear of sounding crazy.

"Uncle Mack was up here cutting logs for the guesthouse firepit. He asked me if I could help, and I said I'd be out tomorrow, but then I got done at work early because of the storm. When I couldn't find him at the farm, I came looking for him. Found him, but I was two minutes too late."

He swallowed hard, choking back the floodgates.

Cora understood. Mack had been the only real father their nephew had ever known, but she needed to know the rest, so she put her hand on his arm, encouraging him to continue.

"It was those fucking cats, Aunt Cora. They're the size of a mountain lion, and they swing those tails and—"

She held her hand up to stop him. Bronson started lumberjacking right out of high school, and almost from his first day on the job, Cora and Mack had listened to him talk about the ball-tailed cats he claimed to frequently catch sight of in the forest. Well, Mack listened more than Cora. She wasn't one to fuss with the fodder for spooky campfire stories, but she did look it up one day. Just as she suspected—urban legend.

According to Bronson, they were dangerous, although at the time, he hadn't been able to put his finger on exactly what they were capable of. But now he knew. They both did, even if Cora was committed to keeping her thoughts on the matter to herself.

ATV emergency lights turned the otherwise dark forest into an overly bright setting. It was a location she would never want to revisit after this. "I need to go home, sweetheart. I need to be around Mack's things. Make some phone calls."

Bronson turned to look in the direction of the expansive green fields that led the way to their family farmhouse. He squinted his eyes. "You really need to consider changing out those crops for something different." His voice sounded eerie. "Uncle Mack should have done that back when I first told him about these damn cats. Maybe they wouldn't be hanging around here if he had."

Cora couldn't cope. The coroner walked up and handed her a clipboard with a form attached. She didn't know what it said, but she had an idea, so she signed it without looking.

One of the cops approached and touched her arm. "I'm so sorry, Cor."

Cora simply nodded and, without another word, started the hike back to the farmhouse, walking away from her nephew, the emergency responders, and her husband's body to get to the place where they had made their life together.

* * *

Sam and Marisa jogged through the fields at the farm, hurrying toward the tree line that would protect them and allow them to shed their disguises.

About a hundred feet from the forest, Marisa stopped to look back at the crop through which they'd run. "Is that what I think it is?"

Sam stopped to look, too. He chuckled. "Yeah, I believe it is. A metric fuck ton of it."

"Good thing it doesn't work on us." Marisa shuddered. "It never occurred to me that someone has to grow this stuff. You see it and think it starts in a factory or something."

"All drugs have a source."

"A field full of catnip proves it." Marisa turned back to the trees. "Shall we?"

A short hike later, after crossing through a line of maples and oaks and partially ascending the mountain, Sam and Marisa found themselves in a needle-carpeted forest among hulking Douglas firs and ponderosa pines. They stopped to listen for the knocking sound, which was easier to track now that they were in the massive reverberation chamber.

Sam transformed as he walked slowly up the mountain, while Marisa did the same and followed, keeping a pace that matched his own. They hadn't gone far when Sam stopped, holding up his hand to indicate they were near the source. Directly in front of them, a felled Western hemlock leaned against a large boulder. The last of the day's sunlight filtered through the treetops, creating a patchwork of light and shadow on the grey stone.

It was there, perched atop the boulder and facing away from the nearest tree, that Sam and Marisa found the source of the knocking—a large cat.

Leaning its head back in agony with a painful whimper, it hammered the trunk with its tail. One, two, three times in quick succession.

Marisa gasped.

Spooked, the cat turned in their direction and jumped off the rock, preparing to run.

"Wait!" Sam called, taking a few steps in its direction. "We're not here to hurt you."

Standing its ground, the feline glanced around, appearing to make sure there was a getaway route, but waited to see what the couple wanted. If this creature was native to the Pacific Northwest, Marisa felt sure this was far from its first sasquatch encounter. She hoped it knew from experience that they typically existed on a live-and-let-live philosophy and that it believed she and Sam weren't there to hurt it.

Sam held his hands up, palms forward in a sign of peace.

Marisa stayed where she was but reached out to grab a clump of her husband's back hair. "Wait," she hissed. "How are you going to have a conversation with a *cat*?"

Shaking her off, he continued forward and whispered over his shoulder. "This isn't any old cat. It's native to the area, and it'll understand me. And I'll understand it because my great-nan grew up out here. She taught me a bit about this species."

"Naturally." Marisa stayed where she was, observing the bizarre interaction between her seven-foot-tall husband and what looked like a mountain lion…with a tail deformity.

Sam talked while the cat replied in growly meows. Finally, Marisa saw Sam cross his arms over his chest, a clear sign that he was pissed.

After some nodding on Sam's part, the furry creature showed a gesture of appreciation and respect by rubbing against Sam's leg. A gesture Sam returned with a pat on its head. With a nod to Marisa, Sam's new friend disappeared into the forest.

Before Marisa could say anything, her husband waved at her, indicating she should follow him. "I'll explain on the way," he said.

As day turned to night, they walked along a lovely path that would have been perfect for a moonlit stroll if it wasn't for the truly unusual tale Sam was about to tell.

"He's a digmaul," Sam started. "Or, more simply put, a ball-tailed cat."

"A digmaul," Marisa repeated as she stepped over fallen branches.

"Right. There's an urban legend that claims there are two kinds of these cats—the digmaul and the silvercat—but that's not true. The silvercat is said to have the same ball on the end of its tail but with spikes. Which is just absurd." Sam laughed. "Could you imagine a cat with a ball of spikes on its tail?" He shook his head at the thought.

With a mocking chuckle and a roll of her eyes, Marisa commented, "Yeah, how insane to suggest a cat would have that."

Sam ignored her sarcasm. "So, this one is the real deal with just a rounded bone."

Marisa stopped in her tracks. "That's *bone*? At the end of its *tail*?" She whistled. "That thing could be lethal."

"Yeah, it could be, and humans believe them to be dangerous, but they're actually very gentle cats."

"I can see why it makes people nervous, though."

Sam turned to his wife. "That's one side of it, babe, but their tails are a defining part of who and what they are. It would be like if I had…small feet. You wouldn't have felt the same about me if I'd shown up at your house with measly sized fourteens."

Marisa's mouth fell open in mock disbelief. "I love how you rationalize nature's mysteries, but are you calling me petty?"

"Not petty, my love. Discerning. You want your Bigfoot to have big feet just like our digmauls feel their ball tails are a significant characteristic."

"'Balls!' said the queen." Marisa smiled.

Sam's head whipped in her direction. "Don't you dare. This is serious!"

Marisa pursed her lips together and put her head down. "If I had 'em, I'd be king," she whispered.

"Leave it to you." Sam frowned.

"So, what exactly is going on here? We're supposed to be getting some R and R, and I'd like to start both of those as soon as possible."

They came to a fork in the path, one direction offering a cleared option while the other presented thick brush and fallen trees. Sam thought for a moment before choosing the road less traveled.

"This shouldn't take long," he said as he stopped every few feet to look and listen. "Then I just have an…errand to run."

Marisa didn't like the way he said 'errand.' "Sam…"

"Yes, I'm pissed." Sam put his hands on his hips, turned to the sky, and sighed. "I won't even bother trying to hide it from you. But I promise I'm not going to do anything stupid, babe."

"Of all the things I worry about, you doing something stupid is not on the list. But I don't know what I'd do if something were to happen to you… if you were to get hurt."

Putting his arms around his wife, Sam kissed her on the top of her head. "Was there a time in my life when I wasn't so careful and protective of my personal wellbeing? Yes. Has all that changed since we met? Also yes. I will never put you in that position, sweetheart. Trust me."

His reassurances made Marisa feel better. "I do. I trust you more than anyone in the world. I just needed to hear it." She rose up on tiptoe and kissed him on the lips. "Okay, can you finally tell me what happened?"

"So, it's mating season," Sam explained. "That one back there is a male, and he's got the serious hots for a female who is around here somewhere." He peeked behind a large pine before continuing. "The knocking is him calling to her. That's how he's letting her know he's looking for her." Turning to Marisa, he gave her a wink. "Kind of like us with banging the sticks. Cute, right?"

Marisa's sarcasm was back in full force. "Precious."

Sam turned serious again. "Here's where it gets tricky. He loves her, and I guess she's let on before that she feels the same, but there was a recent incident that changed all that." Sam turned to face Marisa, his long arms hanging at his sides. His shoulders were slightly hunched, and Marisa recognized the combination of sadness and anger in her husband's stance. "The ball-tailed cat is a native of the Oregonian forests. They mostly keep to themselves and stay out of sight thanks to a long history of being misunderstood by the lumberjacks in the area."

Sam squatted to investigate a hollow log. "As you've seen, they're pretty big and able to defend themselves, but so are the lumberjacks. The cats have their bony ball tails, but the lumberjacks have axes and saws. When the scorecards are added up, the lumberjacks are more dangerous because their human nature tells them to kill what threatens them, whether it's an actual danger or not. The cats, on the other hand, simply want to be left alone.

"There was an accident up here on the mountain a couple months ago. An old man died. The cats had nothing to do with it, but they were trying to help when another human showed up and—"

"—made the assumption that the accident was their fault," Marisa finished.

"Right. The timing of it was…unfortunate."

"But what does this have to do with the relationship between these cats?"

Sam let out a hiss through his teeth. "It's all related because after the old man fell and hit his head on a rock, which is what ultimately killed him, the female was trying to stop the bleeding with her tail. That's when this lumberjack showed up and went off the rails." He gestured back toward where they'd encountered the cat. "Our friend back there jumped onto a tree branch to escape. His girlfriend followed suit, but as she was climbing the tree, the human swung his axe and…"

The look of sheer dread on Sam's face said it all.

"Ohhh, no."

He nodded. "Makes me so fucking mad. Guy didn't think. Didn't take five seconds to evaluate. Just made an assumption."

Marisa looked confused. "But she's still alive."

"She's alive. But she's not…whole."

"Ouch!"

"Yeah, ouch. Now she's hiding and feeling unattractive. Unworthy. Undesirable. Which is why she won't answer the mating call. And it's also why I'm pissed because that guy didn't need to maim her over an accident. You know how I feel about humans harming wildlife."

Sam shook his head and continued to search each hollow log they came across until, finally, a peek in one end of a particularly large conifer elicited a scurrying sound at the other end.

Speaking in hushed tones, Sam made promises of safety and trustworthiness and assurances that he only wanted to talk. In a matter of minutes, it worked, and the female cat stuck her head up over the log.

He talked, she listened. He moved closer, she emerged from the log just a bit more. From a short distance, Marisa could hear Sam pleading with the cat, imploring her to understand how her male counterpart felt about her, convincing her that the brutality of her injury hadn't swayed his feelings.

Marisa knew Sam's mediation skills were working as the cat inched further and further away from the sanctuary of the log. Unable to stop herself, Marisa gasped quietly when she saw her disfigurement and the severity of the injury.

Sam continued with his supportive words until the male appeared from behind a tree. The female hissed and looked at Sam in betrayal. He quickly apologized for the deception, hurriedly explaining that it was the only way to get the two of them together.

"You need to talk to him," Sam begged. "He loves you, and he only wants to make you happy."

The male cat tucked the ball of his tail behind his legs, as if to hide his intactness, and he approached slowly. The female cat didn't move toward him, but she also didn't run away.

Sam backed up toward Marisa. They watched the two cats begin communicating in their own way as they continued their slow retreat, keeping an eye on the potential new couple until they could no longer see them. Finally,

Sam and Marisa found a needle-blanketed nook in an enormous tree where they could sit and talk.

"What happened?" Marisa demanded.

"It was pretty simple." Sam shrugged. "I explained to him that even though knocking is the preferred method for finding a mate, she might not appreciate that since she's now incapable of returning the call. Then I told her that she had no reason to feel self-conscious. He knew about the incident, didn't blame her for it, and was more worried about her than anything else. He actually wants to help make sure she's okay."

"How long ago did you say the accident was?

"Two months ago."

Marisa thought about the raw appearance of the female's wound. "Will she heal?"

"Perhaps. In time." Sam sighed. "But there is *one* way in which we could guarantee her recovery. Somewhere, someone has something that doesn't belong to him."

* * *

He'd seen this coming from a mile away, so it was no surprise to Bronson when Melanie said, "See you around, Bron," right before she threw open his front door and walked out of his life.

Whatever.

Bronson walked over to close the door, but something on his porch caught his eye before it was shut all the way. A pumpkin. A perfectly round, bright orange pumpkin placed just to the side of his front door. He hadn't done any decorating for fall yet, so it could only be chalked up to Aunt Cora dropping it off. Probably trying to remind him that he could use a little festivity in his life.

Bringing his mind back to the reason for the open door, he slammed it shut and stormed through the house. Melanie had a problem with too many factors in his life. Aunt Cora, for one. No way could he be with anyone long-term who had a problem with his beloved aunt.

The farm. Yeah, she had a problem with that, too. More specifically, the crop of catnip. Falsely claiming she had a cat go insane because of the harmless herb, she ranted about the irresponsibility of farming it. Again, whatever. Bronson couldn't care less about her nutty cat, which had probably gone off the deep end because of *her* and not the catnip. He wasn't a cat fan these days anyway.

If those two things hadn't been enough to make Bronson say she had to go, she'd stumbled across his…trophy.

No, that wasn't the right word for it. A trophy had a positive insinuation, like he'd won an award or done something of merit.

What Melanie had discovered was no prize. It wasn't a positive prop that signified spoils for the victor, although the victor he had been. Victorious in terms of revenge anyway.

This was a record. A stark reminder of when he'd been a moment too late to save his uncle's life. The symbol that Bronson kept safely tucked away on a shelf in the back of his closet was the reason he no longer had the only man who'd ever been a father to him, and he was proud to have a physical reminder of his vengeance. Melanie could go around town all she wanted, whispering to others that Bronson was strange. But Bronson knew the truth.

He opened the closet door, parted a section of hangers where his obligatory lumberjack flannels hung, and stepped toward the shelf where his memorial sat.

Gently stroking the fur that encased the hard, round bone, Bronson leaned his head against the wall. As a tear escaped his right eye, he softly sang, "Old MacDonald had a farm…"

What he never expected to happen next was for a seven-foot-tall behemoth with a grudge to enter his bedroom at that very moment. And he certainly wasn't prepared when he heard the deep, eerie voice behind him sing, "E-i-e-i-o…"

ABOUT THE AUTHOR

N/T Anderson is a published author of steamy romance and the co-founder of the publishing imprint Tepris Press. A lifelong lover of the written word, she spent years working in hospitality, restaurant management, and even pole dancing before becoming a full-time writer in 2009. Nikki's first trilogy, The Acts Series, was released in 2021/2022. More books will be forthcoming in 2023.

In addition to writing, Nikki is also a radio presenter with a catalog of shows for the UK-based audio production company One Flower Two Turtles.

She currently lives in the Endless Mountain region of Pennsylvania When she isn't writing, she can be found sipping rum by candlelight and spending time with her pets — two spoiled dogs and an unruly cat.

The Will-O-the-Wisp in the Office

Peter James Martin

The day started innocuously enough. I was browsing the newspaper, looking for any odd stories that may have caught my eye, while Riz was busy gloating about a recent telephone call that had made him, and I quote, 'a load of money'.

I had noticed a bank transfer of a hundred pounds into the account, which is not what I would call 'a load of money' in this economy. It was better than nothing, I supposed, but it wasn't worth the song and dance he was doing while I was trying to relax.

"How long are you planning on doing that?" I finally asked him, folding up the paper before throwing it in the recycling pile.

"A job went smoothly fer me, let me enjoy it!" he snapped back.

I could have turned it into a shouting match if I really wanted, but I just didn't have the energy to deal with the talking rat, well, other than imagining having a fully working rat-a-pult at hand. . I rolled my eyes and turned my attention to my phone instead, doing my best to completely ignore him this time.

"Dat's wat I thought," I heard him say.

I kept telling myself to pick my battles. They weren't all worth winning.

Both of our attentions were caught when our door started to rattle. It did this for a few seconds before returning to normal.

"Well, that was odd," I said before I was answered by the loudest bangs I think had ever been inflicted on our poor office door. Had it been another door, it probably would have shattered, which would have been an odd thing to have to explain, but luckily, we had reinforced it in case our enemies ever came calling.

This was our first thought when the banging started. Riz ran over to me as fast as his four legs could muster and began assembling the emergency Runes.

"Wen wateva it is comes thru dat door, we're gunna blast dem back to where eva it is dey came from!"

Riz passed one of the Blast Runes to me, preferring to keep one of the more powerful versions of it for himself.

"Why are you using that one?" I enquired.

"Cuz I made it?"

"If that's the one I'm thinking it is, you'll blow us all up!"

"If I'm goin' down, I'm takin' everything down wit me!"

"That's super helpful... Wait..."

I stopped the argument short as I became aware of a lack of noise coming from the door. Whoever, or whatever, was banging had stopped. I couldn't be sure of when they'd stopped, but it was all quiet again.

A dreadful silence descended. I glanced down at Riz, who was sniffing the air. I could see his little brain trying to work something out before he gave a shrug of his shoulders.

"Nuthin' dere now, dey must av left."

I wished that were true. A new sound broke the silence, a hissing sound.

"Snakes!" Riz shrieked as he leapt into my arms. "Why did it av ta be snakes?!"

I got up to have a quick look around and confirmed there were no snakes to be seen. I glanced back at Riz disapprovingly.

"Wat? I 'ate snakes."

"Clearly, given that over-reaction."

I rolled my eyes and was about to say something else when I noticed the little wisp of smoke leading up to the ceiling. I followed it up and stared at a ball of smoke.

"What the...?" I started to say before being interrupted.

"'Ello!" the smoke said energetically, turning a pale blue colour. I almost fell over backwards.

"Hello?" I repeated.

"I said 'ello, but close enough!" The ball of smoke started to bob about.

"Erm…" I took a moment to compose my thoughts. "What can I do for you?"

It was really two questions. The first was literal, the second was seeing if it actually wanted me to do anything.

"Ohh!" Riz shouted out from the table. He'd been watching the encounter with a tilted head, no doubt relieved there weren't any snakes involved but surprised by what was floating around the office, doing a merry bob as it did so. "It's a Will-o'-the-wisp! Don't normally get dose in a buildin'."

"He's right! Friends call me Ro, and I need your help! Mr Brennan, please help me!"

It's odd that I can say that something surprises me, even this many years into the job, but meeting a Wisp in my own office and learning that they have names and that one wants my help takes the biscuit in terms of surprises. Well, not bad ones, anyway.

"Well… Ro? What do you need help with?" I braced myself as anything could happen now.

"I need you to save Joy!" Ro turned a yellow colour as he spoke, trembling. "Joy's in trouble! Joy's in trouble!" He started flying around my head at an ever-increasing speed.

"Slow down! Who's Joy, and how are they in trouble?" I moved to try and catch him with my hand, but he flew right through it.

"Joy is like me, and a man is trying to catch her. He's trying to catch us all!"

"A man is trying to catch you?"

I heard Riz do a spit-take at that as he was taking a drink at the time. My eyes wandered over to the rat, who was actively trying to avoid my gaze.

"Riz… What aren't you telling me?"

"Nuthin'! Let's jus' deal wit Ro's troubles, eh? He must really need our help if he waz willin' ta come all da way 'ere from Mulgrave Woods! We 'ave ta help Jay!" Riz shouted in a strange change of tone.

"Firstly, it's Joy. Would you actually listen to the conversation for more than three seconds, you little prick? Secondly, how do you know he's from

The Will-O-the-Wisp in the Office

there?" Again, my suspicions were raised.

"Duh!" Riz blurted out, appearing a little nervous. "Everyone knows dat's where you can find Will-o'-the-wisps up in dis area! Now, let's get in da car 'nd see wat you can do ta help out. Shudn't need me dere fer an easy job like dis!"

"Easy? Bit too early to say that, isn't it? However, we'll help you, Ro. Let's go and save your friend. Riz, pocket. Now."

"Don't ya know how ta get ta Mulgrave Woods? Ya really don't need me ta go wit ya!" he replied, cowering.

"Riz, you're coming with me." I wasn't giving him a choice here, and to make this as clear as possible to him, I grabbed him by the tail.

"I've got soaps ta catch up on!"

I ignored his pleas and plonked him down on my shoulder.

"Follow me, Ro… And try to keep out of sight while we get to my car," I said to the Wisp, which was still bouncing around.

"Okay!"

If only Riz was this enthusiastic.

Together, we got to the car and headed to Mulgrave Woods near Whitby.

* * *

Riz took his usual position on the dashboard, alternating between criticising my driving and looking a bit nervous. Ro hovered in the passenger seat, and there were times that I could have sworn he was looking out of the window, which was odd, as it didn't look like he had any eyes to even look out of. Naturally, this prompted a very curious question from me.

"Urm, Ro…?"

"Yes?" the Wisp seemed to turn around, if such a thing was possible.

"How do you see?"

"I see everything!"

That was a creepy response. And also not a helpful one – I wanted more specifics.

"When you say 'everything'?"

"He's bein' literal. Wisps can perceive everythin' around dem ta sum degree," Riz explained.

"Why do you know that?"

"I know everythin' 'bout Wisps! I'm a frickin' expert!"

I rolled my eyes at Riz, and he glared back. Another usual drive for us, then.

"Any other questions you have?" Ro asked, oblivious to our argument,

"Can you tell me what happened earlier, then, so we can prepare for what might be waiting for us in the woods?"

"Okay! Me and the others were gliding through the trees, like we normally would be. We were invisible because it's not fun to glow during the day. We do our best performances at night! We'll do a special one for you!" Ro answered. "We were flying when people in black arrived, carrying guns that froze my friends! Me and Joy, we fled, but they caught her! We have to rescue Joy!"

As Ro was speaking about this 'Joy', I noticed that his colour was changing again, but instead of changing as a block, this time, his core started out white and turned in a gradient. It went from white to yellow, to orange, and then to red. I also noticed that the temperature was starting to rise. I had an inkling of what was happening, but it wasn't something I wanted to happen in the car.

"It's okay, Ro! We'll rescue her, but I need you to focus, okay? What about these men? Is there anything you can tell me about them? How many were there? Were they all armed? Was anyone leading them?" My quick thinking paid off, and his colour returned to what it had been a few seconds before.

"There were three men, I think. I remember three! No more, I'm sure. Their leader, the one who shouted at them a lot, stood back, watching, always watching."

"Right, two thugs, one rich guy thinking he's a drill sergeant. Should be a pleasant job…" I said through gritted teeth.

Jobs that involved dealing with actual humans were a lot harder to deal with. After all, to get them to stop, I had to either convince them that what they were doing was wrong or incapacitate them in some fashion. If I went that route, I'd have to involve some external agency, like the police, to take them away while letting the Ministry of Otherworldly Business know.

Then there's the third route, which I always avoid where possible, though it does happen with alarming frequency because of people's own stupid schemes. What is that method, you ask? Well, I'm not a murderer, so I'll let you figure that out.

The Will-O-the-Wisp in the Office

Riz took a more cavalier approach to these matters that usually boiled down to 'blast 'em'. It was a constant reminder, if I needed it, that he could very much be an arse at times.

"Ya want da next right, rememba!" Riz shouted at me, completely derailing my train of thought.

"We'll be there soon, Ro," I said, acting like having a Will-o'-the-wisp sitting – or hovering, as it were – next to me was nothing unusual. My life can be extraordinarily strange at times.

I think Ro nodded in agreement, though he could have been doing almost anything else, as it was impossible to tell, but he seemed happy enough. I let a silence overtake us briefly, and as I wondered if there was anything else for me to say, I heard Ro mutter to himself.

"I'm coming, Joy."

"Who's Joy, then?" I asked. I don't fully know why I asked, other than curiosity.

"Joy is fantastic! She makes me happy!"

As if to prove a point, Ro's colours turned bright again, becoming a warm colour that made me feel happy as well.

"So…" I started to say, but I quickly realised I didn't have any way to end the question without coming across as extremely odd.

"Bren wants ta know if Joy is ya girlfriend," Riz blurted out.

"One day," Ro said shyly. "She makes me want to live!"

That last part concerned me, but at the time, I didn't connect it with everything. I was more angry at Riz for stepping in as he had, especially when he followed it up with his next little zinger.

"Oh, Bren, meant ta say, we needed dat left ya jus' went past…"

As if I didn't have enough going on.

* * *

After another ten minutes driving, where to my credit, I didn't launch Riz out of the window at any point for his constant and needless advice, we arrived at Mulgrave Woods, where there were already two big black cars parked up awkwardly in the car park. Didn't take a rocket scientist to work out who they belonged to.

"Dey must be wat dose eejits arrived in," Riz commented.

See what I mean?

I ignored the comment and prepared myself. I'd brought a selection of Runes along in my coat pocket, and there were more in a bag that I kept in the glove box – that is, if Riz had remembered to restock it. Last time I went for it, it was filled with IOUs.

I guessed it had been restocked, though, as the moment I reached for it, Riz already had his head stuck in it, grabbing whatever he could. I let him finish before getting what I needed – from what little was left, of course.

Ro waited impatiently for us to finish, his bobbing up and down getting faster and faster as we took longer and longer. He also started pushing against the window, wanting to find any crack that would allow him freedom from the car.

I was ready first, so naturally, I gave him egress by unlocking the door. He whooshed outside, rushing around in a circle, his colour changing to a pale yellow, but now, without any other prying eyes, he allowed himself to shine brightly.

"Follow me! I'll lead you to the nasty men! But be careful! You might get lost forever!" Ro zoomed off, leaving a slight trail. But I didn't have time to dwell on that as Riz bit me.

"Oi! Ya can't leave without me, ya twonk!" he shouted angrily, busting out one of his less-used swear words. He'd called me worse before.

"Let's get after him, then!" I said, and as I grabbed Riz from the dashboard, he tried to keep hold of all the Runes he'd gathered up. "Do you really think you'll need that many?"

"Ya neva know."

I couldn't argue with that, so I set off to chase the errant Wisp before he caused any other problems. The one we already had was difficult enough.

* * *

It was lucky for us that Ro's trail allowed us something to follow, as he always seemed just that little bit ahead. We were never gaining on him, despite me running as fast as I could possibly manage.

"Mush 'arder!" Riz yelled, prodding me in the neck, as if that was going to make me go any quicker.

"I'm going as fast as I fucking can!" I snapped. I was going to follow up with another remark, but a third voice put paid to that.

"How much longer are we gonna wait, boss?"

The Will-O-the-Wisp in the Office

They received an answer from a fourth voice, someone who had less of a tolerance for idiots than I did.

"I already told you! Don't you ever listen?!"

I had a little empathy for whoever was talking, but I got the impression that the guy who was speaking was who Ro had referred to as 'the one who stood back and shouted.'

"But boss—"

"When the job is done, then you can put your complaints in! Till then, shut up and keep an eye out! I wanted all these Wisps, and I'm going to get all the Wisps!"

"Right, if anyone 'ere says dey know me, dey're nuthin' but a filthy liar!"

"Riz, once this is all over, we're going to have a long discussion, do you understand me?" I whispered as I bent down low.

I peeked through the branches so I could get a closer look at the two men. What I saw was a very well-armed man rocking what looked to me like a machine gun with two rolls of ammunition tied around his body. I would never have guessed he would have been hunting Wisps, as his equipment seemed more suited to hunting a yeti or even a Wyrm. Luckily for us, the night vision goggles on top of his bald head were inactive.

He was standing next to a series of crates that had multicoloured light seeping through. I recognised some of the stones decorating them as Runes, hinting at how they were keeping the Wisps locked up.

The other guy wasn't dressed for outdoor hunting, unless your idea of outdoor hunting is locked to the expeditions of the 19th century. The one who'd been barking orders was a short man with slicked-back grey hair. He also had a monocle because of course he had a monocle.

I glared at Riz.

"Why is it everyone you know is a fucking caricature?" I asked in a low voice, though it would have been easy for me to lose my temper.

"I don't even know wat dat word means!" Riz protested. He then twitched his nose and looked around. "Urm, where did Ro go?"

I went to look around, but I suddenly had a more alarming question to ask Riz.

"Where did the guys go?"

It was at that point we heard the click of guns, and I instinctively placed my hands in the air.

"Well, this isn't what I expected to find... Riz? Is that you? Don't tell me you decided to cash in on these Wisps as well!"

I slowly turned my head the best I could to glare some more at the rat on my shoulder.

"Are you going to answer him, Riz? Or should I? Or are you still going to tell me that you don't know this twat?"

"Yer enjoyin' dis, ain't ya? It's not enuff dat I'm stuck in dis uncomfortable position, ya got ta fuckin' rub it in!"

"I believe this is called karma, is it not? And yes, I'm going to enjoy this, every last bit of it! After that? I'm going to call Valarie and tell her all of this, and then—"

"If you're quite finished, I have places I have to be, and your intrusion is holding matters up," the rich guy interrupted, tapping his foot.

"I suppose we'll have to deal with this mess YOU created." I gave a final furious look at Riz before turning my attention to the real problem. "So, you want to capture all the Wisps, Mr...?"

I motioned for him to give us a name. No doubt Riz knew it already, but I just wanted him to be quiet for the time being.

"Mr Reginald Wendelsham, the third. Charmed, I'm sure. It is true: I want to capture all the Wisps here, and I don't see why you would be sticking your neck out for them. Your little friend there was more than eager to sell me the details, after all."

"Unlike the rat here, I actually have a moral compass. What are you planning on doing? Turning them into an exhibit for your probably massive house? Selling them to idiots as nightlights?"

"I have a business to run, and to run it, I require stock. My clientele expects the very best and the very rare. These Wisps are at least one of those things. What they do with them after I get my money is of no concern to me. Nor should it be to you. In fact, as I've stated, I do not have time, so here you go."

Reginald reached into his pocket and pulled out something that I couldn't see clearly, but I felt it as it was thrown in my face. I looked down at where it landed. It was a wad of cash, multiple ten pound notes bound together by an elastic band.

"A bribe?" I said, raising an eyebrow.

"Take it, and be on your way. Otherwise, my colleagues here will be

The Will-O-the-Wisp in the Office

forced to deal with you. I'm only offering you payment as a courtesy because of your friend's help earlier."

As he spoke, I heard heavy footsteps behind me, and I knew that the other guy was now behind us. Then came the click of a rifle, as if to underscore the threat.

"Why don't he jus' shoot us anyway?" Riz whispered to me. "He'd save money dat way!"

I was going to throttle him for even suggesting that within their earshot, but he was right. It would have made more sense, which meant that he was going out of his way not to kill us.

"So, I just pick up the money and walk?" I asked. "Leaving the Wisps to you, that right?"

"It is," Reginald said. "You get to go home, a bit richer than when you arrived. What could be wrong with that deal?"

I was trying to figure out what his angle was when I saw Riz inching towards the money. I tapped him on the head, then remembered when he'd bitten me in the car, which, in turn, made me think of what Ro had said before he shot off.

"He said we might get lost… You want to follow us out of here, don't you?"

I went to stand, but the thug behind me knocked me down again.

"Shrewd thinking. Do I need to increase my offer? We already tried to leave once we had a few Wisps, but we ended up back here. I then thought capturing all the Wisps would allow us to exit this place. And now, you arrive. I assume the rat led you here?"

"No! We were led 'ere by—"

I quickly clamped my hand over Riz's mouth.

"I made him bring me here so I can fix his mistake!" I declared. "He should never have told you about the Wisps in the first place."

"You're not in a position to really do anything about this though, are you? We'll dispense with the bribe and move on to good old-fashioned threats. Lead me out of these woods, or we'll kill you," Reginald said, putting his hands behind his back.

"You were going to kill us anyway. If I had taken that bribe, I wasn't going to be heading back to my car," I pointed out. It was an obvious ploy: get us to do what he wanted, then tidy up the loose ends with a gun to the back of my head.

"Fine, have it your way. What's a few more bodies to deal with?"

"Wait! He don't speak fer fuckin' both of us!" Riz screamed after he got free from my grasp. "Ya make the price right, 'nd I'll lead ya out. As long as yer not gonna kill me, of course. We've worked well togetha so far!"

"Sounds promising," Reginald mused. "Of course, I could sweeten the deal even further if you help me get the rest of the Wisps into these custom-made boxes."

"Wat's dose things? Neva heard of a way ta confine Wisps before. Plus, how ya stoppin dem from jus' lettin' demselves out?" Riz asked.

I thought it was a peculiar question at the time, but it made sense in hindsight.

"I had them designed in such a way that only a human could open them. The stupid Wisps tried ever so hard to free their friends that it made it easy to capture them. So, Riz, what do you say to two thousand pounds in exchange for your help?"

"Ooh, me likey dat much!" Riz started drooling, but I bopped him on the head to refocus him.

"Riz!"

"Look, I'm jus' keepin' options open, 'nd besides, at least ya know why ya were needed 'ere! I mean, da Wisps would normally handle dis demselves. Anotha reason why I gladly gave 'im da details – cuz he paid up first! Wouldn't 'ave done it if I got money afta," Riz explained.

I didn't necessarily approve of what he'd done, but it made sense. More importantly, I completely understood what I had to do now. I simply had to make the means to get it done.

"Are you going to help or not?" Reginald asked point blank. I think he was having enough of our roundabout discussion.

"What do you think?" I smiled as I flexed my arm, allowing the Rune I had stashed in my cuff to fall in my palm. "Kleuzeur!"

The Rune turned into a brilliant light that I shone in the eyes of Reginald and his hired goons, blinding them for a moment, which was all we needed to get away.

"Goggles down, now! Shoot them! I don't want to see their smug faces again!" I heard Reginald shout.

I hid behind the nearest tree and worked my way right, going from cover

The Will-O-the-Wisp in the Office

to cover. I had to double back to where the Wisps were captured, but I was also getting concerned about where Ro had disappeared off to. Then I saw several lights in the distance, a spectrum of colours dancing towards me.

"I brought the cavalry!" Ro sang out, not that I could tell which light was him. I didn't have time to celebrate as gunfire burst apart the tree just above my head, reducing my cover significantly.

"There you are! And you brought more of those Wisp things!" the first hired goon said.

"Let's get them too!" his friend replied, opening fire on the new Wisps, injuring a couple who couldn't dodge in time.

"Don't forget that twat with the rat!" the first reminded him, putting me in the crosshairs again, which meant I had to run again to avoid being turned into Swiss cheese.

"Dis jus' keeps gettin' worse, don't it?" Riz pointed out unhelpfully.

"Brennan!" Ro called out, floating near me, seemingly oblivious to the danger he was in as gunfire ripped up the foliage behind us. "We're ready for you to lead the charge! Then we can rescue Joy!"

"I've got a better idea. Ro, I want you to lead the charge!" I said in-between breaths. "Riz will be a distraction, and I'll free your friends!"

"Wait, wat's dis now? I'm a wat?" Riz spluttered, but given how fast things were moving, he wasn't getting out of it.

"Lead the charge? No! We rally around you! That's why I got you!" Ro said defiantly.

"No, you only need me to free your friends. You're perfectly capable of handling this chump, you've just got to remember what you're fighting for! Don't worry, Ro, you've got this in hand. Speaking of that…"

I took Riz from my shoulder and put him in the palm of my hand.

"Ro, get all your friends to follow you, and make sure they keep moving to avoid getting hit! Ready, Riz?"

"Ready? Fer wat?! I 'ave no idea wat's goin' on!"

"Remember Richmond?" I asked quietly.

Riz's eyes widened as he figured out what the plan was.

"Oh, fer fuck's sake. Do I get a say in this?!"

"No," I said as I unceremoniously tossed him towards the hired goons, who were wasting a lot of bullets firing into the trees.

"I'll get you fer dis!" Riz yelled out.

I couldn't tell what happened next, but given they stopped firing at me, I think it worked out to plan.

"Ro! Now's your chance! Get all your friends to swarm that guy!" I pointed at Reginald, who hadn't moved from where he'd been standing. "I'll release the others!"

With the way things were looking, I allowed myself to feel confident that everything was under control. As you can probably work out, that was a mistake.

Reginald began to smirk as he held out one gloved hand and caught the charging Ro. The Wisp tried his best to escape, but Reginald's grip was tighter.

"Like it? This glove allows me to hold these things without worrying about my personal safety. They are rendered harmless. Now, I've had quite enough of all this resistance. All you Wisps! Gather near those crates, or I'll crush this one to death!"

Reginald turned to face me, wearing a smug, self-assured smile.

"Same goes for you as well, Mr Brennan. Don't even think of releasing all those caged Wisps, unless, like me, you're curious to see what the inside of these things looks like."

I didn't have much of a choice – at least, not at that second.

"You idiots! Stop playing with the rat and box these Wisps up!" Reginald called out to his goons.

I watched as Ro struggled against his predicament, and I racked my brain for a solution that we desperately needed. I felt something tugging at my leg, and I looked down and saw Riz.

"Riz? I thought you were still over there!"

"Nah, I jus' left dem to it! I don't fink dey're da brightest bulbs."

"Okay then, so we still have a chance to turn this around."

"Ya betta not throw me again!"

"I'm making no promises," I said bluntly. "But—"

"Wat're ya plannin' dis time?" Riz asked me. "Yer last one worked brilliantly."

I wanted to whisper it to Riz, but Reginald still had his glare locked on me, wanting to see if I was going to risk Ro or not. Naturally, I wouldn't if I could help it. Besides, it was Ro that was the answer to this problem.

"Trust me, okay?"

"Are ya goin' ta throw me again?"

"Do you want me to?"

"No?"

"Then trust me."

I nodded at Riz, and I could tell from the look on his little face that he was still confused, but ultimately, he nodded back, though not before sighing. With his tacit seal of approval, it was time to end this.

"Hey, Reginald! Did you capture a Wisp called Joy by any chance?" I asked, much to his surprise.

"These things have names?" he baulked.

"...and feelings," I added.

"Feelings? What are you blabbering about? In a moment, my men will finish whatever stupidity they're engaging in, and then they can finally put you out of my misery!"

"Ro, what was it you liked about Joy again?" I said cheerfully.

At that point, Ro jerked up, almost pulling Reginald's arm off.

"Joy is funny! Joy is brave! Joy believes in me, and I believe in her!"

Every little outburst that he came out with caused him to change colours, just as I'd seen earlier that night, but I wanted to push it even further. This was my trump card.

Riz had made his way back up to my shoulder, though he was keeping an eye on the two hired goons, who seemed to be getting their act together.

"Ya plan finished yet? We're 'bout ta be shot at again!" he complained.

"Ro! How does Joy make you feel?" I shouted, wanting to make sure that Reginald knew what I was saying and that his downfall belonged to the Wisp he was holding on to.

"Joy makes me feel special! Joy makes me happy!"

By now, the air around Ro was beginning to warp as he got hotter and hotter. Steam started to hiss out from the glove Reginald wore.

"Ohhhh, I see wat yer doin'!" Riz grinned. "Heh, guess dat's some nice thinkin'. It's jus' like dat song, ain't it?"

If I wasn't trying to concentrate on getting Ro all fired up, I might have tugged at that thread and asked what he was talking about. Instead, I shouted out what I felt was the final thing I needed to ask Ro.

"Do you love Joy?"

"Yes! I'd do anything to protect her!"

Time seemed to freeze as Ro went supernova, and as he became a miniature sun in colouration and heat, Reginald's glove could no longer contain its prize and was immolated. I think Reginald was able to pull his hand out before that happened, but unsurprisingly, I wasn't too bothered about that.

With the danger to Ro abated, I followed through on what I'd wanted to do initially and freed all the other Wisps, who started to swirl around Ro. I did notice a pink one that bobbed along merrily, flying around Ro like a moon orbiting a planet.

"Boss! What do we do now?!" I heard the hired goons shout in unison.

I turned to see them trying to aim their guns again, but they had the shakes real bad and couldn't aim at anything. I was interested in what Reginald was going to say.

"Uhh…" he murmured, surrounded by the creatures he was trying to hunt.

"Wat's dat? Wisp got ya tongue?" Riz asked. Seemingly, he'd found his confidence to gloat now that the danger had passed.

"R-run, you idiots!"

Reginald scrambled to his feet and went to run but found a wall of Wisps blocking any escape. The Wisps also did the same to the hired goons, who offered no resistance to what was happening.

"What do you think will happen to them?" I asked Riz.

"Dey might eat dem?" Riz shrugged.

As one, all the Wisps spoke together. I even heard Ro's voice as part of the harmony.

"For your transgressions against all Wisp-kind, you are sentenced to wander the lost woods for eternity, never to know peace!"

"Always thought dat law was a bit extreme," Riz whispered to me, as if he'd been expecting this outcome all along.

"Is that because you're afraid they're going to sentence you as well for leading that twat here?" I replied openly.

I had nothing to fear in this, and maybe, just maybe, some punishment for Riz would make him think twice before letting greed cloud his judgement. But the little dork escaped such a fate as the Wisp chorus seemed to part, opening a path to Reginald and his goons into the forest.

"Oh, look! They're letting us go! I thought we were supposed to be lost?" one said, oblivious to his fate.

The Will-O-the-Wisp in the Office

"Yeah, I know the exact way to the car park!" his friend exclaimed.

Reginald said nothing, as he seemed to be the only one totally aware of what was going on. He gave me one last look, almost begging for my help. I smiled and waved. I wouldn't be shedding a tear for him tonight.

The hired goons ran off first, with Reginald walking slowly behind them, and I quickly lost sight of them, the darkness swallowing them whole and their voices dwindling to a whisper on the breeze.

"In time, dey might become Wisps," Riz mused as he climbed atop my head, peering into the darkness. "Wouldn't dat be funny!"

I shook him from my head, and he fell into my palm.

"Dat Ro, eh? Talk 'bout great balls of fire! How did ya know dat was gonna happen? I didn't tell ya anythin' 'bout Wisps bein' able ta do dat."

"I paid attention to Ro when he was talking about Joy before, plus I know stories about the Wisps as well, ones that my mother shared when I was a kid!"

"Alright, cleva clogs." Riz rolled his eyes.

"We didn't even use any Runes for this job," I said, holding the same Runes I'd brought with me from the car.

"I know, I never get ta 'ave fun no more."

"Excuse me!" Ro and Joy both exclaimed as they approached us, separating from their friends.

"Thank you! Thank you!" Ro said, bobbing up and down as he spoke.

"Any friend of Ro is my friend too!" Joy announced, her voice sounding exactly as I'd imagined it would.

"I hope you two are very happy together," I said, smiling.

"Yeh, if ya ever need a babysitta, our rates're very friendly," Riz grinned.

"A what?" Joy asked.

"Don't worry 'bout dat, jus' be happy fer da couple of... err... Wisps!"

"We sing and dance for you as a token of our gratitude!" Ro told me.

As if on cue, all the Wisps started dancing around us in a dazzling display of colours, singing in perfect harmony. Though I had no idea what language they were using, it sounded beautiful all the same.

If more jobs ended like this, I would be one happy fella. I decided to worry about remembering where I'd parked after the light show was over...

ABOUT THE AUTHOR

*P*eter James Martin is Teesside born and bred. He lives for folklore both local and international, often working it into his stories where appropriate. His most well known work is about a long suffering investigator and his talking rat business partner.

Find more musings on his blog at [the strange tales of Peter James Martin.](#)

Firefly Glow

Rose J. Fairchild

"Finally home," I sighed as I reached to close the garage door. I pulled it, and though it was creaky, there was something else—a new sound. I halted, listening.

The sound returned. A meow, and it was close. "Here, kitty," I called, releasing the door and entering the darkness. It yowled again, the sound moving quickly behind my house toward the woods.

I bolted after it, pulling my phone out and switching the flashlight on. "No, kitty! You'll get eaten if you go in there!" My imagination ran wild, remembering cats I'd lost to foxes, coyotes, bobcats, owls, and hawks as a little girl. "Come back!"

I jogged, stopping intermittently to listen for the feline. Each call drew me further from home and deeper into the forest. With every passing moment, fog crawled thicker around my ankles, billowing around my hurried steps.

Meow.

So close. Running further into the trees, I swung my light from side to side, searching for the flash of nocturnal eyes among the trunks. The forest, however, was eerily empty.

"Of course it is, you dummy. You're thundering through the trees like a rabid moose. You've probably scared everything away."

Trees blurred past me, yet the forest was still, quiet, and empty. It held the weighty silence of death cradled in its many branches.

I stopped running, scanning silently with my phone's flashlight.

Again, the cat cried, though I couldn't tell exactly where it came from. There was another yowl, and a many-legged, spiny thought dug into my brain.

How many times has the cat meowed, yet the sound hasn't changed? It's like a recording, played over and over.

Never in my life had I had a cat that consistently made the same sound with every plea, whether for food, attention, or help.

"Something's off."

My heart raced as I searched the trees for the way home. The fog had grown, creeping through the trees at waist height now. I swung my phone, wincing at its glare off the mist. I couldn't see a cat—or anything—in that if I wanted to.

My lungs suddenly felt too small, unable to suck in the air I needed.

"Shit, shit, shit... Which way?" I turned my face skyward, catching fleeting glimpses of the crescent moon through wind-tossed leaves.

Meow.

It was right behind me.

I surged into the trees, tearing through the blanketing mist. Branches slapped my face and clawed at my skin.

Catching my toe, I tipped forward. The fog swallowed me as I squeezed my eyes shut, unable to stop my fall. I crashed to the ground with a grunt, the aroma of earth, pine needles, and rotting leaves filling my nose.

My hands and right shoulder burned from their collision with the ground. Worse, I'd dropped my phone.

Damn it.

Glancing around, I caught sight of its gleam seeping through the fog up ahead. I crawled toward it, listening for the eerie yowl, ready to run without the light if necessary.

Shuffling forward, I moved faster as I neared the phone's light. As I reached for it, I brushed something sticky and damp, wiry fibers protruding from it.

I shuddered, grasping the phone and swinging its glow onto what I'd touched.

I'd found the cat.

It lay dead, mouth wide as though screaming. Its eye sockets were empty, gaping holes in its blood-soaked face.

Acid surged up my throat, the taste of bile coating the back of my mouth as I scrabbled back from the poor, mutilated creature.

The air was too thick, sticking in my throat when I gasped for breath. I choked on the coppery scent of gore.

Pressing the phone's flashlight to my chest, I was suddenly worried it would call whatever—whoever—had butchered the cat to me.

Meow.

Pressing against the tree, I tried to quiet my breath and slow my heart, unwilling to be betrayed by its thunderous pounding.

Meow.

Footsteps padded against soft earth. The animal was quiet but sounded significantly larger than a cat. A whuff of air sounded as though something sniffed, searching.

The meow came again, then lifted into a mix of vixen's scream, hawk's shriek, and the bleat of a fawn.

Fuck, fuck, fuck! Please don't let it find me.

As it drew closer, a rattle-hiss accompanied the footsteps, punctuated occasionally by loud sniffing.

I could hear its breath, which meant it was too close. There was nowhere to go, and my only weapon was a pocketknife.

Dragging it from my pants, I flipped the blade open, tucking my phone in to replace it as two blue-green glowing orbs appeared in the fog ahead. They approached slowly, their light unwavering.

My heart hammered in my ribcage as the orbs drew closer, a jagged horizontal line of light appearing below them.

A mouth. Oh, God, please protect me. Please, please, please!

The creature broke through the fog. Its maw opened again, displaying needle-sharp teeth as its full-moon eyes locked on me. It uttered that unholy mix of cries, exposing a pointed tongue covered in sharp, hooked barbs.

It was a half-decayed abomination—a demonic apparition.

The wolf-sized beast shrieked again, and this time, I heard human screams laced through the animal cries it had stolen. Its voice was many, lifted from its previous victims.

"Holy fuck…"

It inched closer. I brandished the knife with a shaking hand.

"You're not getting my eyes—or my voice!"

A sound poured from its glowing jaws like a thousand laughs in an ocean of tears.

My guts turned to liquid. Unable to afford the luxury of worrying whether I'd shit my pants, I took a breath and roared, rushing the creature.

It danced around me, unearthly fast, swiping at my legs with razor claws. Pain sliced through the side of my calf, but I bolted past it, racing headlong through the trees. I didn't care which direction I was going. All I wanted was to put distance between me and the beast.

Needles pierced my arm, a heavy weight dragging me to the ground. The knife flew from my hand, the sound of it bouncing filling me with frustrated rage. I kicked at the beast latched onto my arm, punching its face with my other hand.

It clamped down harder, twisting. Something snapped in my arm, sending a shot of sharp, stabbing pain through me.

I screamed and swung my fist at one of the creature's glowing, bulbous eyes, connecting with a sickening squelch. The eye popped, a glowing liquid seeping down the beast's face as it released me, shrieking agony into the darkness.

It rattle-rumbled, clawing at its injury as I pulled my phone out and switched the light on, scanning the ground for my knife.

A gleam of metal flashed a few feet away. I raced toward it, praying for a miracle.

Searing pain tore through my heel. I dropped to my knees, maintaining my grip on my phone, and crawled forward until my fingers closed around the knife's hilt. I swung the blade as I spun around, hoping to connect with rotten flesh—hoping it would have some effect when I did.

There was nothing behind me. I spared a second to glance at my heel, groaning at the mangled mess of bloody flesh and exposed tendon.

No more running away.

I debated shutting off my phone's flashlight, deciding it didn't make any difference. I was watching for glowing eyes and listening for the creature's hellish cries, neither of which required additional illumination.

The flashlight, however, was a small source of childish comfort, and there was no worry of calling the creature in with it. It already knew I was here—had already tasted my blood and fear. Light or not, it would keep coming for me until one of us was no more.

Setting the phone next to me on the ground, I fought to slow my ragged breath, desperately trying to calm the pulse of blood in my ears.

Animal cries and human screams echoed through the trees, seemingly from all directions. I backed against a massive trunk, protecting my more vulnerable side from attack while watching for glowing orbs.

Hissing, shrieking, scraping sounds wove through the mist, crawling through the forest to taunt and confuse me.

The woods fell silent, the only sound the hiss of breath over my tongue and my heartbeat pounding at every pulse point.

Sucking in a few pinched gasps, I gathered enough air to hold my breath for a moment, listening.

Deafening silence smothered me with its leaden weight.

The night was pregnant with barely-leashed malice. Dread squeezed cold, clawed hands around my throat, each breath filtering less oxygen to my panicked brain.

As silent seconds ticked by, fear constricted my ribs, stuttering my heartbeat and crushing my lungs.

Leaning forward, I glanced around, unable to see much through the fog. Something warm and wet dropped onto my shoulder. Turning, rancid breath washed over me as bony jaws opened, exposing the creature's glowing throat.

I tumbled backward, yelping as I crushed my mangled heel, narrowly avoiding the sharp snap of fangs where my face had been a breath before.

The beast leaped, jaws wide. I lifted my good leg and kicked it in its bony ribs, sending it sprawling into the mist.

Its claws raked through dirt and over roots as it scrambled to its feet and surged toward me again. I caught its stomach with my good foot and gripped its throat with one hand. Exposed teeth clacking in my face, strips of rotten flesh peeling away beneath my fingers, I fought, gagging against the stench.

Shifting my hold on the knife, I raised it, swinging forward the next time the jaws snapped shut. The blade sank into its undamaged eye, spilling firefly glow down the creature's sunken face as it screamed in a thousand stolen voices.

I pulled it free, luminous drops flying, then falling to paint the forest floor.

I stabbed again and again until the eye socket crumbled and the creature lay, unmoving, on top of me.

Shoving it off, I rolled over and used the pocketknife to saw through flesh and separate vertebrae until the head rolled to the side. Sawing through the remaining corrupted muscle, I hacked, gasping and sobbing until the head dropped to the ground.

Kicking it away, I realized the sun was beginning to rise, and I could finally see the path through the trees.

Glancing at the mangled horror, I watched the sun's rays touch the raw, scabby corpse. A flush of gray spread over it, and then it crumbled into ash. Pale petals of nightmare, now only a memory, drifted on the morning breeze.

Unable to walk, I began crawling toward home.

ABOUT THE AUTHOR

Rose J. Fairchild juggles writing around family, pets, and a library job. She lives in the mysterious Catskill Mountains of Upstate New York, where all things magical (and sometimes terrible) live. She's had short stories published in anthologies by Fae Corp Publishing, Sulk Media, and in Deranged Minds: Campfire Tales, edited and assembled by author Ray Bush.

Rose is the author of the Taste of Faerie series which is currently in progress. Book one, "A Shiver of Rainbow and Shadow," book two, "A Swirl of Smoke and Stars," and a complementary collaborative novella that continues from where book 2 left off called "Faerie Fire & Demon Desire: A Darkly Delicious Correspondence" are all available now. Rose is currently working on another complementary novella called "Born of Blood and Sin" and will begin work on book three once that is complete.

Felons and Freaks

Jon Ford

— Edward Steven Tyler —
— 19:07 Friday, June 6, 2021 — New Chicago —

I fucked up.

There. I admitted it. Time to pay the piper, as they say.

There are two of them, as usual. They always work in pairs. Both enter the room slowly, the picture of cool, calm, and collected. Meanwhile, I'm sitting here sweating like a whore in church, my hands cuffed to the table. It's hot in here. Bad time of the year to be cooped up in an interview room without the air conditioning on. I reckon they did that on purpose. Sweating me in preparation for the inevitable good cop/bad cop routine. The fact that fresher air begins to filter into the room the moment they walk in is a clear indication that I'm right.

They're both dressed in suits. They're nice, but they're off the rack. His is a dark navy blue. Hers is black. Both are wearing white shirts, but he wears a tie. She doesn't. She's got some paperwork tucked snugly under her arm. He's carrying a shoebox. Old. Battered. Says 'Nike Rogues' on the side of the black cardboard in bright red print. Size twelves. I doubt that's *actually* what's in there.

I do have a sneaking suspicion I know what is, though.

"Edward Steven Tyler?" I nod to confirm my identity. "I'm Detective Bruneau, and this is my partner, Detective Watts."

Bruneau sits down first in the chair directly opposite. He puts the shoebox carefully on the table.

I cast my eyes over him. Evaluating him. I can't help it. It's a reflex. An instinct. A need to figure out if I could take him in a fistfight. I doubt it. He's tall. Six two. Maybe more. Dark umber skin. Chiseled jaw and piercing eyes. The dude's probably got about six inches on me, but I've got about fifty pounds on him. The wrong kind of pounds, though. He's sporting an athlete's build, whereas mine is more Body by Ben & Jerry's.

It's a moot point anyway. I'm hardly gonna punch my way out of a police station, am I?

His partner sits down to his left. She's kinda pretty. Elfin looks. A good foot shorter with a shaggy, dirty-blonde hairstyle cut to about shoulder length. Styled to look casual, but definitely styled. She looks a few years younger than him. Mid to late twenties maybe. Him? I'd peg him at around thirty.

But…there's something about them.

Something a little off.

I've been a criminal as long as I can remember. Never found a line I didn't want to cross, a locked door I didn't want to open, or a law I didn't want to break. I was shoplifting before I got into my teens. I had a lucrative school life shaking down geeks for their lunch money. As I got older, I started to specialize my skills. Honing my specific criminal talents.

It's how I got this job.

The one I just royally fucked up.

Anyhow, it's also how I know there's somethin' funny about these two. I've seen cops before. Seen a *lot* of cops. You do in my line of work. I'm good at what I do, but run-ins with the law are pretty much unavoidable. Inevitable, even.

But these two…

She pulls that file out from under her arm. At first glance, it appears to be a pretty nondescript manilla folder. She places it on the table almost casually. Of course it draws my eye. I'm wondering what it is. My rap sheet maybe? It's quite thick. Extensive. But no. It isn't.

There's a police shield logo on the front and the letters NCPD-SCU.

It's an acronym I know real well. Everyone in New Chicago does.

New Chicago Police Department – Super-Crimes Unit.

Shit.

Okay, so, here's the rub for those of you new to the party.

New Chicago used to be just plain old Chicago. Until 2021.

I'll give you the crib notes. Massive inter-dimensional tear in the sky above Lake Michigan. Alien fucking invasion. Superheroes to the rescue. Bad guys defeated. But the radiation those insect-like motherfuckers left behind meant the Windy City got quarantined under this big fuck off energy dome, and the whole kerfuffle triggered potentially active M-Gene candidates in what was left of the city's human population.

Gets worse, though.

Scientists reckon one in ten have a potentially active M-Gene, the genetic code that gives ordinary folk extraordinary abilities. That's one in ten of every fucker in the world. And statistically, of those, only one in ten normally manifests. And of those, only one in one hundred thousand gets a superpower.

They call it the ten-ten-one hundred rule.

The majority that manifest just get to be really good at something. Think Mozart. Or da Vinci. Einstein. Michael Jordan. That one in one hundred thousand? Yeah, they're the lucky fucks who get things like flight. Or laser-beam eyes.

But the Kriitani radiation changed the equation in Chicago. Triggered *everyone* who had an active M-Gene.

Superpowers galore. Superpowers for the fucking masses.

There were a good three million people in Chicago when the Kriitani arrived, which meant about thirty thousand people got superpowers *overnight*.

And not all of them decided to use their powers for good.

That was seven years ago, and now the city is well into a rebuild. Yes, they call it New Chicago, but due to all the supers hanging around, its new nickname is the 'City of Heroes.'

Bearing that in mind, some people might wonder why exactly people like me—criminals—stay in New Chicago. I mean, the city is a fuckin' mess, still

Felons and Freaks

mostly quarantined under a massive fuckin' energy shield. Isn't the risk too high when there's a Superman wannabe around every fucking corner ready to foil any criminal enterprise they stumble across?

And, of course, now there are also thousands of supervillains competing for each and every heist.

But here's the *other* truth about New Chicago. There's money here.

Lots and lots and *lots* of fuckin' money.

You see, it's the *only* place on the planet where aliens have landed. Officially, anyhow. They had a shitload of alien technology with them on their mothership and then crash-landed it into the middle of the city. Which makes this place ground zero for the next scientific gold rush. Tech companies moved in quickly, funding the rebuilding of the city so they could get their grubby little mitts on revolutionary next-generation technology before anyone else.

Companies like my current employer.

So, the villains stuck around. A metric fuck ton of 'em.

City of Heroes? City of Villains, more like.

To police them, New Chicago PD created a special task force of super-powered cops.

The Super-Crime Unit.

Most of us just call them 'The Freak Squad.'

Anyhow, if they're here investigating *me*, then it implies they think *I'm* a cape.

They're going to be disappointed. Wish I was. But I'm not. I didn't have the 'right stuff' in my genetic makeup.

Not that I'm bitter about it.

"Can I get you a drink, Eddie? Water?" the broad asks.

Of course you can! It's been hotter than Satan's left tit in here!

But I shake my head. I notice she's the one who addresses me more informally. I assume she'll be 'good cop' for the purpose of this interrogation.

"I just want my lawyer." Not the first time I've asked.

"He's on his way," Bruneau answers.

Motherfucker is taking his sweet fucking time!

"So, how about you tell us what happened?" Blondie says.

I roll my eyes. "Again? I've already told the other cops everything I know."

"We don't need the details of the robbery, Eddie. We want you to talk us through the escape."

"There was an...accident," I say, turning to Bruneau. "Jimmy crashed the van."

"Did he?" he says.

"You don't believe me?"

Nah. He doesn't believe me.

I'm not surprised. It's a blatant lie after all. Yeah, Jimmy may have crashed the van, God rest his soul, but it wasn't strictly his fault.

"How about you tell us about this?" Bruneau lifts the lid off the shoebox as he asks his question, and there it is. Large as life and twice as fucking ugly.

That fucking orb.

I wish to God I'd never laid my hands on that fucking thing.

"No idea what that is," I lie.

"Then I'll enlighten you." Bruneau leans back in his chair. "You know who the Greek goddess Tyche is?"

I shake my head. Of course not! As previously mentioned, I hardly concentrated on academia when I was at school.

"Goddess of success, luck, and prosperity. Greeks believed that she had the power to determine the fortune—good or bad—of entire cities. Or just individual people."

My eyes are drawn to the gleaming ball in the box. It doesn't seem as... mesmerizing as it did before. Almost dull now. There's a small delicate spiderweb of cracks in the glass that I swear weren't there before. It's no longer the flawless bauble I first laid eyes on.

Abruptly, things start dropping into place. My brain starts to make the connections. I glance down at the palm of my right hand.

"I've seen your rap sheet, Edward." Bruneau taps his finger on the folder his partner put on the table. "You're a meticulous planner. Rarely caught. Never prosecuted."

"What can I say?" I shrug. "I'm good at what I do."

"Which is why we're here." Watts leans in. "We got a van still stinking of river water and two dead bodies in the morgue. Doesn't seem like this one was very well thought out, Eddie. Or did your luck just...run out?"

Quite the opposite actually.

Felons and Freaks

"Fine," I say with a sigh. "I'll tell you what happened."

— Four Hours Earlier —

I did something *really* fucking stupid. I broke the cardinal rule of the craft.

My number one directive. Four little words.

Stick. To. The. Fucking. Plan.

Okay, five words if you put it like that, but you get the point.

I'm a stickler for my rules. Ask any good criminal worth their salt, and they'll all tell you the same thing. The devil is in the details. So, I assemble the crew. I make the plan. And I *never* deviate. Why not? Because going off-script is the easiest way to get caught.

So why the fuck did I decide to just pick up that big shiny ball on a stupid whim?

Fuuuuuuuck!

It had all been going so well.

The job was a high-paying corporate contract. The objective? Steal an item from the National Hellenic Museum. A very particular item. Now, that place is a veritable treasure trove of Ancient Greek-type shit, but I have to admit, the item they wanted to steal was a bit of an eyebrow-raiser. Spoiler alert: it *wasn't* the big shiny ball. Still, I wasn't going to question the exceedingly large payday it was about to earn me.

I'm a planner, see. That's my thing. My specialty. You want a robbery done well? I'm the man who can facilitate it. I'm discreet. I'm meticulous. And my brain is a criminal Yellow Pages. A who's who of the seedy underground world of crime. I know people who can do just about *everything*.

For example, I have a contact at City Hall. Crossed her palm with a little green, and she helped me get my larcenous paws on a copy of the museum's floor plans. Or like my pal who works for the company that arranged the museum's security systems. An envelope full of Benjamins got me the details on what exactly we had to contend with. With those two pieces of information, it was child's play to find a way in. Breaking and entering I can handle.

Two things that aren't on my resume, however, are safe-cracker and getaway driver. So, I let my fingers do the walking.

Enter the first of those. Lizzy 'The Locksmith' Henderson.

I don't think she's come across a lock she can't pick yet. Big safes, like the one the museum was keeping our target in, are her specialty.

Everything had been going so well.

The museum is closed to the public on Tuesdays, so I knew it would be quiet. We bided our time, waiting for the right moment, and only then did we make our move. The alarms weren't a problem, and I spliced in a little looped footage to keep the security guards sitting in their office, none the wiser for the duration of our little heist. That allowed us ample time and opportunity to slink into the basement undetected. Then Lizzy quietly went to work on the safe.

All I had to do was wait. That's all.

She'd have it open in under five minutes—she'd practiced on the same type of lock before the job, so we knew how long we'd need—and then we'd snatch and bag the item and scram before anyone knew we'd even been there.

But there it was.

Sitting on the workbench near the safe looking like a million dollars.

The orb.

'Bout the size of a baseball, maybe a little bigger. Gleaming glass with gold and silver bands looped tightly around it. There was something etched on the encircling metal. Runes or something. Nothing I recognized. Ancient Greek probably.

But it was the glass that drew my attention.

At first, I thought it was my imagination or a trick of the light, but it looked like there was something trapped inside. It moved fluidly, like a cloud. Ink in water. As I watched, it seemed to shift and sway, dancing against the glass. It moved like it was alive.

I inched a little closer as Lizzy continued her work, oblivious to my distraction. I peered into it. Hypnotized. Whatever it was, it pressed against the glass. Imprisoned. Searching. Probing for an escape with smoky tentacles.

It reminded me of something.

Like videos I'd seen of an octopus trapped in a bottle.

And it was calling to me.

I could feel it.

My hand stretched out like it was possessed. Controlled by someone, or something, else. My fingers were slowly closing around the orb before I realized what I was doing. I felt its smooth surface, and I swear to God it started to get hot in my hand. Something tickled in my palm.

I hesitated, suddenly realizing what I'd done.

Fuck!

Stupid, Eddie, stupid. Just your luck—picking this thing up would have set the alarms off!

And then, just about every fucking alarm in the building went off.

Which brings us back to the here and now. A now which has me and Lizzy piling frantically into the back of our escape vehicle, an old 2011 Ford Econoline, while I wonder what the fuck went wrong. Lizzy thinks it's her fault. Me? I'm not so sure.

"Fuck! I'm sorry, Eddie." Lizzy is shaking her head. "I can't believe I set off the fucking alarms. That has *never* happened to me before. Shit!"

"Don't sweat it," I try and ease her conscience. "We got the item, didn't we?"

She nods but still looks crestfallen.

"Then what's done is done," I say as I try desperately to shut the van doors before Jimmy's scorching getaway ends up with us being thrown out the back to become bloody roadkill on Van Buren Street. For some reason, they won't fucking shut. Broken latch maybe?

"Wanna give me a hand here, Lizzy?"

She shakes her head like a disappointed mother hen and finishes jamming our ill-gotten gains beneath the passenger seat. The carry case it's in just about fits. She gives it a kick that *really* wedges it home. Satisfied, she joins me in trying to wrestle the rear doors closed.

Jimmy isn't hanging around till we're secure, though. With alarm bells sounding off behind us, our nondescript black van squeals and vibrates as it shoots out into traffic. In the distance, I can already hear the police sirens.

Fuck!

"Jimmy will get us out of here," I mutter, trying to convince myself more than anyone else. "Best wheelman in Chicago."

"This ain't old Chicago anymore, Eddie. He doesn't just gotta worry about the cops now."

She ain't wrong.

Jimmy swings our getaway vehicle violently around the corner onto Canal Street. The rear tires skip on the asphalt as the van threatens to roll over.

Suddenly, we're heading south.

Which is the *wrong* fucking way.

We need to get up to where the city is still being rebuilt after the Kriitani incursion. Pretty much everything north of the Chicago River was flattened. Even now, seven years later, it's still mostly derelict, and the law has a pretty hard time pursuing justice up there.

"What the fuck, Jimmy?" I shout toward the driver's seat.

He just grunts in response.

As we complete the turn in an acrid cloud of tire smoke, I can see why Jimmy *had* to turn us south. There's a big accident at the junction. Multiple cars are involved in a crazy pileup that's completely blocking the other routes. Looks like it happened only moments ago.

Just our fucking luck!

But back to Jimmy, our wheelman. I should probably introduce you properly.

James Wilburn. AKA Jimmy 'The Wheels'. He's the strong silent type. Doesn't say much, but he's the best there is behind a steering wheel. Bar none.

He, Lizzy, and I have been pulling jobs together for years. They're some of my most trusted crew. I wouldn't have contemplated doing this job without them. It's incredibly important in this game to have people you can rely on. People you can trust.

Trust. You might think that's an odd word to use. We are criminals after all.

But it's true, and there's a big reason for it.

You see, we're old-school felons. A dying breed in New Chicago. And we all fucking hate the fucking freaks who are quickly replacing us. Too many new supervillains on the streets these days, each possessing a different superpower. Each with a shortcut to breaking the law. Fucking cheats!

Who needs to meticulously plan a robbery when you can turn invisible and sneak your way in? Or why spend years mastering the subtle art of picking a lock when you can just bust a door off its hinges with superstrength? Or phase through a solid brick wall. There's a kid up in the wastelands with ears like Dumbo who can pick locks without any of the tools Lizzy has to lug around with her.

She hates that.

Hates it because it's fucking lazy. Doesn't require skill or art.

Jimmy, Lizzy, and I... we're all human. No superpowers here. None of us trust those fuckers whose DNA has been twisted and mangled by radiation or experiments. None of us are freaks. The three of us are just as the good Lord intended—good old-fashioned humans. Which is the way it should be. We earned our fucking reputations in this city.

Shitballs!

Talk of the devil and thou shalt appear.

Freaks. But the *noble* kind. Do-gooders.

I'd been hoping to avoid any superhero entanglements, but as Jimmy swerves around the next bend to take us east onto Harrison, I spot them. Two of them. It's like just thinking about freaks seems to summon them out of thin air. They're both strolling down the sidewalk, minding their own business. One of them is eating an ice cream. Raspberry ripple maybe...

If we're lucky, they didn't see us.

Yeah, right, like the speeding black van barreling down the street with its rear doors flapping wildly while being pursued by a trio of NCPD cruisers is going to sneak by unnoticed.

I watch them both take flight, not even exchanging a glance. They just react. Initially, they follow the police, but it doesn't take long for them to overhaul the cruisers and close the gap to the van.

As they draw closer, I recognize them. Both of them.

Of all the fucking supes in the city, we managed to attract two of the highest-profile heroes of them all. Two of the lauded 'Fearless-Four.' They're the heroes who threw a wrench into the Kriitani's invasion plans seven years ago. These two are founding members of the Femme Fatales.

Well, fuck. What did I do to piss off Lady Luck today?

First up and coming in hot, *literally*, there's the black leather-clad tattooed brunette streaking along with a trail of flame behind her. That's Kasai. She's the one who threw the bomb into the Kriitani portal to close it. Stopped the incursion in its tracks. She's a fire wielder. Nothing she likes to do more than throw a fireball or two around.

The woman just behind her, the one in the raspberry and white bodysuit with the candy-floss-colored hair? That's Knightingale. She's primarily known as a healer and telepath, but she's got mad telekinetic skills, too. And don't be fooled by her youth. She's rumored to be the brains of the operation.

Yeah, I might hate freaks, but I make it my business to know the enemy.

Anyhow, the clear message here is that we're royally fucked.

My hand reaches into my pocket, and I feel the smooth shape of the orb, its glass surface cool under my fingertips. I'm trying to figure out how we're going to get out of this mess. Maybe I should just throw this fucking thing at them. I mean, it's been just one piece of bad luck after another since I picked it up. We could *really* do with some of that bad luck rubbing off on the fuckers chasing us.

Maybe it's my imagination, but I swear the smooth glass got hot for a second...

Anyway, all hell breaks loose.

I spot Kasai corkscrewing through the air. Her arm is cocked, winding up to throw a fireball in our direction. It manifests in the palm of her hand, a tumbling globe of flame about the same size as the orb in my pocket.

Jimmy must have seen it in his mirrors because he immediately swerves to take avoiding action. We've just crossed the river, and Jimmy jerks the wheel, turning us abruptly left. He cuts the corner, bouncing us across the curbs, and suddenly we're heading north on Wacker.

Kasai begins to follow suit. She doesn't see the lamppost till it's too late.

With a melodic clang, she clips the black pole with her shoulder at some speed. She ricochets off, crashing heavily into the road. As she tumbles, the fireball she was preparing shoots off in a random direction.

Or maybe not so random.

I'm not sure if it's her bad luck or my good luck, but Knightingale takes the rogue fireball square in the midriff. The impact doubles her up, and she veers off in the opposite direction from Kasai. A moment later she crashes into the trees on the corner we've just rounded, where she temporarily disappears out of sight.

Lizzy is laughing, flipping the fallen heroes the finger, but it's a premature celebration.

Kasai is already on her feet, and I know she's far faster than our old van. I watch her break into a run, and within a few strides, she's airborne again.

And she looks *pissed*.

Knightingale reappears, breaking through the trees and hovering momentarily above them. After a quick re-orientation, she also re-establishes her pursuit. She's not as fast as Kasai, but she has plenty enough speed to catch up with us relatively quickly.

"Fuck!" I mutter under my breath. "Fucking supes."

We've given up trying to close the doors. Both Lizzy and I are now focused on hanging on for grim death as Jimmy's driving throws us around the back of the van. I smash into the side of the van and hear the orb in my pocket clang against the steel.

"Neither of these two are bulletproof, right?" Lizzy shouts.

"Not to my knowledge," I shout back.

Lizzy pulls out a gun from under her jacket. I don't pack heat myself.

Mainly because I live by the criminal philosophy that if I've done my job properly planning the heist, there shouldn't be any need for the use of firearms. I pride myself on getting in and out without any entanglements…

Okay, so that's a bare-faced lie. I don't use guns because I'm a fucking awful shot. I almost shot myself in the foot at a shooting range once. That was enough to put me off for life.

Lizzy, though? She's pretty proficient.

She lines up her SIG Sauer P365 at the rapidly approaching Kasai. I watch as she squeezes the trigger and fires. As the gun goes off, the van door swings closed again. The bullet hits the door and ricochets back into the van. It narrowly misses my head.

It doesn't miss Jimmy's.

I don't hear the bullet hit him, but I do hear it hit the windshield, which is now shattered and stained with my friend's blood and brain matter.

As Jimmy's body slumps to the left, it jerks the wheel. We're just approaching the crossroads of Wacker Drive and Van Buren. The van is now on a course to miss both, angling directly between them. The engine revs painfully without Jimmy's deft right foot controlling it, and we pick up speed at an alarming rate. A split second later, the van smashes into a bunch of roadworks.

And we're airborne.

The Ford starts to corkscrew as it flies through the air, over the russet-colored steelwork of the bridge. We land upside down in the Chicago River with an almighty splash, and with the doors still ajar, we're immediately sinking, water flooding in fast.

Too fast.

The impact throws me against the van's roof. For a moment, I'm dazed. Confused.

I try to get out of the back of the van, but the inrushing water is fighting me. I'm disorientated, suddenly unsure what is up and what is down. I can feel the van flipping over in the water as it sinks, but I can't track the orientation. I feel like a sock in a tumble dryer.

I sense the van settle as it hits the bottom. It's dark, and my lungs are screaming at me. I never got a chance to draw a breath before hitting the water. Desperately, I stretch out with my arms, trying to figure out where I am in relation to the doors.

I can feel the seats of the cabin above me.

Windows to either side.

Fuck!

I swim down, searching, and find the van doors now finally closed.

Fuck!!!

How on earth could my luck get any shitting worse? Somehow the fucking van has hit the riverbed and is balancing on its rear end. The doors we couldn't get closed earlier are now firmly wedged shut.

I swim up, searching for the driver's door. The van is full of water now, and the pressure equalized. It should be easy to open the door. But all I find is Jimmy's body blocking my way. I can't move him. Motherfucker has his seatbelt on. I scrabble for it but can't find it with frozen hands in the dark.

As my lungs burn, I move for the passenger door, but I'm blocked again. Another body.

Lizzy.

She's dead. Just like Jimmy.

And I'm gonna be next.

But then I feel the van move. Or rather, I can sense it because I start to drift down toward the rear doors. The progress is slow at first, but it starts to pick up speed. It's rising through the water.

How is this possible? They couldn't have got a crane here this fast. Could they?

I can't hold my breath anymore. I fight the urge, but I can't help it. I breathe in. There's no air, just the dirty river water. It floods into my lungs.

This is it.

Felons and Freaks

I shudder and convulse uncontrollably as the van breaks the surface. I briefly see sunlight streaming in through the splintered windshield before everything goes black.

I'm not sure for how long. I have no concept of the time I was gone, but the next thing I know, I'm coughing and spluttering and looking up into the dazzling emerald eyes of a woman with pink hair.

It takes a minute for my brain to get out of neutral and start to put the pieces of the puzzle together.

Knightingale.

"It's okay," she says to me. Her voice is soft. Kind. British. "You're going to be fine."

She holds her hands over my chest, and I watch as a green glow spreads from her palms and travels across my sodden body. It feels warm. Wonderful. I take a deep breath and smile.

I'm alive.

"Yes, you're alive." Another British voice, but this one has an accent I can't place. "And you're fucking lucky. If Gale hadn't been here to pluck your van out of the river and heal your delinquent arse, you'd be lying in a body-bag next to your friends."

Kasai. Her voice has a much harder edge than her companion's. Still, she's seemingly not without compassion. I can feel her warmth drying out my soaking wet clothes.

I turn my head to the side, and I can see the crumpled wreckage of the van sitting on its ruined wheels. My addled brain starts to put two and two together.

Knightingale lifted the van from the river telekinetically.

Then she healed me. Brought me back from the brink of death.

"What now?" I rasp, my throat raw.

"Now," Kasai says flatly, "you're going to be arrested."

* * *

Just as I'm finishing up with my heist tale, the door bursts open. Finally! A couple of faces I know. I breathe a sigh of relief but try not to show it.

"Thank fuck!" I mutter under my breath.

Yeah. That might have given it away.

The first guy to push through the doorway is Detective Stabilos. He's like the anti-Bruneau. He's everything the cop sitting across the table from me isn't. Short, overweight, and managing to make the expensive suit he's wearing look like a crumpled hand-me-down. I know him well.

Everyone who works for Gray Corp does.

He's a cop on the take. A Gray Corp fixer.

Allegedly.

There's *never* anything that connects him directly to his puppet masters in the gray suits. But we all know that if you've got a problem with the law, he's the man who can make that shit disappear. The look on the faces of the two freak show goons tells me they know his reputation, too. Not that they can do anything about it.

Stabilos fixes me with a look as he walks past.

A look that says, "Shut the fuck up before you say anything really stupid."

Honestly? It might be a little late for that.

The chick with him is Alisa Watkins from one of New Chicago's premier law firms, Madison, Stone, and Watkins. She's one of Gray Corp's lawyers, one of those classy bitches who looks every bit as expensive as she costs. Her suit *definitely* did not come off the rack. It's bespoke. Tailored to her trim gym-rat figure. The blouse is silk, and the shoes are Jimmy Choos. Probably. Not that I know what Jimmy Choos look like, but it's the only expensive brand I know, so let's roll with it, yes?

She's carrying a gleaming black leather monogrammed briefcase in one hand and a drinks holder in the other with two Starbucks cups from which wafts the odor of strong coffee.

It's Watts who gets up first. "Excuse me, we're conducting an interview—"

"An interview that shouldn't be happening at all without my client having suitable legal counsel," Watkins interrupts.

"We're not interviewing Mr. Tyler about the crime itself," Watts continues.

"Alleged crime," Watkins interjects.

Watts ignores her. "We're here because, during the escape, there were a series of unexplained events—"

Felons and Freaks

"That's irrelevant." Watkins shakes her head as she places the coffees gently onto the table. "Let me be totally clear. My client will *not* be answering any more of your questions on the advice of his legal counsel. Me."

Watts is about to make another rebuttal, I can see it dancing on the tip of her tongue, but Bruneau stands up and gets in first. You can tell by the look on his face that he ain't happy, but he's also smart enough to know that the jig is up.

"We're done here. For now," he says. His voice is deep. There's a hint of threat as his eyes flick toward Stabilos. Clearly, no love lost there. "But he doesn't leave here till we're done with him. Is that clear, Detective?"

Stabilos shrugs noncommittally. Honestly, I'm not sure what the hierarchy is here.

"Take it up with the Captain, Bruneau," he shoots back with a snort.

"Don't worry. We will," Watts responds.

Yeah, these guys have definitely either clashed or fucked before, and as both Bruneau and Watts look very much out of Stabilos' league, I'm putting money on the former.

Bruneau carefully puts the lid back on the shoebox, covering that fucking orb. He picks it up, and he and his partner vacate the room without another word.

Stabilos turns to Watkins.

"You need some privacy?" he growls while running his fingers through his greasy hair.

"Please." Watkins nods and sits down in the chair Watts just vacated.

The detective grunts and heads out of the room as the lawyer removes the coffees from their holder. One for her and one for me, I assume, though I can't reach mine due to the cuffs.

"So, Mr. Tyler, did you say anything about the purpose of your job?"

She doesn't beat around the bush. Time is money with people like her. Fuck knows what this is costing the company.

I shake my head. "No. Those two were more interested in the escape and that shiny fucking bauble."

"Good." She nods.

I suspect that Stabilos had been able to keep the regular cops off my back until Watkins arrived, but there wasn't much he could do about Bruneau and Watts. NCPD-SCU has their own jurisdiction, you see. He probably didn't even know they were coming till they arrived.

"Did you manage to obtain the item our employers requested?"

This time it's my turn to nod. I lean forward across the desk, my voice dropping to a conspiratorial whisper. "It's in the van, in a small case secured under the passenger's seat. I imagine they'll need to tow it back here to the impound."

"It's already here," Watkins says flatly. "I checked. It's not been searched yet."

"Good. That's good." I'm relieved.

"I'll tell Stabilos to retrieve the item. Though, if it's water damaged after your little swim in the Chicago River—"

"It's fine. The case is waterproof."

"Okay, then." Watkins looks pleased.

"What about me?" I ask. "Can you get me out of here?"

She leans back in her chair and takes a sip of her coffee. Her eyes flit toward the other cup, which she pushes across the table till I can reach it. Eagerly, I cradle it in my hands and take a long slurp of the warm liquid. I sigh a little as the bittersweet hits my taste buds. I've always loved a decent coffee. This isn't it, but beggars can't be choosers.

"Don't worry about any of that." Watkins smiles at me. It's not a warm smile. Not at all. In fact, it gives me a chill as I look down at the coffee cup I've just sipped from. "Gray Corp will ensure that you're taken care of."

My hand tingles. A warm feeling spreads up my arm, starting at my fingertips.

My eyes dart toward the coffee cup in Watkins's hand.

I smile.

Maybe I don't have the M-Gene in my genetic makeup. Maybe it doesn't matter. Maybe you *can* get special gifts in a totally different way.

And maybe, just maybe, my luck is about to change for the better.

ABOUT THE AUTHOR

Jon Ford lives in Worcestershire, UK.

He lives with his awesome Wifey, their loveable puppy, Vixen, and their demonic hell-hound, Lyssa. All of them under the watchful eye of their cat-overlords Lana and Gale.

Currently writing two series of books.

The Ballad of the Songbird is an urban fantasy saga with sci-fi overtones. It was the winner of a 2023 Queer Indie award. Hunters, Blood to Earth, and Tooth & Claw are the first three of a planned seven book series. The fourth, DragonSong, is due out late 2025.

The Femme Fatales is a sci-fi superhero series in the form of novels and tie in character novellas. The first novel, The Scorched Sky, came out in 2023 and was followed quickly by the first novella, Knightingale. The next book, The Broken Ground, is due out early 2025 and will release alongside the next novella, Kasai.

To find out more about either series—and for my other random musings—please visit my website: www.JonFordAuthor.com

You can also find me on the various social medias.

X (we all know it's still called Twitter really!): @_Knightingale_

Instagram (this one is jointly run by myself and my wife: JonFordAuthor

TikTok: @Knightingale71

Facebook: Jon Ford – Author

Feel free to look me up and say hi!

Promotion Day

Kayla Hicks

"Are you excited for today?" Regina asked, her blue eyes peering over the cubicle's gray divider.

Turning to face Regina, Todd smiled. "I am."

Regina scooted her chair backward across the rubbery floor mat, the wheels squeaking as they went. "The first one to get the new bonus. You're the office big shot right now."

"What do you think it could be?" Todd asked.

"Not sure. A coveted parking spot, a raise, an employee of the month award…" Regina pondered aloud. "But you deserve it the most, having been here ten years. As soon as Becky heard, she started calculating how long she'd been here in case it was a ten-year milestone or something."

"I'm not sure about that," Todd countered.

"Oh, stop it," Regina scoffed, waving her perfectly manicured hand in Todd's direction. "We work hard crunching these numbers, often working overtime to make deadlines. They can spare some good things our way. I just can't believe it took them so long to do it."

"Eh, it may have been the mini strike that was thrown two weeks ago when they made us work until midnight on Christmas Eve," Todd responded, his dark eyes searching their surroundings for any eavesdroppers.

"Very true," Regina said. "When is your meeting again?"

"At ten."

"Okay, you'll have to tell me all about it at lunch. And I better not open my lunch box to find any surprises in there this time."

"Come on!" Todd chided. "You loved that rubber snake. I haven't pulled any pranks on your lunch in a long time."

"Exactly why I said what I said. It's a big day for you, so I thought you might try to sweeten the pie."

"Todd Triffin?" a woman's voice called from the other side of the room.

Regina and Todd exchanged puzzled looks before Todd rose from his chair, raising his hand.

Across the room stood a woman dressed in a white blouse and gray pencil skirt with red-framed glasses perched on the end of her nose.

"Come with me, please," she instructed, her look expectant.

Todd offered a small nod in response before making his way around the cubicles toward the aisle that led to the exit of the large room.

"Hello," Todd greeted her. "I have a meeting in an hour with—"

"Oh, I'm aware," the woman responded as she spun around and began walking down the short hallway lined with a few executive offices. "That's precisely why I'm here. Your meeting was moved up."

Todd remained silent as he followed the woman to the end of the hall and into the glass elevator, which rose to the third floor.

"I thought I was meeting with Harken?" Todd questioned.

"He called in sick today, so you will be meeting with the CEO," the woman responded curtly.

Stepping out of the elevator, the woman led Todd across the glass-encased bridge joining the two business buildings at Hewett Incorporated, her low heels making dull thuds with each hurried step on the thin black carpet.

Todd's heart hammered in his chest so loudly that he swore the woman heard it, proved moments later by the loud sigh she emitted as she turned the corner.

"Please relax, Mr. Triffin," the woman commented. "This meeting is a good thing for you. After all, you have been an exemplary employee for ten years. It's well deserved."

"Thank you," Todd mumbled.

The woman led Todd to a final staircase crafted from light-colored concrete and adorned with dark carpeting at its base. At the top, a shimmering rock waterfall cast a spellbinding allure.

"Walk up the staircase," the woman instructed, her pointer finger gesturing. "His door is the only one up there."

Without another word, the woman quickly pivoted and headed to the right, disappearing around the marble-walled corner to go and be vague with someone else.

Todd took a deep, shaky breath and placed his foot on the staircase, his footfall sending a soft echo around the large room.

No one in his division had ever met the CEO before. Todd's division was a small budgeting sector that handled the foreign accounts for the company, meaning they dealt with the numbers and then sent memos and reports to their managers and similar departments. Not important enough to meet with the CEO by anyone's standards.

When Todd reached the top of the staircase, he looked left and right before he saw a large oak door to his right, a golden nameplate with CEO: David Cross beside it.

Worried he'd stumble and make a fool of himself, Todd approached the door. His hand, trembling and slick with sweat, hovered before him before he mustered the courage to knock twice.

"Enter," a commanding voice stated.

Todd opened the door, immediately shielding his eyes from the blinding light inside.

"Close the door," the commanding voice instructed.

* * *

"Have you seen Todd?" asked Regina, standing just beyond Becky's chair.

"Todd?" Becky questioned, her blonde bob swaying as she turned to face Regina. "I'm sorry, I don't know who that is."

Regina paused. "Becky, you helped me throw his twenty-ninth birthday party a few months ago."

Becky shook her head, her eyebrows pinching with confusion. "I'm sorry,

Felons and Freaks

you must have me confused with another Becky."

Regina slowly walked back to her desk, feeling uneasy after her conversation with Becky. Maybe Todd was playing a trick on her. He was known to do so from time to time. Like the time he'd told her they had an after-work meeting and secretly gathered the employees from their division for an impromptu barbecue. But it was strange that he'd disappeared for the rest of the day yesterday and hadn't returned any of her text messages.

"Hi, Becky," a male voice said from Regina's left. "New haircut?"

Regina booted up her computer, its harsh whooshing sound adding to her irritation.

"Hi, Regina," the same male voice said to Regina.

Regina turned right to say hello when she saw a stranger pulling out Todd's chair and taking a seat.

"Um, that cubicle is taken," Regina stated. "By Todd Triffin."

The man scooted backward until he was facing Regina, his perfectly combed black hair and crisp suit everything Todd wasn't.

"This has been my cubicle for a while now," the man said. "It belongs to me—Chris. Wait, is this like the prank you played on me last week? You told me I had to rush back because my cat needed rescuing from the tree in my backyard… except that I don't have a cat."

"No," Regina replied. "That didn't happen."

"Let me get you some coffee from the break room," Chris offered. "That always cheers you up. Just one of those days, I guess."

Chris wandered away with a relaxed smile on his face, leaving Regina more perplexed than before, causing her to stand and head toward her manager's office.

Walking around the cubicles, Regina made her way toward the exit hallway but stopped in front of her manager's door, surprised that it was closed.

Raising her hand, she knocked sharply twice before a woman's voice called out for her to enter.

Regina opened the thin gray door to see the woman who'd called Todd over yesterday sitting behind the black desk instead of her manager, Harken. Her red curly hair was pulled into a ponytail, and she was dressed in a black business dress and bright red heels.

"Yes, Ms. Urban?" the woman asked, peering up from a stack of documents laid out on the desk.

"Where's Harken?" Regina asked, looking around the room to see Harken's children's photos removed as well as the hand drawing of four stick figures his son had made of their family.

"Please close the door, Ms. Urban," the woman stated, folding her hands together on top of the open document she'd been looking at.

Regina did as she was asked, then turned back to face the woman for an explanation.

"Feel free to take a seat," the woman said, gesturing to the metal chair with thin red padding on the opposite side of the desk.

"I'm fine, thanks."

The woman's lips formed a tight smile, only just big enough to appear friendly. "I'm afraid to tell you that the company has let Harken go."

"Why? He's been here for thirty years."

"Well, after the strike, the CEO thought that this sector needed a firmer hand, so he has placed me in Harken's position."

"I see," Regina stated, feeling as if the rug had been ripped from underneath her.

"I'm sorry to have to relay this information, but we were going to announce it later today," the woman continued. "But from what I see in your file, you are a great employee. I think we'll get along just fine. I'm Sarah Hoffman."

"Did Todd Triffin call in sick today?" Regina asked, remembering the real reason she'd come here in the first place.

"No, I don't think so," Sarah said. "But then again, I don't think a Todd Triffin works here. I haven't seen him in any of these files."

Regina's thoughts swirled at the new information. Her forehead was suddenly sticky with sweat, and she reached out with a shaky hand to grab the back of the metal chair to steady her before she took a seat.

"Is something the matter?" Sarah asked, her previous smile forming into a frown.

"Um… yes. Yesterday, Todd Triffin, who has been here ten years, went with you to receive some sort of bonus, and I haven't seen him since."

Sarah's frown deepened before she leaned back in her chair. "I think I would remember if something like that occurred. If you aren't feeling well, you can go home for the day. You're looking quite pale."

"Uh… okay. I think I'll do that," Regina conceded.

Rising from the chair, she stepped out of the office, heading back to her cubicle to grab her items.

"Got you that coffee!" Chris chippered on as he heard her approach, his smile beaming with pride before slowly receding as he took in her appearance. "Whoa, are you okay? You look pale."

Without a word, Regina collected her purse and coat and headed for the exit.

Once in the parking lot, Regina pulled out her phone and tried to call Todd's number. This time, she received the notice, '*The number you have reached is no longer in service.*'

Her heels began to ache as she stomped in her blue high heels toward her car in frustration, a sharp pain becoming increasingly noticeable with each step. She reached for the door handle with a shaking hand but froze when her eyes fixated on the red sedan parked in the corner of the parking lot, a baseball player bobble-headed figure sitting on the dash.

Todd's car.

Running over to his car, she tried the handle to find it unlocked and searched inside for any clues as to where Todd was. But there was nothing, and popping the trunk didn't reveal anything either.

Moving back to the front of the car, Regina hastily opened the glove compartment to find Todd's registration and insurance, nearly crying with relief at having found evidence of his existence.

This had to be enough evidence to prove there was a Todd.

Feeling surer than anything, Regina pulled out her phone again and called 911, hoping the police could get some answers.

Regina waited fifteen long minutes before a squad car arrived and a young officer stepped out of the vehicle.

"Are you Regina Urban?" the officer asked.

"I am."

"You want to report a missing person? A Todd Triffin?"

"Yes," Regina replied. "See, he was at work yesterday and never returned from a meeting, and he hasn't returned any of my calls. And then when I came into the office today, no one else remembered him. At first, I thought I was imagining things, but when I came out to leave in my car, I saw his car sitting there. I checked the car to see if he was in it, but it was empty. I did manage to grab his insurance and registration, though."

Regina handed over the paperwork, feeling hopeful.

"Miss, were you in a romantic relationship with this coworker, Todd Triffin, and did he try to end it?" the officer asked.

"What?!" Regina exclaimed in surprise. "No, absolutely not. We've worked together for five years now, he's just a friend. Why would you say that?"

"Romantic relationships in the workplace are fairly common, and when they go wrong, it can be awkward for all involved. And if that were the case, Mr. Triffin could have been avoiding harassment."

Regina's cheeks flooded with warmth at the accusation. "No, that's not the case whatsoever."

"Very well, let me run these through my system and see what we can pull up," the officer stated before returning to his vehicle.

Regina leaned back against Todd's vehicle, feeling the cold metal through her blue dress, and released a pent-up breath, hopeful that this would lead to Todd's disappearance.

After five to ten minutes, the officer returned, and his mouth formed into a hard line. "Ms. Urban. It would seem that Todd Triffin has been dead for ten years now. I'm actually not sure why his vehicle is still here."

"No, that can't be right," Regina stammered in disbelief. "He's worked here at Hewett Incorporated for ten years!!"

"I'm sorry to tell you this, but my records show that he's deceased. I'll call someone to have his vehicle towed," the officer explained. "Would you like me to call someone for you?"

"No… I'm fine," Regina said.

"Dispatch, this is Officer Cowen. I need a tow truck here at Hewett Incorporated for a deceased person," the officer said into his radio as Regina slowly wandered back toward her car.

This can't be right, Regina thought. *Maybe he's at home.*

Regina started the engine of her car with a newfound sense of purpose and set off toward Todd's house.

Nestled on the outskirts of town, his small condo was a remnant of his brief marriage to Donna, his high school sweetheart. Donna, sweet but restless, had sought greater pursuits, none of which included Todd.

Todd was probably sitting on his couch, more than likely accompanied by his faithful companion, a small dog called Gunther. Regina had been to the condo a few times to help him move furniture and let Gunther out when Todd had gone to visit a relative last summer.

For the entire drive over, all Regina could think about was how a person could just disappear and no one remembered him. It was unimaginable. To be simply erased.

When Regina slowly drove along the quiet street lined with identical condominiums, her heart sank a little when she saw a blue vehicle sitting in the driveway and a heart-shaped wreath hung on the white front door.

Easing her car to a stop near the curb, Regina put it in park, shut off the engine, and paused. Everything inside her screamed that this wasn't right, that something was off. However, she tried to push the thoughts aside as she exited her vehicle and walked on unsteady legs up the driveway, past the blue vehicle, and onto the front stoop.

Taking a deep breath, a cloud of warm air appearing before her, she raised her finger and pressed the doorbell.

The sound of a dog barking sparked new hope as she waited for Todd to open the door and tell her he was just sick and that this had all been some elaborate hoax. Instead, the door swung open to reveal a little tan Gunther barking beside a smiling Donna.

"Hi, can I help you?" Donna asked.

"Donna? Did you and Todd get back together?"

"Uh... I'm sorry, have we met before?" Donna asked, tucking a lock of brown hair behind her ear.

"Yes, I—"

"Who's at the door, Donna?" a male voice asked.

A tall man appeared in the doorway. His blonde hair was a little unkept, but his outfit, a tucked button-down and slacks, was professional.

"I'm not sure, exactly," Donna replied, her gaze swiveling back to Regina with confusion.

"I apologize, I must have the wrong house," Regina stammered. "Have a wonderful day."

Not wanting to provide any further opportunity for Donna to question her, Regina quickly made her way back to her vehicle, driving away from the quiet street before she pulled over to the side of the road and stopped the car.

Gripping the wheel tightly only made the shaking in her hands extend to the rest of her body as she tried to wrap her head around her current predicament.

Todd was gone. And there was no getting him back and no one to explain his disappearance.

The last thing Regina knew, he'd gone to meet with Harken. But Harken was gone now, so she couldn't talk to him either. Who else would remember Todd?

"What about Bobby?" Regina said aloud in the silence of the car.

Knowing that this was her last shot at finding Todd, Regina pulled back onto the road and headed in the direction of the highway that would take her back to Hewett Incorporated. Back to Bobby, the security guard, whom Todd knew well.

Even if he didn't remember Todd, Regina could come up with something to get a look at the security cameras.

* * *

It was nearly lunchtime when Regina re-entered the Hewett Incorporated parking lot. Half the cars were gone, likely from employees going out for lunch. Regina managed to find a parking space close by and hurried toward the entrance, feeling her frantic heart pound against her lungs.

Stepping through the revolving door, Regina's gaze scoured the well-lit lobby, its lights reflected on the marble flooring. The receptionist's back was turned as she stirred a cup of coffee at a small coffee station behind the desk.

All the while, Regina tried to think what floors she'd seen Bobby patrolling, remembering she'd met him somewhere unfamiliar.

The third floor.

Trying to appear casual despite her uneasy state, Regina walked at a near-normal pace across the lobby floor toward the elevator, her heels clacking across the smooth surface.

As the shiny metal elevator doors parted, several suited employees spilled out, ready to head out for lunch. Regina stepped into the now vacant space, pressing the third-floor button as the doors slid closed.

Taking deep breaths as she prepared her story, she stared at her smeared reflection in the metal of the doors. She was indeed pale, which would help add authenticity to any story she concocted to get into that security room.

A gentle rocking motion signaled the elevator's stop, followed by the doors gliding silently open, revealing an upscale side of the office. The hall was filled with lush green plants planted in marble vases and painted portraits of high-ranking employees, none of whom she'd ever met.

The canned lighting above bathed the elegant setting in a dim light. And as Regina peered up and down the hallway, she felt uncomfortably lonely in the silence surrounding her.

Slowly turning in a circle, she tried to remember where the security office was on this floor, feeling nothing but utterly lost.

"Can I help you?" a voice asked from behind her.

Regina spun around and nearly cried out with relief when she came face to face with the man she was trying to find—Bobby.

"Oh, thank goodness!" Regina sighed. "I was looking for the security office, but I wasn't sure where it was."

"Do you work here, ma'am?" Bobby asked, his hands resting on his belt as he squinted in her direction.

"Yes, I do, on the second floor," Regina explained, trying to think on her feet. "You see, I have a huge problem. One that could get me fired."

"I'm not exactly sure I can help you with that," Bobby said, reaching up to scratch the small patch of stubble on his chin.

"You see, I went to get some coffee and we were out of filters, and someone said I could come to the coffee station on this floor and get more. They had done it before or something. Anyway, when I went to get the coffee filters, I placed my annual report on the counter, and someone from this floor must have grabbed it."

"I still don't see how this involves me."

Regina could feel tears spring free as her half-assed plan fell apart in front of her. "You see, I was supposed to deliver that today by five, and it went missing yesterday when someone else accidentally grabbed it. I was… I was hoping you could let me look at the security feed from yesterday to see who took it?"

Bobby stepped closer, placing a hand on her shoulder. Confliction was clear on his face as he shifted on his feet and looked around them for any bystanders.

"I'm sorry," Regina stammered through her tears. "I shouldn't have asked.

Just pretend this didn't happen."

"No... I just..." Bobby began. "All right. You can look quick, but in and out. I could get in trouble for this."

"Are you sure?"

Bobby sighed and nodded curtly. "Follow me."

Bobby led her down the left side of the hallway and around the corner to a gray door that read *Security* in gold lettering. Swiping his keycard, he unlocked the door and ushered her into a small room.

"You said yesterday on this floor?" Bobby asked, typing on the keyboard. "What time?"

"Around nine am."

A sharp knock on the door caused them to freeze, both of their gazes sliding to the door in fear it would open.

"I'll see who that is. Look through the feed here—and do it quick," Bobby instructed.

Rising from the chair, he cracked the door open and stepped out into the hallway. A woman's voice could be heard just outside the door.

Regina immediately took a seat and began searching for the feeds of the second-floor cameras in the office hallways. She paused the feed when she saw Sarah Hoffman walking down a corridor in a white blouse and a pencil skirt with glasses.

Fast-forwarding the feed, she saw Sarah walking away with Todd toward the elevator.

"Where are you going?" Regina mumbled.

"I'm about to do my rounds, and then I can come down for a meeting," Bobby said from the other side of the door.

"One more thing," the woman said.

Taking a deep breath to steady her nerves, Regina clicked through the cameras on other floors until she saw Sarah and Todd appear on the third-floor camera feed. They were coming from the right side of the hallway.

"Where is this?" Regina mumbled.

Sarah said something to Todd and pointed forward before walking away from the camera and disappearing.

Todd placed a foot on the first step before gradually climbing the staircase and out of sight.

Clicking out of the camera feed, Regina frantically searched through the feed icons as she heard the swipe of Bobby's keycard, finally finding what she needed and clicking on the correct icon.

Regina was on her feet and making a show of wiping away tears when Bobby opened the door.

"Thank you," Regina whispered.

Bobby nodded and opened the door to let her exit.

"I won't forget this," Regina said, giving Bobby a meaningful look.

"Don't mention it. I hope you find what you're looking for," Bobby said. "If you'll excuse me, I need to start my rounds."

As Bobby headed off in the opposite direction, Regina took her opportunity to find where Todd had gone.

Heading back the way Bobby had led her, she wandered quietly down the hall, her head on a constant swivel for any potential bystander or sound. Passing the elevator, she moved around the corner at the other end of the hallway and found herself facing a long white hallway with doors on either side. At the other end of the hall, however, it looked like the space opened up into a larger area.

Moving quickly through the hallway, she heard occasional mumbles from behind closed doors, but otherwise, the space felt vacant.

As Regina neared the larger space at the end, trickling water could be heard from somewhere beyond her field of view.

"Yes, I will have them to you right away," a woman's voice stated.

Lightly placing her hands on the corner of the wall, Regina leaned forward ever so slightly, peering around the corner to see Sarah Hoffman standing alone, her phone held to her ear. She was standing in the middle of a wide area with dark carpeted floors and a set of concrete stairs that led up to the source of the sound of trickling water.

"The two problems we had yesterday have been taken care of, and I'm currently working on the third. It won't be long until we have a clean slate," Sarah continued before she started walking away, her footfalls but light thuds against the carpet.

Once Sarah was out of sight, Regina rechecked her surroundings before stepping out of the hallway and into the open space, the sound of trickling water louder as it echoed around the room.

Regina took in her surroundings, her eyes searching the ceiling for the camera that had shown her where Todd was in yesterday's feed. Thankfully, she spotted it down a short walkway about twenty feet away, tucked in the corner.

Trying to stand where she'd previously seen Sarah and Todd stand, she found herself positioned between a set of stairs coming from a bridge encased in glass that branched the two buildings together and a set of concrete stairs leading up to a trickling, shimmering rock waterfall at the top

Now or never.

Regina climbed the concrete staircase as quietly as she could, trying to keep her heels from clacking on the stairs as she went.

Stopping at the top, Regina looked left and right. She saw wood paneling covering the walls surrounding the shimmering rock waterfall and a single large oak door to her right with a golden nameplate reading *CEO: David Cross* beside it.

Todd had been asked to see the CEO, and then he disappeared. Unless he got a huge promotion no one is supposed to talk about it yet.

A muffled thud reverberated from behind the door, igniting Regina's curiosity and urging her to investigate further. Stepping closer, she positioned herself directly in front of the door, pressing her ear against the cool wood grain.

Another thud echoed from behind the door, causing her to jump back in surprise, her hands instinctively flying up to stifle the gasp that escaped her lips.

Suddenly, the door began to creak open, each agonizing inch accompanied by more and more blinding light from within that spilled over Regina.

"If you plan to snoop, you might as well see what's inside," a male voice stated from somewhere within.

Regina's body froze with fright, her feet unwilling to propel her forward into the unknown.

No one had ever met the CEO, and no one spoke of him. If Todd had gone to meet him, it had to be serious. And now he was telling Regina to come inside because he had caught her snooping.

Am I going to disappear too?

"Regina? Go!" Todd's voice called out.

"Todd?" Regina asked, lifting a hand to shield her eyes from the bright light.

Wanting to see Todd, she stepped forward until she was in the room. The large door closed with a loud thud behind her as the lock set in place.

Regina tried to look around the room, but everything was too bright, causing her eyes to tear up with pain.

"Todd, where are you?" Regina asked.

"Silly girl," the male voice said. "Snooping where you shouldn't have been! Time to remedy that!"

Regina felt something large and warm wrap around her waist, lifting her into the air.

"Put me down!" Regina screamed as she balled her hands into fists and pounded at whatever held her.

Prying her eyes open ever so slightly, Regina caught a glimpse of a giant tentacle wrapped around her, its large blue underbelly suction cups gripping her with something slimy.

More tears sprang free as the blinding light continued to sting her eyes, causing her to clam them shut once more.

"What have you done with Todd?!" Regina begged.

"Todd has given his ten years to the company, so it was time he served his higher purpose," the voice explained. "But it would seem that our memory swipe worked on everyone but you, so you will be serving your higher purpose early."

A rumble sounded in front of her, shaking her from head to toe. Prying her eyes open once more to try to see her surroundings, she found the source of the blinding light—and the giant tentacled arm—was a huge white orb in the corner of the large room. And with every second, Regina was being pulled closer.

Feeling dread pool in her stomach, Regina leaned down and bit the tentacled extension, drawing a purple liquid from it and causing the creature to cry out in agony, loosening its grip enough for Regina to wriggle free.

Regina plummeted to the ground, landing hard on a mahogany desk, causing the wind to be knocked out of her.

Gasping for breath, she rolled off the desk and onto the floor, which was covered with something sharp. Opening her eyes to a squint revealed thousands of bones of various sizes piled on the floor.

"Oh my God!" Regina screamed, rising to her feet as she tried to scurry through the debris to the door.

"Not so fast!" the voice screamed louder than ever, shaking the room, the bones rattling on the ground.

Regina lunged forward, her fingertips brushing the door handle before a tentacle wrapped itself around her ankle, throwing her off balance and down to the ground.

Quicker than Regina could react, she was being dragged backward across the debris, her hands scrambling for anything to hold onto. When she was just inches away from the white orb, she managed to grab the back leg of the desk, crying out as the tentacle pulled harder, making Regina's shoulders and arms scream in pain.

With one final tug, Regina's grip slipped, causing her to hit her head on the ground before the tentacle pulled her up and into the bright white orb.

ABOUT THE AUTHOR

Kayla Hicks is mostly known for The Backup Superhero series, but she is a multi-genre author with works also in Young Adult Dystopian, Contemporary Romance, Horror, and Children's literature.

To find out more about Kayla Hicks visit: kayla-hicks.com/

August Shaw and The Orb of Destruction

Alex Minns

The six stood equidistant around the plinth. Their eyes flicked between each other and the object of their desire. The golden orb sat on its throne in the centre of the subterranean hall.

August Shaw, or Shade as he was known in sidekick circles, looked to his left. Todd stood rigid. He wasn't necessarily a man of action, but he wasn't afraid to get his hands dirty and was by far the slyest of the group. His shirt sleeves had been rolled up: that was never a good sign. His face looked paler than usual in the flickering glow of the wall sconces.

Todd's eyes were firmly fixed on Sandra, or was it Rita? It really was hard to keep track of who was in control of Sandra's body – the plucky girl detective or her demonic roommate that lived rent-free in her brain? In the low light and this far away, Shade couldn't see what colour her eyes were. Rita or Sandra – he never could tell – was Todd's off again, on again flame.

But today, her interest didn't lie with Todd. Instead, she was looking around the room, a frown creasing her usually sunny features. She tugged down on her blue cardigan before pushing her glasses back up her nose.

"Does something seem off about this to you chaps?"

"I'm not falling for that one!" Godley flicked his cape out behind him for effect. "You're just trying to get the orb for yourself."

"Yeah!" Harix stomped his foot in agreement, making the entire chamber shudder. They all paused for a moment to check the orb wasn't about to fall.

"Godley, dear heart, we both work for heroes. We are on the same side trying to stop that lot from stealing it." She pointed dismissively in Shade's general vicinity.

"I feel like we should be offended," Todd muttered to Shade.

"She's right!" Harix yelled again, turning towards Shade and Todd.

"She's right about me, you twit. You work for a bad guy, remember? Well, you did." Godley put his hands on his hips, fluffing out his cape as he did, which Shade thought looked ridiculous. Not that he had an outfit. His boss, Balthazar, wasn't really strict about all that; he wasn't really strict about anything.

"You don't have a boss either." Harix rounded on Godley.

"He's going to come back!" Godley tried to square off against Harix, but his head didn't even draw level with the beast of a man's armpit.

"Guys!" Sandra snapped, her voice starting to waver. "Focus. The writing, it's all gibberish." She pointed at the runes circling the plinth, painted in a suspiciously blood-red substance.

Shade didn't recognise the writing. Balthazar was as lax in training as he was in providing uniform. It wasn't surprising, really, considering his status as a bad guy. Every time he and Shade tried to carry out an evil deed, it went wrong. Attempt any heist, they end up thwarting someone else's; kidnap someone, end up saving their life; try to take over the City, end up improving all public transport for residents.

He still wasn't sure how that last one had come about, but no one really seemed to mind, not even the Syndicate, the ruling council of baddies. It hadn't stopped them from sending an improvement notice.

But this job couldn't fail: he had to get that orb.

It was a shame Balthazar was currently tied up on one of the upper levels after getting caught in an angel trap. In fact, none of their bosses had made it this far; only sidekicks had made it to the final chamber.

Now the friends all stood facing off against each other, failure not an option for any of them. This was really going to put a dampener on the next RPG night.

"Todd. You know I'm never wrong about these things." Sandra glowered at him, and Shade could hear the others take an audible breath.

Todd's jaw flexed nervously. "True. But I also know you're good at misdirection too."

"You sod." Rage took over her features as Rita took control. Cinco, stood between Todd and Sandra/Rita, started beeping erratically as her defence systems came online.

Harix leapt into the air, arms lifted high. Godley attempted a forward roll but got tangled in his cape. Rita's hands twisted into claws as she homed in on Todd.

"Oh crap." Shade muttered.

Then all hell broke loose.

2 hours earlier.

"If you could just pop through there." Balthazar pointed at the brick wall and smiled encouragingly.

He stood a good foot taller than Shade and was always immaculately dressed. His long velvet coat hung off his frame like a cloak, billowing out at the waist despite his hands being clasped behind his back. His hair was slicked back and ended just shy of his shoulders. Shade had asked long ago if he'd ever met Anne Rice, but he'd just looked at him blankly.

Shade took a deep breath and looked back at the wall. Getting into the building had been easy. It was an old Victorian edifice where two levels of converted offices hid the secret lower levels and a multitude of sins, including a hidden level that supposedly had no stair access. Shade was certain there were stairs somewhere, but sending him ahead was just quicker, and Balthazar did love cutting corners. The wall looked sturdy and thick.

"What's behind there?"

"A room, one would expect."

"I thought your source gave you plans of the place?"

"Did I say plans?"

"Yes."

"More of a gist of the layout. You'll be fine, just pop on through and…" He made a popping gesture with his hand towards the wall and grinned.

"If this is like that Tuscan vault…" Shade shuddered, remembering the ten-foot-thick wall he'd had to navigate through.

"Would I do that to you again?" Balthazar looked hurt, and Shade believed him. Balthazar was never knowingly unkind; he had saved him, after all. He was, however, a bit lame.

"Not on purpose."

Shade focused and let the air leak out of his lungs. Slowly, he breathed in again and readied himself. He stepped forward and felt the familiar sensation as he went out of phase. He had no better explanation for it. Ever since Balthazar had brought him back from beyond, he could do this. It was as if he was already half ghost.

His body buzzed, fighting to get back to reality as he moved into the wall. He could feel the resistance: a shadow of the bricks trying to scratch at his corporeal self. He kept moving. If he stopped, he would get disorientated, and that could be disastrous. Being lost inside a wall, forever turning around and not knowing the way out, had quickly become his deepest fear.

It could only have been seconds, but it felt much longer before he emerged out the other side. His body snapped back into phase, and he fell back against the solid brick in relief. It was short-lived.

He turned his attention to the room ahead of him. The tastefully decorated corridor reminded him of a museum: all dark wood and tiled walls. But before he could try and figure out exactly what he'd landed in, he was going to have to address the two goons staring at him.

Though staring wasn't quite the right word, seeing as they didn't have eyes. Their faces were completely blank, but they knew where he was. Being an experienced villain's sidekick, Shade did what any other self-respecting sidekick would have done. He screamed.

As soon as the shrill, fear-laced noise left his throat, the goons sprang forward with unnatural grace. One even dropped to all fours and charged like a wolf. They were dressed in grey suits. For a moment, Shade watched as the surreal creatures closed the space, terror freezing him to the spot as he wondered how the faceless creatures would kill him.

At the last second, self-preservation kicked in, and he jumped to one side. The goon on all fours leapt up, planted all four limbs on the wall and pushed away, twisting in mid-air to face Shade's new direction.

"Balthazar!" he screamed.

It was useless. Unless he found a way to let his boss in, he was alone. He scrabbled backwards, searching for some hidden door, but the creatures were too fast. The one on all fours was in the air again and about to land on top of him.

Instinctively, Shade phased out, and the goon skittered through him. The things were utterly silent as they moved, their blank faces tracking him perfectly. He snapped back into phase and pushed himself to his feet.

There were cabinets dotted around the hall: plinths with glass cases on top. Shade darted behind one, putting it between him and his assailants. He found himself lamenting, again, how Balthazar never trained him to do anything except phase. Would self-defence classes have hurt? Even Todd had done some of those, having somehow worked it into his contract. However, he'd also managed to work private medical insurance, a company car, and a lifetime Netflix subscription (without ads) into his contract.

The two goons started moving in a pincer movement around the cabinet towards him. Inside it was some kind of rod that just looked like a stick to him. They were on either side of him now. Despite their lack of faces, he was certain the one on two feet was looking at him smugly.

Shade took a deep breath and went out of phase again. Doing it this frequently was exhausting. He had to focus this time as he passed through the case, willing his hand to regain phase for an instant as he grabbed hold of the artefact.

The upright goon smashed his hand down on the glass, spraying shards everywhere. Shade spun round to face them as he wheeled backwards. The one on his feet straightened its grey tie. Definitely smug. As the other readied itself to pounce again, Shade looked down at the mystery rod. He held it aloft, and both creatures paused.

"Fetch!"

He flung it as hard as he could down the hallway, and the one on all fours spun and chased after it. Both Shade and the other goon watched in disbelief as it scampered away.

"Huh."

Shade was slower to regain his senses, and the goon was quickly at him again. Shade yelped. The goon was going to slam him into the wall. Shade reached out and grabbed the creature's head, grimacing as his thumbs squelched into where its eyes should have been.

His body protested as he flickered out of phase again, the goon's momentum taking him backwards into the wall. He heard a click as the pair of them launched into the brick. Shade let go and carried on falling backwards before tumbling out the other side and landing at Balthazar's feet. Shade lay on the floor, panting heavily, as his boss looked down at him.

"You alright there?"

Shade just stared at him. Then something to his left whirred. It sounded like something was dragging.

"Oh well done, you found the door!" Balthazar clapped, striding into the room.

Shade hauled himself up, straightening his t-shirt and baggy jeans, before following his boss in.

"What happened to him?"

Balthazar was peering to the right. The goon was sticking out of the wall, everything above his shoulders hidden inside the brick.

"He found the door switch."

"Helpful chap then." He grinned at Shade, who felt the sudden urge to leave him in a wall, although he was fairly sure his boss would be able to get out on his own. Todd had often asked what the man's deal was, and after seven years, Shade still knew barely anything about him.

"There's another one somewhere he…" Shade trailed off as he heard the thing galloping down the hallway towards them.

"Ooh, bit off-putting, isn't it?"

As Shade sidestepped behind Balthazar, his boss held out his hand. Words that Shade couldn't understand echoed down the hallway as Balthazar unleashed his magic. Thunder shook the corridor as the power raced towards the creature. The thing hung suspended in the air for a split second before it snapped out of existence. Something dropped to the floor as it disappeared.

"Ooh, is that the Staff of Zeus?" Balthazar picked up the stick. "Ugh, it's soggy… Drool." He shook it off.

"But it didn't…" Shade's mouth twitched as he pointed to it. Balthazar just gave him one of those looks that said he was missing the obvious. "Where did it go?"

"Oh, who knows? Not here." He shrugged. "Right, let's go find this orb, shall we?"

Balthazar started marching off in the direction the dog goon had come from before stopping, spinning on his heel, his coat flapping dramatically, and heading in the opposite direction. Shade had to walk double the pace to keep up with Balthazar's long strides.

"What exactly is this orb MacGuffin? And why are we after it?"

"Well, it's an object of great power, obviously."

"You haven't got a clue, have you?"

"Details Shade, details. Look, the tip-off said it would be worth it and that everyone else would be after it too, so there's no time to waste! Especially before that blasted detective gets to it." He was talking about Sandra's boss, not that her boss did any actual detecting. "Come on, August, where's your sense of adventure?"

"Must have left it in the wall."

They spent the next half an hour wandering aimlessly up and down corridors, hitting dead ends and frequently pausing when Balthazar was distracted by the contents of various cabinets. He'd gotten Shade to grab two medallions, one mystic letter opener and a pair of sunglasses, which Shade was fairly sure weren't supposed to be in the cabinet. Balthazar was now wearing them despite the old light fittings only providing a low-level glow.

"Look, maybe this tip-off was a dud, boss." Shade's legs were weary. Going out of phase had sucked his energy reserves dry and left him hungry and tired.

"Here." Balthazar threw him a chocolate bar and carried on. Shade fumbled it and dropped it to the floor. As he was picking it up, he glanced up and saw Balthazar hurrying forward. "Ooh look, a stone of…"

Shade didn't hear what else he said – his spidey senses were screaming at him. "Wait! The rug!"

The whole place had wooden floors, why on Earth would there be a Persian rug in the middle of an open space?

When Balthazar stepped onto the rug to grab at the stone sitting conveniently in the centre, beams of light shot up to the ceiling from all around its edges.

"Ah." Balthazar looked around him, and Shade dropped his head in dismay. Balthazar, dragging at one corner of the rug with his foot, pulled it away from the edge of the cage of light, revealing the symbols on the floor beneath it. "An angel trap. Blast."

"Angel trap?" Shade looked up at him suspiciously.

"Just a name." Balthazar waved it away. "But quite an effective device all the same. I, um, well, I need to work on how to get out of this, so…" He turned on the spot, one arm behind his back, the other tapping a finger to his chin. "Be a good man and go find the orb while I sort this out."

"Balthazar…" Shade was already shaking his head.

"Now don't make me order you, August, please."

Shade unwrapped the chocolate bar and angrily gnawed a chunk off the end as he carefully moved around the edge of the cage, refusing to look at his boss as he muttered, "I want a pay rise."

* * *

The place was a warren. Either the underground section sprawled much further than the footprint of the building above ground implied, or there was something funny going on. Shade was inclined to believe it was the latter. He started scratching marks into the walls at junctions using the mystical letter opener to keep track of where he had been.

"That, sir, is wanton destruction of public property."

For a second, Shade was gripped by panic at being caught. He hid the letter opener behind his back before his brain registered the voice.

"Todd?"

He was grinning as his friend stepped around a corner, a sly smirk on his face.

"Had you for a second."

He sauntered over, his shirt and tie as immaculate as always. His friend had ended up as an assistant completely by accident. He'd walked into an interview thinking he was applying to be an office admin person in some bland, undefinable conglomerate and ended up in front of a self-titled supervillain who made Shade's boss look thoroughly competent.

Todd had never had any villainous leanings, not outwardly at least, but decided a job was a job. The fact that he'd ended up being quite good at it and was the first assistant who had lasted longer than a week meant he was now the company's most valuable asset. Shade never really understood how a company could be based purely on criminal behaviour, but, as Todd put it, there were hundreds – his was just the only one admitting to it.

"What are you doing here?" Shade asked, trying to shrug off his embarrassment.

"Oh, you know, stealing a piece of fancy technology that will... Well, I have no idea what it's supposed to do, but He's got to have it, hasn't He?" Todd paused. "You're not after it too, are you?"

"We're after an artefact or something." Shade shrugged. "He's gotten himself trapped back there."

"Mine too. I told Him not to go in the vault until we'd checked for sensors, but no." He shrugged as they started walking together down the next corridor.

"Vault? In this museum?"

"Yeah, was a bit surprised myself."

A roar of frustration made them both stop where they were. "Did that sound like...?"

"Harix?" Todd finished. Tentatively, they stopped just short of the doorway to the next room and looked at each other.

"Nah, you can go first." Shade waved his friend forward.

"Fine." He sniffed and dug in his pocket for a small cylindrical device. He clicked a button, and Shade instinctively ducked. The objects from Todd's R+D lab were not known for their reliability. Todd sniggered. "Don't worry, bought it online." Shade stood up as Todd extended the mirror on the end of the rod round the edge of the doorway. "What the hell is that thing?"

Shade moved to stand beside him and peer into the mirror. Harix, in the centre of the room, had hold of the grey creature that had attacked him and was repeatedly smashing it into the floor.

"Bad, bad, grey dog thing." Each word was punctuated by the thing hitting the floor again.

"So that's where it went..."

"A friend of yours?" Todd asked, retracting the mirror.

"It's not getting an invite to the next RPG session, let's put it that way."

They wandered into the room and waited for Harix to let the creature drop to the floor.

"I was going to ask you about this year – are we sticking to the same system?" Todd asked. "My character could do with a refresh."

"Todd! Shadey!" Harix bounded over to them and scooped them both up into a bearhug before they could protest. The big man's arms fitted round the pair of them easily and managed to squeeze the air out of them within seconds. Thankfully, Todd's tapping on his arm eventually had the desired effect, and Harix let them both go. "I can't believe you're both here, that's awesome! Did I forget something? Are we playing a session? Shadey? Is this part of the game?"

Shade didn't reply for a second or two. He liked to think that it was to let them both imagine for a moment he was clever enough to have pulled that off, but in reality, he still couldn't breathe. He shook his head weakly.

"On a quest, buddy," Todd replied. "Boss wants some new tech, and Shade's after an artefact. What about you?"

"I have an interview for a new boss! He heard about this device that can trap your enemies and said if I can get it for him, I can be his new sidekick! Isn't that great?!"

"A new boss? Cool. Who is it?"

"Doctor Shark."

Todd and Shade said nothing, trading a sideways glance.

"What?"

"Nothing," they replied in unison.

Harix pouted.

"Well," Todd began. "You know why he's called that, don't you?"

"The rumours aren't true. They are vicious lies made up by The Wonders to discredit him." Harix folded his arms and half turned away from them.

"Look, man, we just want to make sure you get hired by a boss that deserves you." Todd patted him on the back.

The big man's mood changed instantly. "Aw, you guys do care, don't you? You're the best." He moved to hug them again, but they both scooted away. Instead, Harix ran his big fingers through his mop of sandy-coloured hair. "Well, don't suppose you've seen an orb anywhere about, have you?"

Shade froze. Then he noticed Todd had too. They looked at each other, suspicion colouring Todd's face.

"Your trap is an orb, Harix? And I suppose your artefact happens to be an orb too, Shade, does it?" Todd asked as he started edging nonchalantly towards the exit.

"Todd, what does your new tech look like?" Shade asked.

"Oh, a cubey thing, I think." He waved his hand. "I'm just going to…"

He turned and started running.

"That was weird," Harix commented.

"We're all after the same thing, Harix," sighed Shade.

"Oh." He blinked a few times, and then realisation dawned on his face. "Oh!"

He started chasing after Todd. Shade felt guilty letting Harix take the lead, but he knew Todd would never do anything that would seriously maim them. He paused as an explosion rocked the hallway and then carried on.

He rounded a corner, revealing Harix struggling to get out from under a heap of rubble. Shade took a deep breath, phased yet again, and ran straight through, hoping to catch his villainous friend.

The hallway led to a fancy doorway to a large chamber. Todd was sat on the floor, massaging his jaw. Shade slowed down, giving him an inquisitive look.

"Apparently everyone got the memo." Todd nodded towards the centre of the room where Sandra was standing next to the plinth holding the orb, her arms folded defiantly. Cinco was lurking ominously by the back wall. "That really hurt, Sandra."

"I am sorry, sweetie, but you know I have no choice." She shrugged. "I cannot allow you to steal this orb."

"This is because of your birthday present, isn't it?"

"No, it was perfectly lovely."

"So why aren't you punching Shade?"

"Hey!" Shade gave him a light kick in the leg. Todd just shrugged before climbing back to his feet.

The floor shook as Harix entered, shaking brick dust from his hair. "Todd! You're okay! How did you get through that boobytrap so quickly? Oh, hey Sandra, Cinco. Cool, is everyone here?"

"Godley is just securing the back entrance so the police can get in and secure the orb," Sandra replied.

As if on cue, the caped sidekick trotted down a set of stairs and took a position behind the plinth. He waved enthusiastically.

"You called the police?" Todd let out a groan.

"Godley did." Sandra folded her arms in triumph.

Godley's smile dropped. "I thought you did?"

"Oh for…" Sandra rolled her eyes and turned to their robot friend. "Cinco, can you get a connection to the police?"

Cinco tilted her silvery head. "Negative, we are too far underground for me to be able to get a signal."

Todd looked at his phone. "Really? I've got two bars."

"Be a dear and phone the police, would you?" Sandra smiled sweetly.

"Sorry, forgot the number." He circled around, trying to get a better angle on the orb. "Well, this is nice."

The last time they had been together had been the last sidekick convention. After thwarting an attempt by Harix's old necromancer boss to replace all the sidekicks with zombie minions, they had messaged regularly, but this was the first time they'd all been in a room together.

Shade couldn't deny the twinge of sadness he felt at them being at odds. Despite having different bosses (and being on different sides of the law), work had never come between them before. Godley looked like he was spoiling for a fight. Harix was still looking bemused about seeing all his friends. It was impossible to tell how Cinco was feeling, seeing as her face could only flicker between a few preprogrammed expressions. Todd was staring at Sandra, his expression as unreadable as Cinco's.

Sandra, however, was frowning.

"Does something seem off about this to you chaps?"

* * *

Ten minutes later

Shade phased and passed through Harix, who was holding Godley in the air by his cape. Godley's mask had half slipped off his face, and he was torn between trying to replace it and lashing out pathetically at the giant. Shade shifted back into phase in front of the orb just in time for a book to thump him on the head.

"Sorry!" Todd called out as he ran from Sandra – no, Rita, judging by the bloodcurdling battle roar she unleashed.

Cinco shot a laser from a nozzle protruding from her palm that sizzled over Shade's head and burned a hole through Godley's cape, making him fall to the floor in a heap.

"Hey, that's my best cape!"

Shade patted his head nervously, feeling a singed hair or two from the laser. "This is my best head." He ignored the giggling coming from a dark corner where Todd had last been seen, which was followed by a howl of pain.

"Shade," Cinco declared, "you must retreat from the orb. The weapon must be destroyed."

"Weapon? Don't you dare, metalhead! I need that to get my boss back!" Godley leapt up and ran at Cinco.

"Metalhead. This is an insult, yes?"

Godley faltered as he reached the robot, suddenly unsure of how to proceed. He looked down at the laser pointing at his chest. "Noooo, more a term of endearment…"

Shade ignored them. Something was sparking in his brain.

"Stop," he called out. They all ignored him. "Todd, stop! You all have to stop!"

Nobody even looked in his direction.

Shade spotted a gong in a nearby display. He scrabbled forward on all fours, keeping low, zigzagging around flying objects. He grabbed the beater and hit it with all his might.

Everything in the room vibrated, and Shade curled into a ball, covering his ears. Still, the sounds of fighting had ceased. Either that or the ringing in his ears was just too loud.

"What the actual hell, man?!" Todd yelled, hands over his ears.

"We can't touch the orb."

"What?" Godley shouted at the top of his lungs – apparently his ears were even worse.

"Why can't we touch it? It's a trap." All of his friends looked nervously at each other. "We've all been told different stories about the orb, all tailored to get our bosses here. Who are… where?"

"Vault."

"Locked in his own van."

"Missing."

"Reading my CV."

"Right, all absent. And here we all are. Now, who tipped everyone off? I say we figure that out first because I'm that certain if we touch that orb, something bad is going to happen."

"This orb?"

Shade didn't like the sound of Harix's voice. All heads snapped to him. He was standing next to the plinth, the golden orb in his hands and an expression of horror on his face.

"Crap," Todd muttered.

"Nothing's happened, though. Maybe it's all—"

Godley was cut short as barriers suddenly slammed down over all the exit points.

"You had to say it, didn't you?" Sandra rolled her eyes as she helped Todd up.

"To be fair, Sandra, I didn't actually get to the end of my sentence." Godley folded his arms and backed away from Harix.

"Ah, Harix is the victor, I see!" a voice boomed out of nowhere.

"My name's not Victor," the giant mumbled as he spun on the spot, trying to locate the voice. The sidekicks all gathered closer together – well, five of them did, away from Harix.

"I know, I meant you were the first to…" The voice sighed. "You know what, never mind."

At the end of the chamber, a projected image appeared, a head floating in the air. The face was masculine, with a square jawline and perfect teeth, but the upper half of his visage was covered by a black eye mask and a hood.

"I knew you'd all get to the final chamber. Your worthless bosses are trapped, helpless in my cages. Now their precious sidekicks are about to be buried under tonnes of rubble, leaving them forever trapped."

"What was that about rubble?" Todd leaned forward.

"Err, guys, the orb is ticking." Harix waved it closer to them, and they all yelled and recoiled as one.

"A bomb, really? How run-of-the-mill," Sandra tutted, but Shade noticed her grip Todd's arm a little tighter.

"What exactly did we do to you?" Godley yelled at the face before throwing a pot he'd found through the hologram.

"Really, Godley?" the disembodied voice asked.

"He can see us," Shade muttered to Todd, who gave him the slightest of nods in reply.

"You did nothing except keep those blithering idiots out of trouble and in my way."

The sidekicks shared confused glances but kept quiet, knowing full well that masterminds love to ramble on about their plans if given enough room.

"All your petty squabbles and warring keeps everyone in their place. No one rules over the others. They're saying these are the calmest, most peaceful days we live in! It's a disgrace!"

He paused, getting his breath back. "I tried to unite them, but no, they didn't want to be led by one person. They couldn't see that my way would create utter mayhem! I would have rioting on the streets, people turning on each other. I would turn this city into the dystopia it was meant to be! No more superheroes saving the day, no more villains dividing up the minions to keep each other just weak enough.

"But they couldn't see it, not while they had you lot holding their hands, making them feel important. If only Thaddeus had swapped you all out for zombies at the convention like I told him to."

"And you would have gotten away with it…" Todd began.

"Don't you dare say it," Sandra warned.

"I'm talking!" the voice boomed.

"Cinco, can you trace where the projection is coming from?" Todd whispered.

"Of course." She gave a curt nod and a manic grin before her eyes turned red and she started scanning.

"Once you rotten lot are out the way, along with the rest of the sidekicks, your bosses will have no choice but to follow me! I shall rule the City."

"You and whose army?" Todd shouted. "Or have you got a sidekick kicking around somewhere like a hypocrite?"

"I do not need sidekicks! I will have henchmen – much more pliable, no independent thinking!"

"Does the voice sound familiar to you guys?" asked Harix, who was still holding the ticking bomb, tilted to one side as he chewed his lip in thought.

"Now you mention it…" Shade nodded.

"I calculate the signal for the projection is nearby, the other side of the wall." Cinco's eyes flashed as she scanned.

"What did she say?" The voice twisted slightly as if looking at her. "Stop it, pay attention to me."

"Shade, you reckon you can post that thing if we find him?" Todd grinned and nodded towards the orb.

"Guys, it's getting warm." Harix was starting to sound frightened.

"Give it here, I'll take a turn." Godley took the orb from him and looked at the surface of the sphere. "I don't know what these numbers are, but they look small."

"Shade?" Todd pressed.

Shade nodded. "Let's just hope he's not under a load-bearing wall."

"Fine, be like that!" The voice yelled petulantly. "Maybe you'd like another friend to play with."

A shimmering haze appeared just beneath the floating head, and another grey creature materialised.

"Are you kidding?" Shade backed away instinctively as it dropped to all fours, its grey tie dragging on the floor.

"It's got no face." Godley's voice rose in pitch. "And it's looking at the orb."

He was right – the thing was pointed right at the orb. Godley reacted and threw it straight at Todd, who deftly caught it.

"Hey!"

The creature turned to Todd and started running at him. This one was faster than the last one, its limbs even longer as it galloped forward.

"Rita!"

Shade watched as Sandra shuddered, willingly letting Rita take control. Her eyes changed colour, and a wicked grin spread across her face. She smoothed her hair back and whipped off her glasses. Strange, unearthly words started coming out of her mouth as the demon inside Sandra started incanting.

In front of Todd, a small purple ring appeared, and the creature fell straight into it. Shade's head snapped up as he heard a rushing noise.

The creature had reappeared in the air above the head and fell to the floor with a thud. Harix chuckled. The creature righted itself and ran again. Harix stopped laughing.

"Shade, Cinco, find where he is!" Todd threw the orb over to Harix just as the creature got close to him. "I think we have to play pass the bomb."

Shade ducked out of the creature's path and fell in line beside Cinco. He quickly glanced back. Rita started hovering in the air just to infuriate the creature even more.

"Tick-tock, you two," Rita called. Shade followed Cinco to the giant head.

"The projector is up there, but there is a signal coming from…" Cinco turned in small jerky increments. "This way." She launched forward, the pistons in her legs pumping as Shade scrabbled to keep up. "It is within five metres of this point."

"Better check."

He took a deep breath and let his body phase. He plunged his head into the wall, hoping it wasn't thick. His ears popped as he emerged without having to put much of his torso into the wall.

"You?"

A hand swiped at his head, but he was still out of phase, and it passed straight through. Shade hauled himself backwards, his hands braced on the other side of the wall.

"Over here!"

Harix had the orb. His eyes lit up, and he wound his arm back to throw the orb to him. Shade's eyes widened in horror. It was going to take his head off.

"Cinco, duck!"

Harix let the orb loose with a roar, and it flew towards him. The giant nearly tripped himself up with the effort. The orb caught Shade in the midsection. He yelped as he phased out, his feet flying up in the air as he was carried backwards through the wall.

As Shade passed into the small cubby hole their attacker was hiding in, he let go of the orb, dropping it into his lap. The momentum carried him straight out the other side of the room.

There was a small generator just outside the door to the hideaway. Shade pulled the cable from it before tumbling to the floor into a heap. It wasn't long before he heard footsteps coming down the corridor.

"Shadey!" He didn't have time to react and stop Harix from squeezing the life out of him. "Good catch, man."

"Has it gone off?" Godley asked, rubbing his hands together with a little more glee than Shade suspected a good guy should have had.

"I think he's disarmed it." Shade shrugged as they stared at the door.

"Did you get a good look at him?" Todd asked.

"Oh yes," he nodded. "We should have figured it out when he said, 'you rotten lot'."

"No…" Sandra's jaw dropped in disbelief. Her demonic side must have expended too much energy and gone back to sleep.

Shade gestured for Harix, who was only just letting go of him, to open the door.

"Marvin Postlethwaite," Shade said as the door swung open. Their quarry was sat in the corner of a cupboard, a laptop and microphone in front of him. "Never were content with being a sidekick, were you?"

"You're still on about all this? I thought once we discovered your plot to overthrow Mr Splendid and become number one, you decided to become a reality TV star?" Todd asked, leaning against the door frame.

"You didn't discover anything, I told you," Marvin said.

"Yeah, when you were trying to impress Sandra," Todd narrowed his eyes at him.

"You guys suck. And I nearly killed you all!"

"Um," Shade looked round. "Guys, where's the grey thing?"

"Oh, he lost interest in us when you took the orb," Todd said.

They looked at Marvin. His eyes widened in horror as he realised. He tried to give Harix the orb, but the big man just shook his head. Heavy smacking noises echoed down the corridor towards them.

"No, wait!"

The sidekicks parted in the middle just in time for the grey creature to launch itself through the air towards Marvin and the orb. Marvin let out a massive scream as the thing jumped up and down like an overexcited Saint Bernard. Marvin was pinned beneath it, the orb trapped between them.

"Bye, Marv," Todd waved at him.

"Is it wise to leave him there?" Cinco asked as they turned and walked away.

"That creature won't let him go, and I reckon each of our bosses will want a turn with him." Todd shrugged.

"And then mine will definitely want to deliver him to the local police. Justice needs to be done." Sandra took Todd's arm as they wandered back through the corridors, looking for the scratch marks Shade had left.

"But they'll just stick him in the asylum. They keep sharing diabolical plans in there and they have the worst record for escapes." Godley shook his head. Despite being on the same side, he never tended to agree with Sandra.

Todd let go of Sandra as she argued with Godley and dropped back in line with Shade. He cocked his head enquiringly at Shade's smile.

"I just don't like it when we fight," Shade answered as Todd patted him on the back. "You ever think about being in charge?"

"Take over from The Boss?" Todd's eyebrows skyrocketed. His boss didn't really have an inventive pseudonym. He had thought it would just be easier for all henchmen if his name was The Boss – no awkward nicknames to learn then. "Nah. Who would want that? Come on, we all know us sidekicks wield the real power, and they take all the flack."

"I suppose we better free them." He stopped, and the others stopped too. He was almost certain Balthazar was round the next corner.

"It would be the expected course of action," Cinco agreed.

"Or…" Todd began.

"Or?" Shade asked.

"Or… there's a pub just round the corner. Come and get them in the morning?"

They all stared at each other.

"I do have my games manual in the van. Could do a one shot over a few drinks."

Shade tried to look coy and pretend he didn't have them pre-written just in case something like this ever happened. Todd smiled at him, seeing straight through him.

"Oh, goodie!" Harix clapped his hands together. "Last one to the pub is buying!"

Harix disappeared at a rate of knots. The others sighed in dismay before falling silent. Then, as one, they turned and ran.

ABOUT THE AUTHOR

Alex is based in the East of England and is a self-professed Jack of all trades (and still a master of none). Having asked for a typewriter when she was four years old, she ended up in a variety of careers including forensics, teaching, PR and wielding custard flamethrowers. Always writing into the wee hours of the night, she writes fantasy, scifi and steampunk stories (occasionally all these genres at the same time). You can find her all over the shop through https://linktr.ee/lexikonical

The Radiant Star

Anya Pavelle

Graniteport, Massachusetts, October 15, 2024

Lou Reed's "Perfect Day" blasted through Valerie's earbuds as she watched the sun creep over the harbor of Graniteport, Massachusetts. The singer crooned, "Just a perfect day, problems are left to know. Weekenders all night long, it's such fun."

Fuck that. This weekend was shit, she thought as she downed a sip of some kill-a-yak-from-20-yards-away-strength coffee. She'd had enough of death and demolition.

Valerie stared at the Wheel of Fortune tarot card on the wall near the cash register. Last week, she mounted the print on indigo paper and placed it in a distressed copper frame. The cycle of the universe repeated itself in tarot cards and people's day-to-day shit.

The weather did, too. As much as everyone on Cape Ann wanted to tether summer to the granite bedrock, they knew that the earth would continue to spin on its predetermined axis and revolve around the sun. The perennials in the flower box outside the window had shriveled, but they'd return with warmer weather. Summer meant money. Tourist money.

The early autumn morning was a bit too chilly for Valerie's liking, but she could deal with it. Her piping-hot coffee radiated from her grandmother's old blue mug. For once in her thirty years of life, Valerie welcomed Monday. This Monday meant renewal and, potentially, an end to her grief.

As Reed droned on, she surveyed the activity through the large bay window—her and her cousin Willa's new bay window to be nitpicky. It was almost as if, way back in 1884, the builder of the original fisherman's shack had placed the window here so that influencers of the future could capture Instagram-worthy snapshots of Graniteport's famous harbor.

In 1934, a painter transformed the shack into an artist's studio. Then, Valerie's grandmother, Lorelai, purchased the building in 1968 and christened it as the Radiant Star—a perfect name for a New Age shop. Willa had wanted to call their shop Radiant Star, 2.0, but Valerie convinced her more spontaneous cousin that they didn't want tourists to think they updated iPhones or Androids.

Plus, the 2.0 looked shitty in the antiquated font they chose for the new sign. Branding *mattered*. The Radiant Star remained true to its roots.

To the left of the composition and bathed in pink morning light, lobstermen hauled traps aboard their boats. A stream of fog drifted atop the green sea and dissolved into the air above. The harbor had, for lack of a better phrase, awesome energy. Huge blocks of granite formed the perimeter of the harbor and breakwaters. Over a hundred and fifty years ago, locals had hauled these same blocks from a quarry not one mile away.

This place was iconic, historically and aesthetically. When late morning hit, the village's businesses would open, and tourists would descend upon the quaint coastal New England streets for trinkets, food, and art. The busiest season was summer, of course, but autumn was a close second. Graniteport was only half an hour from Salem, which descended into beautiful chaos on Halloween.

A flurry of activity caught the attention of her right eye. A party of ten or so people tumbled off a bus and ambled up to a larger vessel called *Graniteport Whale Watching Tours*. Kind of a long-ass name for a boat, but whatever. The name did its job. Tourists needed clarity about where to go next, and signs and cell phones worked. Valerie and Willa could make a killing if they tapped into the whale-watching market. They needed all the money they could get.

Valerie pulled her phone from her pocket and texted Willa, who'd procrastinated on getting their business cards ready for today—opening day. She was at a 24-hour print shop in Danvers. Apparently, they printed on-demand business cards for an added fee. At least there was that.

Valerie: *Hey. I think we need a QR code on the back of the business* card.
Willa: *Good idea!*
Valerie: *Is it too late to add one?*
Willa. *Nope. We're going over specs now.*
Valerie: *For once, your procrastination paid off. Do you know how to make a QR code?*
Willa: *Of course. I'm offended you even asked me. See you soon!*

Soon? Perhaps. Willa always ran at least thirty minutes late.

Valerie closed her eyes and envisioned a smooth opening morning, with tourists and locals alike eager to see the revamped store. Bikini Kill's "Ocean Song" kicked her neurons into high gear as she pictured a steady stream of patrons buying coffee (Italian or Cuban espresso), incense (well over thirty scents to suit all tastes), art (mostly of fishing boats and rocky shores), or tarot cards (ten varieties, of which Valerie preferred the Celtic version). Inhaling the scent of white sage, she could feel that energy from the future as if it sparked around her.

Someone tapped Valerie's shoulder, causing her to jump. She spun around to see her realtor, Maryellen, standing behind her. The older woman's smile wilted.

"Oh dear. I didn't mean to startle you."

Valerie pulled out the earbuds. "It's totally fine. I was just manifesting."

"Manifesting success?" Maryanne asked.

Cracking a weak smile, Valerie nodded. "I sure hope so."

She and Willa had just borrowed $500,000 from Graniteport Regional Bank to buy their grandmother Lorelai's shop. Unbeknownst to everyone on the damn planet except for Maryellen, Lorelai had taken out a mortgage against the property to cover a shitshow of issues. First, the pandemic had cratered business for two years. Then, a nor'easter had damaged the stone foundation. Without those repairs, the shop would've slid right into the harbor.

And last in that horrible trifecta—Lorelai had gotten sick. Sick enough to need experimental treatment in Mexico. Not that it'd done any good. She'd died three months ago, leaving Valerie and Willa, her only grandchildren, devastated.

Grieving people often made rash decisions. Sinking a quarter of a million dollars each—plus the half a million mortgage—was well on the extreme AF end of rash. But the women couldn't let their grandmother's landmark shop get turned into another store that sold Graniteport sweatshirts or lobster rolls. So, they took out their own mortgage.

Failure wasn't an option. It just wasn't.

"Don't worry," the realtor said.

"Are you reassuring me as a realtor, family friend, or psychic?" Valerie asked.

Maryellen scanned her surroundings. "Right now, as a customer. You've done a marvelous job on the renovations." She paused. "And now, as a psychic, I can tell you that she's proud."

Tears clustered in Valerie's eyes. Maryellen had been one of Lorelai's closest friends, so she helped Valerie and Willa finagle the shop from the bank's clutches.

For the past four weeks, they tirelessly renovated the old two-story building with a crumbling 1960s vibe into a multifaceted business. Valerie and Willa had refinished the wood on the exposed beams, added new paint, and spent a small fortune on furniture and fixtures.

The first floor had one large open space with two levels. On the street level, they installed gallery lighting to feature emerging local artists. Patrons could purchase these unique works of art for a fair price. Tourists, not locals, usually bought art as souvenirs of their trips.

The cousins also put their classic New Age supplies in that part of the shop. Lorelai had carried a wide array of incense, crystals, divination items, herbs, and statues of various deities. When she became too ill to run the shop, though, she shut her doors for all but one day a week. Valerie wondered why Lorelai hadn't asked for help or—goddess forbid—told her family members that she was even sick!

The old woman always did have a fiercely independent streak.

The least Valerie and Willa could do now was maintain her legacy. To start, they renewed contracts with her local suppliers. Valerie and Willa also added an espresso and tea bar in the store's harbor-level section. Guests could enjoy a cup of their favorite beverage at a table by the large bay window overlooking the town's famous harbor.

Valerie loved the harbor-level part of the store the most because of its stone floors and massive granite fireplace. Those iconic features gave the place some quintessential New England character.

That space additionally had room for Graniteport's more talented individuals to share their gifts. On Mondays, Maryellen would give psychic readings with her tarot cards. Tuesdays belonged to the palm reader, and the local astrologer booked Wednesdays. On Thursdays, a medium with thirty years of experience would channel the dead. And on Fridays, the village's most famous witch planned to craft unique spells for her clients' needs. The Radiant Star would keep twenty percent of the profits from these bookings. The talent, thankfully, felt this split was more than fair.

All of those activities would take place during regular business hours. Most shops on Deerskin Neck, the most popular section of Graniteport, closed at 5:00 p.m. But the Radiant Star would stay open until 10:00 p.m. so that people could rent the space for seances, Dungeons and Dragons tournaments, or other private events—maybe even intimate weddings for the gothic crowd who wanted to get married on a moonlit night near the sea.

Valerie knew they had to capitalize on the shop's unique vibe. The new rustic-industrial aesthetic married the old and new and was best described as "techy-artsy-witchy-New England." They would make it a thing if it wasn't already a thing!

Hopefully, the diverse business ventures would keep the store in the black. As long as the cousins could pay the mortgage and meet expenses, they'd be fine. To save money, they had even terminated their expensive Boston leases and moved into their grandmother's old living quarters on the second floor of the building.

"Thanks for telling me that," Valerie said. Then, she noticed the weathered Stop & Shop bag in the realtor's arms. "Did you bring something for the opening? I already have cookies, but I don't mind adding to the pile of goodies."

"Not quite." The realtor removed a present from the bag. "A gift for good luck."

Valerie gasped as she studied the wrapping paper, which had mermaids swimming across the surface of the robin-blue paper. The nymphs had elongated bodies and flowing hair, almost as if they'd emerged from a Pre-Raphaelite painting. Where had Maryellen found such a unique print? Certainly not Walmart.

"You shouldn't have. Really," Valerie said.

"Pish posh," the older woman said. "I'm actually returning this to your family."

"Come again?"

Maryellen's eyes crinkled with mischief. "Open it."

Valerie rested the box on the table and untied the twine knots. The package was almost too pretty to open. Valerie carefully pulled back the scotch tape. Underneath the paper, she found a simple cardboard box. And inside that, three heavy glass spheres tied together with braided rope.

"Floats?" she asked, holding them up to the light. Fishermen used these glass spheres as buoys for their nets—and as decorative flourishes on the side of their shacks. There were three balls in total: ruby, seafoam, and sapphire. Jeweled light scattered on the floor as the morning sun crept through the orbs.

"Not exactly. These are mermaid balls," Maryellen explained. "Your grandmother gave them to me years ago when I opened my brokerage."

Valerie frowned. "Mermaid balls? I don't get it."

The realtor-psychic offered her a patient smile. "The day before she opened this store, she bought two sets of buoys from a local market, thinking they'd look pretty in her shop. The morning she opened, she saw a mermaid right here in the harbor. She always thought they brought her luck."

"You're kidding."

"No, I'm quite serious," Maryellen insisted.

It took all of Valerie's self-control not to burst into laughter. What a preposterous thought. Mermaids didn't exist. SCUBA divers and marine biologists would have found evidence by now. But then again, her grandmother used to leave out milk for fairies and summon spirits. Did Lorelai believe she saw a mermaid? Perhaps that was the more important question. Valerie scanned her childhood memories for any mention of a mermaid sighting. Her grandmother had told her countless stories about sailors and sea nymphs. With Graniteport's maritime history, that was a given. But she'd never mentioned seeing a mermaid herself.

"Gram would have told us," Valerie said.

"Would you have believed her?" The psychic's question had a biting tone.

"When I was five," Valerie admitted after a few moments.

Back then, she and Willa had believed in fairies, mermaids, Santa Claus, and a whole host of otherworldly beings. But their fathers, who had married into the family, had discouraged such childish beliefs. To be frank, they dismissed Lorelai as a crazy old hippie.

Despite that judgmental belief, though, neither man had argued when their wives sent the girls to Graniteport during the summer. All four adults worked full-time in Boston, so they sure as hell took advantage of three months of free babysitting.

It was during those warm, sea-scented summers that Valerie and Willa learned how to sort incense, run the cash register, and help clients pick the perfect stone for their needs. Rose quartz for love. Hematite for grounding. Amethyst for healing. Those memories were some of the best of Valerie's childhood.

Valerie studied Maryellen, who was close to seventy. She stood tall and proud, and her eyes glittered with intelligence. Was the realtor suffering from some early cognitive decline? Old people didn't always know when their minds began to slip.

Maryellen raised an eyebrow. "I have all my mental faculties, thank you very much."

And this is why you don't question a telepathic psychic, Valerie thought. "Sorry. It's just that I don't even remember seeing the balls."

"They fell and broke when your grandmother was dusting them years ago," Maryellen said. "She buried the pieces in the flower box outside the bay window for good luck.

"Luck?" Valerie asked. "Yeah, right."

The older woman rested a hand on Valerie's shoulder. The pressure felt comforting, like one of those weighted blankets that cured anxiety and insomnia. "My dear girl, it was your grandmother's time to go. The balls brought her luck—not immortality like one of those stones in the Avenger movies."

"Avenger movies? Those are your thing?"

"I'm partial to Thor. He's quite handsome."

Valerie giggled as she imagined Maryellen swooning in front of a cardboard cutout of Chris Hemsworth in his Thor gear. The solemn air cleared from the room, almost as if she'd smudged the place with five incense sticks.

Valerie wiped her eyes. "I needed that."

"There's always time for laughter," Maryellen said, shifting her gaze to the glass orbs. "Anyhow, I'm retiring from the real estate business next month, and I think you two should have these. Whether mermaids or your grandmother brings you luck, it doesn't matter. They'll look pretty in here."

A rush of warmth flooded Valerie's heart. What a kind gesture. She doubted her grandmother had seen an actual mermaid in Graniteport Harbor all those years ago. But Valerie did believe in cherishing one's family treasures.

"Thank you," she said.

The women spent the next fifteen minutes finding the perfect place for the buoys—no, mermaid balls. Next to the bay window, the glass orbs would capture the light and vibe of the harbor.

"This feels right," Maryellen said.

"Yep," Valerie agreed.

"And who knows? Maybe you or Willa will see a tail splash right outside."

That thought earned a chuckle from the younger woman. "Then I'd better have TikTok ready."

"TikTok?"

"Social media."

"Ah. My interns handle all of that." Maryellen glimpsed at her watch. "I should probably be off. I have real estate agents to supervise."

Valerie enveloped Maryellen in a hug. "Thank you for the lovely gift. Can I make you some tea before you go?"

The real estate agent nodded. "That'd be lovely."

A few months ago, Valerie had worked in software design, a gig that paid her bills but didn't inspire passion. More than anything, she understood tea and how to harmonize various herbs to an individual's needs. Maryellen Lewiston, with her prim tan pantsuit and tall stiletto heels, gave off an aura of lavender and vanilla. She was also feisty, so a hint of caramel syrup would be perfect.

When Valerie dropped the lavender flowers into the hot water, the pattern caught her attention. A whale's tail. She swirled the tea around, but a similar pattern emerged from the stormy cup. Her eyes darted up to the mermaid balls.

"Maryellen?" she asked. "Do you see this?"

The older woman peered into the cup. "Huh. What do *you* see?

"A whale's tail," she said, not wanting to sound ridiculous.

"Really?" Maryellen prompted. "Be honest."

The mind was a powerful thing, especially for the grieving. Valerie couldn't accept that her grandmother was simply gone—reduced to the pile of ashes that she and Willa had poured into the ocean on a gray, windy day. Lorelai used to say that everything held a spirit that would travel to an afterlife that welcomed all.

Valerie wanted to believe, too. For the past months, she had studied every license plate for a sign from her grandmother. The sea of cars that clogged the roads had mostly gibberish numbers and letters. But she once came across LOR-I46, which must have been from Lorelai, who'd been born in 1946.

Then again, a grieving brain could spin anything into a message from the beyond.

"Maybe a mermaid tale surrounded by stars," Valerie said, shoving aside her doubts.

"Keep an open mind, my dear." The realtor cleared her throat. "But right now, you have a store to open. Focus on that."

Valerie handed her the tea. "Gotcha."

"Do you need help with anything before I go?"

"No. Willa should be back with the business cards soon."

"One hopes," Maryellen said. "But I *will* see you soon. I might be selling my real estate business, but I won't sit on my old-lady couch and watch Avengers movies all day in my retirement. I'll be here every week—and more if needed."

That promise brought down Valerie's heart rate after Maryellen left. The antique clock on the wall struck 8:00 a.m. One hour until the grand opening. Valerie scanned the open expanse of the shop. What to do? What to do? Pull the cookies out of the fridge, but not until 9:00. Wouldn't want them to get dry. So, she checked the espresso and cappuccino machine. They seemed to be in good working order.

All in all, Valerie could relax until Willa returned. The business cards were the last thing on the list. When she lived in Boston, Willa had worked as a graphic designer and marketing specialist, so a simple business card was in her wheelhouse. She used to design everything from album covers to Instagram templates. Time management was not one of Willa's skills, though. Hopefully, the printing process was going smoothly.

Time was Valerie's thing. She loved lists and spreadsheets—even for charting her laundry schedule and optimal caffeine levels throughout the day. She even binged Marie Kondo videos on YouTube to relax.

As she waited for her procrastinator of a cousin, Valerie attended to last-minute details to keep her mind from spinning out of control. At 8:45 a.m., when her nails were almost bitten down to the quick, she heard the doorknob click.

"Finally…" she said as her cousin tumbled into the store, a long cardboard box in her hands.

Willa rolled her violet eyes. "Come on. I'm not *late*. I'm *efficient*. If I'd printed the cards two weeks ago like you wanted, we wouldn't have the QR code."

"Good point," Valerie conceded. "Can I see?"

As Willa pulled one of the cards from their box, the scent of fresh paper filled the air. She handed one to Valerie. "I took a few liberties with the design. I hope that's cool."

As they'd agreed last week, an intricate star covered the left side of the card. The business name, address, and phone number sat in the center. But the design on the right caught Valerie's breath. Swimming across the northeast quadrant of the card was the upper half of a stylized mermaid. Her hands shaking, Valerie flipped over the card, only to see the mermaid's tail continue onto the backside right next to the QR code.

"Oh my God," she said as tears clustered in her eyes.

Willa cocked her head, tilting her bubblegum-pink pigtails. "Shit. No good? I'll go back to the shop."

"No, no. It's perfect."

"Why are you upset, then?" Willa asked. "You're freaking me out, and it's not even Halloween!"

"I need to show you something." Valerie ushered her cousin to the bay window and pointed at the glass orbs. "Maryellen dropped these off a while ago. Do you recognize them?"

"They're buoys?"

"Not just buoys." Valerie sat at one of the window-side tables. "Can I ask what inspired this design change? I mean, I love it, but I have to know why you chose this before I ramble on and on."

Willa slid into the chair opposite her cousin. "Well, the shop has wicked mermaid energy. We're on the harbor. What better way to communicate an *ocean* theme than a pretty mermaid? It also works from a design perspective by balancing the composition and texture. The star felt lonely on the left."

Valerie nodded. "Agreed."

"Plus, I think Gram would have liked it," Willa added.

Tears streaked down Valerie's face unabated. Out of millions of license plates, she could understand how LOR-I46 was a coincidence that she'd translated into a message from their dead grandmother. The lavender flowers, too, could be dismissed as a product of her grieving mind.

But Willa's spontaneous design choice? That was something real. It had to be.

"She would."

"What's going on?" Willa asked.

Valerie pointed to the glass balls. "Maryellen told me that Gram used to have buoys just like this. She bought some for her and Maryellen to celebrate their new businesses. When Gram hung hers up, she apparently saw a mermaid in the harbor. Her buoys broke later, and she buried the glass pieces in the flower box. Maryellen brought us her mermaid balls as a good luck gift."

"Sounds like Gram was smoking something strong." Willa laughed and snapped a picture of the balls. "The glass is pretty in the morning light. I'll make an Insta post about them later."

"Maybe Gram *was* on something," Valerie said. "But I've been seeing mermaids all morning. In tea. On the business card."

Willa rested the phone on the table. "You're really buying this mermaid shit? Think about it, Val. We used to spend every summer here. She taught us how to leave offerings for fairies. Don't you think she would have mentioned seeing a mermaid?"

"All I know is that I've felt close to her today," Valerie replied.

As she savored the play of light the glass orbs cast on the floor, Willa stared out the window. They had to open the store in less than fifteen

The Radiant Star

minutes, but Valerie sensed that both of them needed a message to confirm what Maryellen had said.

"Should we ask for a sign?"

Willa shrugged. "I suppose it couldn't hurt. What do we do? You're better with herbs and rocks than me."

"We need to be intentional. I know that much."

As soon as Valerie uttered those words, a childhood memory jumped from her past, demanding her attention. When she and Willa first arrived at the shop at the beginning of each summer, their grandmother had them make a wish for the next few months. These requests to the universe had to be logical—no magic lamp with a fully functional genie, for example.

Valerie once wished for a boyfriend, and that very autumn, she'd gotten her first kiss on a field trip to the planetarium in Boston. The relationship with Spencer only lasted two weeks, but the universe had granted her an age-appropriate version of her wish.

She took Willa's hand. "We need to make our wishes. Remember?"

Willa nodded and grabbed her cousin's other hand. "Let's say it together."

"We wish for a sign. So mote it be." Their voices weren't in perfect unison, but the universe surely wouldn't hold that against them.

Both women turned to face the harbor. Valerie's hopeful side believed a sea nymph would jump right out of the water and plop onto the harbor's edge. Nothing happened at first. How long should they wait? Not more than five minutes if they wanted to open the store on time.

They held their breaths, eyes locked onto the fogless sea. A few moments later, a dolphin's fin pierced the water's surface. Was that it—the sign they wanted? Dolphins usually avoided the harbor because of the boat traffic.

"Thoughts?" Valerie asked.

"I dunno."

Valerie sighed. "Let's give it another minute."

As if it could hear the women's conversation, the dolphin flashed its tail, offering them a perfect view from the window.

Willa traced her finger along the curve of the mermaid's tail on the card. "Holy shit. Its tail is in the same position as the mermaid. Look!"

Valerie grabbed the card in her clammy hands. "You're right."

Just then, a child outside yelled, "Look, Mama! A mermaid!"

The two women followed the sound of the voice to a whale-watching boat that had just left the dock. A young girl of perhaps five was jumping up and down as she pointed at the dolphin. The cousins sat in silence as the clock struck away their precious seconds. Valerie's heart raced. Expecting a literal mermaid was too much. But this?

"Wow," she said, exhaling her long-held breath. "I think we just got our sign."

"Same," Willa replied.

The scent of cinnamon filled the air. Lorelai used to bake them cinnamon-nutmeg-apple cookies at the beginning of summer. As Valerie worked to slow her thumping heart, the moment seemed to stretch far beyond the seconds allotted by the universe.

She didn't need to dissect everything the universe sent her way—not when some things were beyond human comprehension. Lorelai could exist in the Radiant Star and her version of the beyond. Her essence could infuse the polished wood beams, linger on the scent of incense, and visit new dimensions if she wished—all simultaneously.

On the day when Lorelai hung the glass orbs in her shop, had she seen a mermaid or dolphin?

It doesn't matter, Valerie thought.

A cloud of peace settled over the shop. Somehow, she knew that everything would be okay. The clock struck at 9:00 a.m. It was best to greet the day with an open mind and a hefty dose of confidence. Their bank accounts depended on it.

"Ready?" Valerie asked.

"Let's do it," Willa said.

The cousins glanced at the mermaid balls before heading to the front door. Whatever the day and upcoming weeks brought, at least they resurrected their grandmother's shop from ruin. Hopefully, the locals and tourists would appreciate these efforts.

Valerie gripped the door handle with all her might and threw it open. At least twenty people waited in line on the granite cobblestone street to see the Radiant Star emerge again.

Success.

ABOUT THE AUTHOR

Anya Pavelle was born in Massachusetts but eventually settled in Florida, where she lives with her husband and dog. Although she usually writes historical fantasy and dystopian fiction, she enjoys experimenting with tales of magical fisherman floats. When she's not writing, Anya loves traveling the world, SCUBA diving, and curling up with a glass of wine and a new book.

To connect with Anya, visit her webpage at anyapavelle.com

The Shadow Trials

SJ Covey

The blazing orb of the sun dipped below the horizon as Beth climbed the famous hundred and ninety-nine steps from her cottage's door towards Whitby Abbey. For centuries, the abbey had loomed over the town, its watchful gaze staring out to the sea, immense and unmoving.

The stone steps slanted and were mismatched in size, having been worn away by time and an untold number of footsteps. While some had been replaced, others shifted and tilted under her feet, in need of some attention before another frost snuck underneath them and expanded, causing them to loosen further.

Beth's legs ached. It had been a long shift. But she needed the peace the view over the cliffs gave her. The abbey grounds sat high up on the hill next to a cemetery, silent and foreboding. Sea fog drifted over the clifftops, rolling over the cemetery like a velvety blanket.

The unusually still water of the sea gleamed and glistened like thousands of precious stones with a million shades of pinks and oranges embracing the setting sun. There wasn't the drama of the spring tides from a few years ago tonight. Back then, the high tides had summoned waves that had seemingly increased their intensity with each roll ashore until people, frantic and concerned about flooding, began to hastily fill sandbags and lay them like a pitiful wall against Mother Nature.

A bat flitted at high speed, switching direction at the last moment.

Ironic cliché. Bat-Whitby-Dracula.

Beth shrugged at the bat as it headed off over Whitby, the home of Count Dracula's legend. Beth had firsthand knowledge that the legend was a lie, a cover-up. Indeed, Beth was a part of the conspiracy. The conspiracy that Dracula, although he was portrayed as the villain, had in fact been a protector of the supernatural world. Now, Beth joined his descendants to continue that task.

The bat's high-pitched squeaks forced Beth to pull her long dark hair, its sapphire blue streaks matching her dazzling blue eyes, over her ears in an attempt to shut out the sound. The bat swooped in low, and she felt the wind of its passage caress her cheeks. She instinctively threw out her arm and suspended the bat in an energy field.

"Not on my watch, you don't, buddy."

Pushing her arms out, Beth helped the disoriented bat on his way in the opposite direction before releasing him from the invisible energy field she'd created around it.

She couldn't stop the smile from taking over her face; although new to her, her powers were ancient, gifted to her by the Egyptian god Osiris. He had bestowed upon her the magical powers of Isis, his powerful wife. In her time, Isis had been the source of all magic and was said to have been more intelligent than a million gods.

Beth swiped her right hand in the air, and an orb of white light glowed from the centre of her palm, illuminating the heaviness of the thick night air engulfing her. Something caught her eye, and she squinted through the fog and at the ground before her. Beth bent to pick up the feather lying next to her foot.

No way… is that…?

She picked up the feather, spinning it between the forefinger and thumb of her right hand. The bat's squeals still floated through the air but became more distant with each circle it made.

H— Horus?

Her breath caught in her throat, questioning the distinctive, zebra-like stripes of the feather in her grasp to be that of a peregrine falcon—the animal persona of the god Horus. She wondered if the ancients were trying to contact her from their static point of time in ancient Egypt.

Beth had returned to this plane from her coma to come to terms with the gift she'd received before accepting her fate: to fight alongside Dracula's descendants.

She placed the feather carefully back where she'd found it.

'Your guess is incorrect,' a deep, echoing voice resonated in her head.

The mist had continued to creep in from the sea and up the cliffs, skulking its way across the clifftop cemetery and covering the gravestones furthest away from Beth. The closer it came to her, the thicker it seemed to be, yet there was a warmth to the fog.

Beads of perspiration gathered in her hairline, and a bright yellow light glowed in the midst of the fog. Her palms felt clammy, and her light linen shirt clung to her back.

What's causing this heat?

"Ra? Is that Ra?" Beth felt her eyes widen in awe at speaking directly to the creator of all Egyptian gods and goddesses.

A thrumming filled the air. Beth's hair whipped about her head, switching from left to right. Automatically, she took on the fighter's stance that she'd learned from her friend, Travis, and leaned into the fog, which appeared to be growing denser with every passing moment.

A figure approached. Beth couldn't make out their form immediately, only determining that it was a human form and that they were taller than her.

Her eyes strained, and she wanted to wipe away the thick, oppressive fog that clouded her vision and made her feel like she was looking through a veil.

"Hello?"

The fog cut her words dead. It encompassed them. All the sounds of the evening died away.

Before Beth stood a man with hair and eyes the colour of night. His thin, pinched face somehow glowed ethereal in the muted light of the fog. He wore a rich, dark suit that appeared to absorb any light. The only brightness was the gold adornments of his buttons and cufflinks. Beth bowed her head reverentially.

"Please raise your head." He nodded enthusiastically.

She did as he bade her, locking her eyes with his.

"What? How?" Beth managed words, but whole sentences were elusive.

"Had you not seen the feather, had you not connected the signs and named me, this would never have been possible. Do you understand?" Ra tilted his head to the left in a bird-like motion.

Beth slowly nodded.

What kind of trouble am I in for Ra to be involved?

"You're not," he replied, stealing the thoughts from her subconscious.

Beth gulped, processing Ra's words.

"Osiris has been condemned."

"What does that mean, 'condemned'?" Beth winced, unsure she wanted to know the answer.

"He granted you the knowledge of the ages. Of course there would be consequences."

His dark eyes and stillness lacked emotion, but Beth felt the accusation in his words.

An owl hooted in agreement.

"Osiris has been imprisoned, and he must select a mortal." Ra's words felt like a stone landing on Beth's chest.

"And he chose me?" she interrupted, running her fingers through her hair and then rubbing her eyes.

"You're the reason for his condemnation."

"I didn't ask for any of this. I was unconscious." Beth's tone shocked her.

"True, but you can't deny that your powers have saved those you love. And will continue to protect mortals." His tone was that of a teacher who wasn't annoyed, just disappointed.

"What do you need?" she sighed, resigned to the fact that nothing in this life was free, and although she'd not asked for this, she seemingly had a debt that needed to be paid.

"Osiris is incarcerated in the prison of the gods." Ra's shoulders rose, making him appear even taller than he was. "He granted you the knowledge of the ages and Isis's powers. That wasn't playing by the supernatural rules that govern us."

Ra turned his face to the moon, a soft smile on his lips.

"Okay." The word hung to her lips, drawing itself out. She felt sure there was more to this, more to being stood in a foggy cemetery at night with Ra. "But the rules are pretty woolly, and everyone seems to change them to suit their agenda."

Beth stared into the fog as her thoughts drifted to her father. Her sworn enemy. He was a master manipulator in this world of the supernatural.

"There are trials which he must face." Ra's words dragged her out of her reverie, and she gave him her full attention, shifting her focus from the horizon. "And he needs a mortal to conduct them on his behalf. That is you. He chooses you," Ra finished.

"I already have a job." Beth flung her arms out from her shoulders with the most pathetic reason she could give not to be involved. "What happens if I say no?"

Her voice held no enthusiasm for his answer. Yet again, Beth didn't want to know what it was. Her eyes simply squinted into thin blue lines.

Ra's eyes were unblinking, watching her irrational reasoning.

Then Ra shrugged.

Beth jutted her head towards Ra. She imitated his shrug, exaggerating the action.

"What does that mean?" Her words were clipped, and she spoke them carefully, as if she were treading on eggshells.

"It would be bad… very bad." There was Ra's infuriating shrug again.

"Bad?" Her shoulders almost touched her ears with the question. Beth was trying very hard to keep her cool, but the god before her was being more elusive than dark matter or a giant panda in mating season.

"Very." Ra nodded slowly. His chin touched his chest, then rose back up so he could use his sharp eyes to lock her with that steel stare of his.

He pursed his lips together and began to whistle, his hands sweeping the fog around him in circles. It danced and swayed in time with his tune like he was conducting the elements.

Beth strained her ears, trying to identify the tune, mesmerised by his display. She picked up the song and joined her base to his rhythm by manipulating the light breeze that brought the scent of the sea over the cliffs to them and wrapping it around his dancing fog.

"Patience," Beth whispered. Guns N' Roses—great tune.

Ra's mouth twitched at the left corner. "Shall we?"

The fog swirled faster until it resembled a tornado inside a glass jar, a brilliant glowing sphere of light emanating from the centre of this whirlwind. Beth stopped manipulating the sea breeze but could still taste the salt on her lips.

The sphere's luminosity grew, becoming almost painfully bright in contrast to the darkness that engulfed them in the cemetery on top of the cliff.

Ra's hand extended into the brilliance at the centre of the maelstrom of fog; the light seemed to spark and flare at the edges. Beth entered the void without a second thought, entering an eerily silent world.

The air was thick with the scent of a dry heat that scorched the insides of her nostrils, catching in the back of her throat. Tiny specks of light twinkled like stars in her peripheral vision; it seemed like these heavenly spheres were guiding the way through the vortex Ra had created.

Her ears pulsated with the rhythmic thrumming, and her eyes became slits as she squinted while her face was pelted with tiny grains of something.

What is this? Beth couldn't place the sharpness pricking her face.

"It's a sandstorm," she whispered, but her voice was whisked away, stolen by the ever-increasing storm. She was forced to shut her eyelids entirely to avoid them being filled with the sand that stung her cheeks.

The storm passed as abruptly as it had started, allowing Beth to finally take in her surroundings. She could do nothing to stop her jaw from dropping open and her eyes from stretching wide.

"Welcome home, Isis."

Ra's words showed genuine affection, and his eyes twinkled when he smiled at her.

The sun's brilliance was sinking, turning the sky into an inferno. The Great Pyramid on the Giza plateau before Beth glowed in its flames, which sent a thick purple hue around it, giving it an air of mystery.

"This"—Beth spread her arms wide in disbelief—"is the god's prison?"

Ra stared with that now familiar unblinking gaze—the falcon's gaze.

An owl's call broke the silence, and she wondered at the sight of a Pharaoh eagle-owl's expansive wings gliding through her line of sight, encompassing the Sphinx, pyramids, and setting sun.

"So, what now?"

Beth looked around in the failing light. Most of the tourists who'd thronged the plateau were making their way back to their coaches, turning to get a last look at the magnificence of the structures that defied man and time. They reached for their cameras as one, the synchronised swimmers of the photography world. They continued to happily snap away, oblivious to the two people standing in the background who'd appeared out of thin air. Unseen and unnoticed.

A woman, Beth couldn't determine her age, stood on tiptoes, her finger outstretched, while a man, also of indeterminate age, directed her, seemingly to catch the perfect hilarious shot of her touching the top of the pyramid or holding the sun in her hand. Various other distant tourists were clearly doing the same thing from minutely different angles but for identical holiday shots.

A glint caught Beth's eye, and she was drawn to a camera lens standing apart from the main group of photographers. *Now that's a photo I'd like to see*, she thought, chuckling to herself. *Someone taking a picture of everyone taking the same picture—that's pure gold.*

Beth's shoulders dropped with a sigh. Looking back at the couples and families trying to catch a funny photograph reminded her of the time when she and her best friend, Ian, had fooled around trying to catch similar hilarious shots on a rainy weekend when he'd come to visit her in Whitby. She must have been about eighteen at the time and had only recently arrived in the town herself.

Eleven years. Beth sighed, her eyebrows hitching up in surprise that so much time had passed. So much had happened in her life. It seemed like a lifetime ago.

While she'd been thinking, the tourists had traipsed back onto their coaches. The sounds of the dry engines struggling to start assaulted her ears, and the smell of diesel fuel made her nose twitch. It was the smell of childhood summer outings and walking past idling ice cream vans.

Beth watched the coaches drive away until they were the dots of worker ants in the distance. The few remaining locals smoked and talked, making their way home for dinner.

"Now."

Ra's whisper shivered down Beth's spine.

Another vortex opened, tiny circular lights guiding the way, and she stepped inside.

It was dark, not pitch black, but the kind of darkness that made Beth glance here and there, convinced she'd seen something or someone. The air smelt stale and musty.

What was that?

"Hello?"

Beth felt the weight of the ancient stones of the pyramid pressing down on her; she knew Ra had transported her into the prison of the gods. She didn't understand his need for theatrics. Why hadn't he transported her straight inside, and where had he gone?

'She's here, she's here, she's here,' a thousand voices whispered as one directly inside Beth's head. Dark shadows ran, flew, and swooped around Beth.

If I'm the only person here, how do I know if the voices are in my mind? she pondered for the briefest of moments.

"What is your challenge?" Her voice projected with confidence.

'She thinks there's only one, she thinks there's only one—hahaha."

Beth clasped her hands over her ears, blocking out the cacophony of laughter that made it feel like the stones above her moved.

They are my challenge, Beth realised.

Beth felt movement all around her. There was a grating sound coming from somewhere she couldn't determine. The darkness was playing tricks with her senses.

Better rely on my superpowers.

She tried to make light of the circumstances to spur her on. Closing her eyes, the room went dark, then slowly her other senses gave her a sightless internal vision of the situation. Huge blocks of stone were lining up in the vast space above her and heading towards her. She could feel their weight in the air. Fine hairs prickled their way up her arms.

She dropped to the floor, opening her eyes and holding an enormous, perfectly square block the size of a small car in a pure, brilliant white energy ball. The light she'd produced allowed her to see the other blocks heading her way.

Dark shadows clung to the corners, and an unseen wind rushed around the room, shrieking, distracting Beth from working out what the test was.

Then she saw it: although the blocks she held above her looked the same size and shape, there were differences. Beth twisted her left wrist, making one cube spin and rotate. The wails from the shadows and wind continued.

"Silence," she demanded.

Instantly, a silence worse than the shrieks descended on her.

"There, it's a jigsaw."

Quickly, Beth manipulated the blocks above her head while she continued to lie prone on the dusty floor.

Above her in the high vaulted ceiling, her outstretched hands manoeuvred the square blocks, spinning them, trying to align them even as more joined the puzzle. There were now nine blocks rotating above her.

That's it.

Beth pinned the four corners in place, hovering but static, before rotating her left and right wrists simultaneously so that the remaining pieces slotted into place. The image revealed a snake whose body folded over and over on itself, creating repeating figures of eight.

Now what?

Her arms remained outstretched, and she rolled sideways to get to her knees, then gained her feet. Beth allowed her arms to drop. The faceless shadows shrouded the blocks. They consumed them, almost devouring her completed jigsaw.

The sound of rock grating on rock to her left took Beth's eyes from the jigsaw. A whoosh of air blasted through the newly made gateway, causing the hairs on her neck to stand to attention. Then came another whoosh, and her eyes caught sight of a dense orb the colour of the midnight sky flying from behind her through the gap where a flickering light could be seen.

Guess you want me to follow.

Adrenaline surged through her and every one of Beth's fight-or-flight triggers was firing, but she knew that beyond this room lay the reason she was here. What she had to do. Floating images of her friends and her sister, Alice, flashed through her mind.

The sooner she got through this, the sooner she'd be back with them, fighting alongside them and protecting them against the evils of the supernatural world they were all a part of.

Beth glanced at the shadows; they seemed to pause in their writhing to watch her enter the labyrinth. The walls of the narrow, twisting corridor were rough and damp. The uncertainty of what lay ahead slowed Beth down. She tentatively placed one foot carefully in front of the other, waiting for the next surprise. The air was thick with the smell of decay mixed with the dampness of the earth.

Every ten metres, the open flame of a flickering torch warmed Beth's face as she stepped past it.

Who lit the torches? How long have they been burning?

The flickering light crackled and cast ghostly shadows up the walls of the narrow tunnel and onto the ceiling. Burning oil rose from the flames, filling the air with a not-unpleasant smell that masked the dampness and decay. It was the smell of antiquity, and Beth rather enjoyed it.

The flames seemed to dance and sway in the darkness to a soundless tune, the main beat of which was the sound of Beth's footsteps on the sloping floor, which led her deeper into the heart of the Great Pyramid. Finally, she reached the next obstacle. A pit. Beth peered down to see scorpions climbing over each other and snakes interweaving over and over. She shivered in disgust.

'You will fail,' the voices taunted.

"Disperse." Beth's hands were wrapped in an ethereal white glow. She positioned the light, showing the creatures their paths to freedom. They scurried and slithered through the gaps and holes in their pit that Beth had created for them.

'You cannot defeat us; Osiris is one of us now,' the voices claimed.

Their dry whispers sprinted up and down the corridors like the breaths of unseen creatures breathing down her neck. Beth ignored them and forged through the labyrinth until she was suddenly plunged into darkness, like someone or something had blown all the torches out.

Beth cast a shining ball to hover above her.

"*Guide* me to Osiris," she commanded. The shimmering ball floated along the tunnel, casting shadows in its wake. Beth followed. The shrieks behind her intensified behind her, turning into pitiful moans of…

Of what? Are they anguish? Sorrow? Am I getting closer?

Abruptly, her progress was blocked by a living shadow creature coalescing out of the darkness before her. Beth approached it warily. Unlike the others, this one seemed almost human in shape and structure. Its sightless eyes and lack of any distinct features made it even more menacing.

Thinking quickly, Beth summoned an energy wave of brilliant white light and pushed it down the tunnel. Light conquered shadow. The screech from the creature faded into nothingness.

Beth sniffed, drawing in a new yet familiar odour.

Is that smoke?

The air had an acrid tinge, with the telltale shimmering of heat haze and thin wisps of smoke. Beth wrapped herself in a protective bubble of healing energy to avoid harm and carried on the way the pyramid's passageways led her into the labyrinth.

It appears my next challenge is to find my way through a maze. How many bleeding challenges are there? Beth stiffened her spine, poised to take her next determined step.

"Lead me through this challenge," she commanded, and her glowing orb appeared again.

From the corner of her eye, she saw a dark orb, its dense obsidian hue the complete opposite of her own conjured helper. Her feet turned towards the darkness, unable to resist.

Just one step. Just to see…

An unseen force pulled her towards the darkness. Like a cartoon character, she put on the brakes, screeching to a halt before her foot touched the ground. Beth sensed, with everything she was, or was yet to become, that it was the wrong direction. Turning back to her own bright light, she turned away from the lure of the dark orb.

She felt the heat before seeing the tunnel ahead lighting up. The distinctive crackle of flames attacked her ears. In the next corner of the maze, a wall of fire gave a crimson, orange, and yellow war dance, daring her to cross it and be consumed by the flames.

Beth's balled fists rubbed at her eyes, making them water and fill with more tears as her eyes tried to protect themselves from her environment. She blinked repeatedly, attempting to remove the foreign objects of smoke and soot. Within the flames was a figure; her streaming eyes could have been deceiving her, but she didn't think so.

Is that…? she asked herself before diving into action.

Without a second thought, she rushed into the flames and hooked her arm under Ra's shoulder, trying to wrap him in the safety of her protection spell. She smelled her skin fizzling and burning when a flame penetrated her cocoon of safety.

"Argh!" Beth cried out, almost losing her grip on Ra. "Goddammit!"

She heaved with all her might, and eventually, she made it to safety on the far side of the flames.

"Why… why didn't you leave me? Ra spluttered. His voice sounded

The Shadow Trials

scorched.

"How long were you in there?"

Beth placed her hand on Ra's heart, and a brilliant white light glowed soft and steady. This was a giveaway that she was letting her healing powers wash over him.

Then, as an afterthought, she brushed over the burnt skin on her left arm. The faintest of glows emitted from her hand, and the blistered skin returned to its smooth, unblemished texture and light summer tan it had had before she'd entered the flames and rescued Ra.

"I used the last of my energy, the last of my power, to project my image to you." Ra's eyes were softer than when she'd seen him in the cemetery.

He sees himself as harsher than he is, Beth reasoned.

"You weren't really there?"

Ra nodded, his eyes locked on hers.

"But how—"

He cut her off, placing a delicate finger onto her lips, sealing them shut with the most delicate of touches. Beth felt a shiver run down her spine.

I've been touched by a god, her inner voice screamed, unable to contain its excitement.

"Magic, my dear. Your kind of magic. That's what led me to find you."

"The magic of the ancients…" Beth grinned despite the situation she was in.

His lips turned up at the corners, and his eyes looked to be watering, as if they were filled with tears.

He's proud of me. Beth grinned with pride.

"Yes, I am, Isis—excuse me, Beth. I mean Beth."

Although Beth wanted to ask a million questions, she was also aware that they may be up against a deadline. No one had told her a deadline existed, but in her experience, one was usually implied in these situations. She always felt like she was on the back foot in trials, tests, and battles. Playing catch up with the older kids who knew and played the rules to their advantage.

"Why are you here?" Beth asked, trying to unravel how the father of the gods had been imprisoned.

I mean, trapping Osiris was bad enough, but Ra? The Ra, for fuck's sake!

"And Osiris? What of Osiris?"

Beth looked around the room they occupied. The flames were beginning to die down now that they were no longer fuelled by the sun god Ra.

"*I* defended Osiris and his faith in you. I think I was, perhaps, a little too enthusiastic." Ra's face beamed with a wide smile.

"You're both here because of me?" Beth sighed, her shoulders dropped, and her usual proud, ramrod-straight back folded in on itself in defeat.

"I might remind you that you never asked for this." Ra's tone was like that of a teacher to their willing pupil. "You sacrificed yourself for me."

His voice was softer than a feather drifting slowly to the floor on a summer breeze. A summer breeze that was abruptly snuffed out and turned to twilight. The air around them thickened, and thrumming filled their ears once more.

The time for talking had passed. The time for action was now upon them.

The shadows that had been ever-present inside the pyramid formed behind them. They merged, creating a solid form, a prison cell of bars, not made from forged steel but from their beings, whatever they may have been.

Osiris appeared inside the prison they'd formed, incarcerated yet resplendent in his dual crown of Upper and Lower Egypt, holding his mace and flail. Like Ra, he appeared in his human form.

"You came." Osiris's regal voice reverberated around the walls.

Beth wasn't sure, but she thought she felt the shadows shrink back from him, cowering within themselves for fear of what he'd do to them if—or when—he escaped. Beth was certain of one thing, she would free Osiris, lord of the underworld, or die trying.

"Release him. I've done your bidding." Beth's voice almost matched Osiris's in its strength. "I came to Osiris's aid. Release him."

Beth's eyes searched the cavernous room for who she should address. But bar the shadows, there was only Ra, Osiris, and herself.

'You are yet to complete your challenge.'

A dark fragment split away from the cell they'd structured. The breakaway shadow spun to a stop next to Osiris's place of detention.

'You must work out how to free your god.' The phantom spat the word 'god' like it was a dirty word. 'He'll be freed if you're dependable and worthy of his trust in you. If not…' The shrouded creature ended with a cackle worthy of a Grimm's fairytale witch.

"If not… what?" Beth clutched at Ra's arm, shaking it. Her awe of being in the presence of gods had vanished in the desperation of their predicament.

"The worst thing that could happen to a god," Ra answered with a slow, determined edge to his voice. He seemed to be stalling.

"Which is?" Beth nudged him with her elbow. She needed the ugly truth and to know the odds she was up against.

"Invisibility."

Ra's answer did nothing to clarify or satisfy her inquiry. She nodded, encouraging him to continue.

"Our immortality, our names being spoken for millennia after we have left this plane for the next. If you fail Osiris," Ra paused, "we will fail to have existed. Our memory will be lost, all trace of us erased for eternity."

Beth couldn't help but gulp. Although she'd fought before, she'd never fought alone or with the stakes being the elimination of not one but two gods. And not just any gods. These were two of the most recognised gods in modern times, having left the earth in ancient times.

That was no mean feat, and what was there between them and oblivion? Beth, a barmaid and artist who'd lost her way and stumbled onto a path of supernatural and otherworldly beings.

If Osiris never existed, he'd never have given me Isis's powers, and I'd know nothing. Plus, I wouldn't be here, so… I can't fail. I've got this.

This understanding made her more determined to beat the shadows and free Osiris and Ra. Losing simply wasn't an option.

All bets are off, there are no rules. Dammit all to hell.

The breakaway shadow swirled high above their heads and screamed around the room.

'I am the foundation of all that you know.' It screeched to a halt an inch from Beth's nose.

'Yet you may never see me directly.' The shadow vanished only to reappear instantly, resting against Osiris's cage nonchalantly, its bent elbow resting on a shadowy bar.

'I am solid and unyielding but can also be shaped and moulded.' A fluidity flowed through it, making the speaker look like a dark lava lamp.

'Show me your answer with your magic, keeper of Isis's powers,' the creature demanded.

Beth's eyes moved from Osiris to Ra and back to the shadowy creature.

With a slow blink, she took a deep cleansing breath and carefully wrapped protection spells to cover everything beyond the walls of where they stood.

"Geb!" Beth shouted at the top of her lungs for the god of the earth. Her arms launched forward from her body towards where Osiris was imprisoned. Osiris placed his hand on his crown moments before—

A giant rumbling followed Beth's outstretched arms, and the floor of the pyramidical room rolled like a stormy sea, sending rippling waves crashing into the shadow prison holding Osiris in place. Several of the shadows faded away to howls and moans. They flew limply at Beth, ragged and somehow torn before disintegrating in front of her.

'I am a force of transformation, a creature of paradox, a bringer of light and darkness.' The words hissed from the shadow like a snake in Beth's ear. 'You cannot defeat ussssss.'

"Give me the rest of your riddle, spectre," Beth boomed, the power of her voice surprising even her.

'A beacon of warmth and a harbinger of pain. A tool and a weapon that can be harnessed yet cannot be contained,' the shadow sneered at Beth.

"Sekhmet!" Beth raised her arms to the ceiling high above her, swirling around in a circle, her sparkling, luminating white power sparking from the tips of her fingers.

Ra sighed, "Ah, my beautiful daughter, Sekhmet." His eyes took on a faraway look as Beth continued summoning Sekhmet, the vengeful manifestation of Ra, the sun god's power, and his daughter.

The answer to the riddle was fire. Flames leapt from Beth's fingertips, and the air in the room became singed. With her left arm, Beth wove a pattern around Osiris and secured another copy of the same pattern to the walls to protect the pyramid's interior.

Flames dashed across the space between Beth and Osiris's prison. An explosion of red, orange, and yellow flames were licked by dancing blue and green coils of immense heat that collided with the shadow's structure holding Osiris. Beth and Ra fell to their knees, their hands clasping their ears to block out the high-pitched squeals from the shadows that remained to form the cage.

"I know your next riddle," Beth said, getting to her feet and helping Ra join her. Her hands went to her hips.

"You bring life and destruction, calmness and fury. You can carve out vast, expansive channels, yet you are invisible."

Beth's voice rose over the crackling of the flames.

"Shu, you are Shu. The air."

As the words left Beth's lips, a tornado of power built, whipping the flames higher and higher. The screams of the shadows intensified, and more of them crumbled.

"No more riddles."

Beth could feel the frown pulling her eyes together in concentration.

"Let's finish this—Djet!"

With that, Beth summoned flowing water. A tidal wave smashed through the room, destroying the weakened cage and freeing Osiris.

Finally, the last trial was completed. Osiris and Ra were free, and the gods welcomed Osiris back to rule over them. He bowed his head to her in thanks before he and Ra shimmered out of existence.

Well, I'm glad there were no sentimental goodbyes and gushing appreciation, although a 'thanks very much' wouldn't have gone amiss.

Beth felt a sense of relief and accomplishment wash over her. She'd helped to bring about redemption and had proven herself a worthy conduit for the power of Isis. Every day, she doubted her worthiness and convinced herself they'd made a mistake and that, one day, someone would come to reclaim the powers, but today—today—she knew she'd proven herself to be a rightful possessor of the title 'goddess'.

'You did well. He was right to trust you with the mother of magic's powers. Let me send you on your way.' The shadow spoke with respect in its voice.

"I can find my way, thanks."

Beth began chanting words, low under her breath. A glowing orb, the colours identical to mother of pearl, formed itself into a portal opening before her, and she stepped back into the cemetery.

As Ra's perfect orb pierced the darkness, the first rays of sunlight appeared and the veil of shadows began to recede, leaving Whitby bathed in the warm glow of the new day.

Beth walked back towards Whitby with a newfound sense of purpose. The wind rustling through her hair and the sound of the sea crashing against the cliffs were constant reminders of the magic and wonder that lay just beyond the mortal world.

"Hey, babe, what you doing up here?"

Doubled over and sucking in great gulps of air at the top of the hundred and ninety-nine steps that led from Whitby town centre to the remains of Whitby Abbey at the top of the cliff was Travis.

"Bit early for a workout, isn't it?" She felt her lips twist and tried to control the flirty nature of her words—without success.

Man, he looks good when he's worked up a sweat. Beth mentally fanned herself to calm her thoughts down.

"Bit late to be coming home from a night out, isn't it?" he retorted, a frown covering his forehead, making his eyebrows bunch into one big fat hairy caterpillar across the bridge of his nose.

Beth snorted. "Sorry, Dad."

She clapped her hands over her mouth, realising not only that she'd referred to him as Dad but that her dad was not only Travis's but his entire family's mortal enemy.

"Sorry, Trav, I didn't think."

"Don't worry, babe."

He's got his breath back remarkably quickly, she thought. *Vampires catch all the breaks. I'd be out of action for months if I ran up those steps.*

Beth walked towards the top of the steps, pausing only to peck Travis on the cheek.

"Fancy a coffee? I'll tell you all about my night out in Egypt and hanging with Osiris and Ra."

She made her way down the stairs, not needing to check that he was following.

ABOUT THE AUTHOR

SJ Covey is a talented young adult fantasy author who weaves intricate tales of adventure, emotion, and self-discovery.

With a flair for creating vivid, compelling worlds where the narratives often challenge traditional notions of good and evil, presenting a more nuanced view of the world. SJ's novels captivate readers, drawing them into the lives of unforgettable characters who must face extraordinary challenges.

Influenced by a love of mythology, magic, and the complexities of human nature, SJ Covey's writing resonates with both teens and adults who seek adventure beyond the ordinary.

When not writing, SJ enjoys immersing themselves in fantasy lore, exploring the outdoors with her exceptionally proud husband, and equally proud Labrador Bauer, who also features in the book, where they enjoy finding inspiration in the everyday magic of life.

Covey's work is celebrated for its imaginative depth and ability to engage readers on a personal and emotional level, ensuring a lasting connection with fans of her five part book series "The Order," which follows the journey of characters Alice and Beth as they navigate an unknown world filled with myths, truths, and intricate bloodlines.

Visit her website SJCovey.com and please swipe a copy, you'll be glad you did.

Untapped Potential

Melissa Rose Rogers

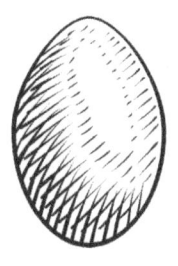

32nd Day of the Month of Nordi in the Year 5004
The Manse of Count Horymír Podrosov in the Southwest of the Lands of Wulkei

Though the sun shone in a cloudless sky, flowers bloomed, and the winds were fair, it was the season of lean longing for young, nearsighted Jutta. Flowers were not yet fruit, and the contents of the storehouse were less than agreeable. Even the odd cabbage sent by the crofters had withered or gone to blossom.

Food fatigue and confinement festered within her, so she took refuge in her library of grimoires. These had been copied at her father's commission, employing a league of scribes at the library in the capital over several years.

"Won't you come down? Had I known you'd imprison yourself, I would never have commissioned all those books." Jutta's father Horymír crossed his arms as if in anger, but his brow betrayed worry.

"There's nothing to do and nowhere to go." She looked up from *Spells of Hermod*. Stacked with books and a decanter of summerberry wine, the table was a perfect barrier between her and her father's cumbersome anecdotes.

Her father pursed his lips on his sunburnt face. He spent as much time as possible overseeing the crops, visiting crofters, and discussing different techniques for irrigation and fertilization. Agriculture was the lifeblood of his fertile lands. Mud stuck to his boots and clung to the crevices of his hands.

"We have a guest," her father said, standing taller and letting his arms fall to his sides.

Jutta tried to recall any gossip from the manse. No preparations had been made. The guest chambers were unaired as far as she knew. As she considered, her father held his tongue, and she couldn't quell her curiosity any longer.

"We're not expecting anyone. Who could possibly be here when the roads are mushy?"

"A traveler from down the river bearing gifts from afar."

Jutta's stomach knotted in suspicion. "No one comes down the river. There's nothing down the river."

"Let's not insult our visitor." Her father's eyes glinted. "Why don't you ask him about his travels yourself?"

Having said his piece, he limped down the wooden stairs.

His old jousting injury must be bothering him more than usual, she thought.

She glanced over the page before her—an illustration of henbane with a description of its uses—and her interest fled. Shutting the book, she fought the urge to follow her father, whose footsteps had now faded beyond hearing. Raw stubbornness kept her on the horsehair chair, staring out the large, triangular window.

Her attic library was pure indulgence, an addition of wood upon fired brick. Bricks, common to the area, made up the rest of the manse. Trees were scarce in these flat lands of crops and cattle, so paper and wood were treasured. What few trees grew were bastions of splendor against the horizon, sacred emblems inviolate and untouchable, and she was privileged enough to notice several—albeit blurry—along the river flowing through her father's lands.

The Greater Moon shone as an indeterminate blob hanging in the afternoon sky. The wind rushed against the fortress, and in the distance, great ripples formed among the reedy, green oatgrass. *It looks like the ocean here,*

Father had often said. Travel didn't suit Jutta, who had never seen a lake, much less the ocean.

Curiosity at her father's announcement overtook her. No horns had sounded from the guards, and there had not been the frenetic compulsion of order typical of a visitor's approach. Gathering her skirts in one hand and gripping the railing with the other, she made her way down the stairs until she came to a door opening to faded tapestries and high, lancet windows that provided thin rows of light, not unlike dungeon bars.

Tension coiled around her from the moment her leather slipper touched the floor. It was too quiet without the clanging of cutlery, or the armorer's hammer, or even the muted laughter of servants.

Where is everyone? It's as if they've vanished, she considered, surveying the gallery. This room formed the hub between the living quarters, workspaces, and the Great Hall. Two fireplaces stood parallel at either end, between which were large, vibrant rugs overlapping in haphazard rectangles. The logs hunched low on each grate, their flames sidling lazily to and fro.

Father would receive a guest in his study, Jutta decided.

Opening the towering, arched door into the corridor to his study, she hesitated in the sudden black. Where the thin windows of the gallery had displaced darkness, this corridor held but a few torches and three doors leading to the servants' passageway, the Great Hall, and the study.

Murmurs filtered from the study, so she listened for more clues about the staff or the visitor.

Hearing no more, she knocked, creating a decisive interruption.

"Enter," her father called through the thick, studded door.

After turning the latch, the door creaked in protest as she opened it with smooth deliberation.

"Jutta. Good of you to join us. This is Bořivoj. I mentioned he'd traveled from the *desert*. He went by way of the ocean and the river."

What nonsense.

Jutta stared at her father, trying to see how this man, presumably a merchant, would see him: weather-beaten but in fine clothes in a resplendent home. Horymír formed the picture of a simple man tied to the dirt, ripe for profit, a fertile field for scams.

Next, she glanced past the brazier, past the window of imported glass, to the tufted chair in which the visitor sat. With chestnut hair and pallid skin like her own but icy blue eyes, this *Bořivoj* had coloring typical of her countrymen. Her eyes were the less-lauded hazel, uncommon and indistinct from the neighboring countries' inhabitants. His physique seemed average, though it was difficult to assess his frame under his stiff and expansive cloak.

"Good afternoon, Lady Jutta. It's a pleasure to meet you. I must say… you're as lovely as your portrait."

The words chilled her. Her father sending her portrait would mean a marriage arrangement. *But I haven't sat for a portrait.* She turned back to her father, who took on a sheepish grin.

Instead of pressing this issue, she asked, "Where are all the servants? It's as empty as a crypt."

Bořivoj answered for her father, making her heart lurch. "Why, unloading your bride price."

Her insides quailed, and it took every scrap of resolve not to flee the study. She made her way, in awkward steps, toward her flesh and blood and away from this stranger. Her mind reeled as she searched her father's face

Once stood behind her seated father, with her back as stiff as the chair's wooden frame, she studied Bořivoj again. His eyes shone bright, his raiment appeared quite fine, and his face was freshly shaven. His strong chin and high forehead with groomed brows gave him a not unpleasant, rectangular face. He returned the gaze with confidence, a smile tugging at his lips.

Her father cleared his throat, not turning toward her. "I had meant to speak with you about this, but the time was never right, and he made better speed down the river than expected."

Bořivoj's blue eyes burned over Jutta's face, measuring her reaction, but she kept her expression neutral. *I hope to speak with my father first and find out his line of reasoning. I should have expected a match would be arranged for me after I turned down Gesdow. I'm nineteen, after all, and my cousins were married off by my age.*

Horymír stood, sunlight catching on the silvers in his dark hair. "I suspect you will have much in common, much to speak of. For now, let's see how the unloading goes."

Bořivoj moved his attention to her father and nodded, rising from his chair.

Jutta felt relief to be leaving this stifling room, yet nagging questions pulled at her mind. *Where will we live? How long can I put this off? Why me?*

What do I have to offer? Father's lands, eh?

The courtyard, a muddy patch surrounded by bulky brick walls, held unfamiliar men in vibrant turquoise livery alongside Count Horymír's servants as they unloaded crates from the riverside. The river elsewise brought nothing but grindylows and minuscule trout.

She stood upon the wall-walk and watched, the wind harassing her skirts and picking at her braid like an ill-behaved child. Her father stood an arm's length ahead on the left, and the surprise visitor about the same to her right.

"They're making quick progress," Bořivoj said, closing the distance between them.

For just a moment, she glanced at him, then looked back ahead, clamping her jaw. She thought with annoyance, *I'm very precious with my personal space.*

She had studied grimoires over the past couple of years, incorporating skills in her routine, passive repertoire, such as noticing proximity. It helped compensate for her poor eyesight. The downside was that reducing said awareness was a challenge.

Undeterred by her silence, her groom-to-be asked, "Curious about what's inside?"

"I'm sure you and my father will inspect them in great detail." Frost rimed her tone, and then regret and worry rose within her. *What if I make him angry? He might be the vengeful sort.*

"Certain items will pique your interest, if I'm not mistaken," he said, voice softening. "I have gifts for you."

A lengthy trunk, long as a coffin but taller, caught her eyes, or rather its locks did, as did its magenta blobs of wax seals over parchment with wisps of black ink. From her periphery, her intended followed her gaze. The men unloading it shifted it to adjust their grip.

"Careful not to rip the parchment," Bořivoj called down.

Straining, they focused on him for an instant before making adjustments. Another worker approached, then another. Three people proved awkward, but four worked well enough. In the end, they carried it one corner each, almost as if they were pallbearers.

"Well, I've seen enough," Horymír proclaimed, stepping past her and Bořivoj.

Jutta turned toward her father, shakiness flaring in her hands.

"The entire staff will make an adequate chaperone for your honor, my dear, and I'd like to give you two a few moments to speak candidly."

"Thank you, sir." Bořivoj lowered his head, and the deference struck Jutta as sincere.

"Think nothing of it," said her father, making his way downstairs.

Wasting no time, Jutta's suitor stepped closer. "I am told, from your father's writing, that you have an interest in the arcane."

"Yes. My father indulged my interests, and a few years ago, he commissioned a team of scribes to copy grimoires from Jednal. Over the next couple of years, key books were copied by a host of scribes, and that's not counting the originals purchased from booksellers and peddlers. My collection is the land's second largest."

"I'd like to see this collection. I, too, have an interest in magic, as you will see from my gifts for you."

"Is that what you sell? What kind of merchant are you, eh?" She studied his cold eyes as long as she could stand before turning back toward the courtyard.

"We can't always choose how we begin. That path formed me, but now I will make myself into a new man for a new world."

"Whatever do you mean?"

Though the cold fire of his eyes bore into her, freezing and consuming, she didn't turn back.

"Things will change for us. You'll see soon enough."

Her eyes narrowed for an instant, not that he could see, but she forced her gaze to relax anyway. A shiver wracked her frame, though a timely gust of wind offered the pretense of cold.

"You're trembling. I see gooseflesh along your neck. Let's head back inside and open your gifts."

His manners were attentive and gentlemanly as he led her back into her home. *He's putting me at ease, or at least trying to, but I'm like a discarded bister seed spinning toward the decaying forest floor.*

Where before the manse had been too quiet, now it was full of clanging, banging, and the steward conducting the household, laden as they were with crates and trunks. Before, it had felt crisp and clean, but now, it was stuffy with the bustle and baggage.

Her father watched it all from the corridor leading toward his study, though she couldn't gauge his expression.

The trunk caught her eye. Jutta whirled toward it and ran a finger down the length of the parchment. The parchment felt brittle, but its black ink looked unfaded.

"A sealing spell, eh?" The magenta wax bore the imprint of some symbol of power unknown to her. Brushing a circle with her pointer around its edges, she considered the spell. It was the dead Yona script, which wasn't surprising given that her father had said this man had journeyed from the desert. "This line's about emanations? Is that correct?"

"I had hoped we would have less of an audience when we discussed this trunk."

"Tell me when the time is right for opening it. I am curious."

The irony jolted her—her father hadn't found the timing to tell her something important, but now she was expecting a stranger to grace her with knowledge.

Bořivoj only nodded.

Soon, they were swept up in the bustle that Jutta would have expected: the airing of the guest rooms, the parade of linens being scuttled down the side halls, the cellars and larder delved into for the best remnants.

Once the servants dispersed, Jutta was alone with Bořivoj in the long gallery save for an elderly woman serving as a chaperone before the opposite fireplace on a spinning wheel, its humming a constant refrain. Jutta couldn't quite tell who it was, and the woman kept silent.

Crates and trunks and boxes formed a meandering maze over the carpets between the two fireplaces. The aromas of wood and river tickled her nostrils as Jutta and Bořivoj made their way through them all.

Perhaps I should be excited, she thought. Her cousins would be. Instead, annoyance and numbness cycled through her: annoyance at her father for not preparing her for this, annoyance at herself for not being more grateful, and numb resignation that this was inescapable.

Bořivoj put forth predictable gifts: fine silk and dishes so thin that firelight passed through their painted rims. Then he produced unfamiliar spices from the improbable land her ancestors had legends of escaping from. Many boxes remained unopened, though Bořivoj, eyes flashing, insisted he would be pleased to show her more.

She moved toward the mysterious trunk. "What's in this?" Meeting his piercing blue eyes, she thought, *he's assessing my worthiness.*

"This holds keys to the future. Instruments of change. I've brought these from afar and faced untold dangers to share them with the right person. I think that's you."

She almost rolled her eyes at *untold dangers* but stopped herself. Was it melodrama? She couldn't tell, so Jutta simply let slip, "But you don't know me."

"I know enough *about* you to want to know more, to build a future with you, and not just for us. Now, are you ready for what's inside?"

Jutta nodded, a knot of dread pulling her guts taut and silencing her. From someone else's mouth, the comment about building a future might mean heirs and a legacy, but his statements earlier about a new world and their future being *not just for us* echoed through her.

He whispered words of power in an unknown tongue, blanketing them in quiet as he used an athame to cut a circle in the air around her and the trunk. He made the motion seem smooth despite the awkward path necessitated by the maze of crates.

He's created a caim, what should be a safe place but for me it's a trap, she decided.

Bořivoj pried the sealing wax from the lid in a swift motion, then lifted the parchment pieces one at a time and unfastened the locks with an array of keys off a small key ring. When he flung back the lid, golden silk caught her eye. Vibrant as a sunrise, fine embroidery stretched over all she could see.

Much better than what I could produce.

Jutta took a halting step closer. The muted hum of the spinning wheel across the gallery grounded her as she inspected the three spheres before her. Perfectly round, smooth, and flawless, they reminded her of snake eggs, except they were unlike anything she'd seen outside of a book and as large as goose eggs. These eggs, in delicate hues of blue, brown, and pink, were spaced with such care on the gold-colored cloth that they might have been artisan pottery on display.

"Lindworm eggs, eh?" Jutta turned away from the spheres, meeting Bořivoj's captivating eyes.

A smile pulled across his face. "Try again."

A traveler down the river, bearing gifts from afar, her father had said.

"Dragon eggs? Great dragons? As in, you crossed the desert with these? They can't be. Are they seaworm eggs?"

"Dragon eggs. I stole them. That's why I took the precautions of the sealing spells, the caim, and the locks."

Legend had it that eons past, the four mortals Paullté, Halvo, Eyas, and Wulkei led groups of fellow escaped slaves across the desert and away from the tyranny of the dragons. There were factions among the groups, and they formed four different areas.

The country named for Wulkei was the first to be settled. Afterward, areas named for Eyas and Paullté were settled farther to the west and south. Then, lastly, the small, secretive nation of Halvo was formed from dissenters in Eyas.

But those were tales dating back nearly a thousand years. No one actually believed in *dragons*. There were rare lindworms and small salamanders, but the idea of great dragons or the mass migration across the desert was absurd. Nothing but fool's gold from a charlatan.

"Touch them," he instructed as if daring her.

Annoyance flooded her, but she wouldn't quail. Jutta reached forward and caressed the pink one. It felt warm and brittle. The texture reminded her of a duck egg, but it had to be thicker, surely. A moment afterward, it glowed from within, and a shadow formed inside the opaque treasure of a tiny creature curled up.

She gasped and snatched her hand back, studying the dimming shadow. Then her vision snapped to darkness. She gasped again, but this time, she felt embraced.

Who are you? You are not like the other, a voice said within her mind.

"I'm Jutta. Who are you?" She wasn't sure if her words came out of her mouth or were only inside her head.

I don't have my name yet. After I break free from this captivity, I will, he told her, and she knew it was a he.

Captivity, what an odd way to describe being in a shell, she thought.

The light from the fading sun and the glow of the hearths increased behind her eyelids, her vision steadily returning. She opened her eyes to see the man whom her father wanted her to marry was chuckling at her.

"Typically, the dragons push their will on people, who obey mindlessly. You *spoke* to it. Not everyone can. You are exceptionally perceptive and strong-willed." His expression struck her as smug.

She ignored his comments to make her own. "They communicate with their minds. That's what the line about emanations meant. That's why you're using suppressive spells."

"Among other reasons."

Jutta said nothing, dread squeezing her belly, so she moved her attention to the old woman spinning.

Bořivoj followed her gaze and said, eyes sparkling, "We'll discuss it more later." He released the caim, and sound rushed back.

The now frenzied servants returned to their duties and quickly prepared the guest rooms for Bořivoj and his cadre.

Dinner was the best storehouse remnants prepared in the quickest way: good appleberry wine, though not their best; hard cheese with rinds washed each day since last summer; cured ham with savory gravy; and crusty bread.

Served at the long table in the Great Hall, it proved awkward. Being a rural county far from the capital, they didn't receive many guests. While her father was intolerably cheerful and Bořivoj feigned bashful, she couldn't bring herself to chat. Thoughts of the egg pulled at her.

Could the voice be a trick of his? What if it's real? I must examine it again more closely.

Her father regaled them with local gossip of the sort that would mortify her cousins. It did nothing to cast their lineage in a venerable light. These anecdotes were the grotesqueries her father had been accumulating all winter—tales of succubi and grindylows and wicked witches, tales of demons and paralyzing spirits in the night. Bořivoj listened, eyes twinkling, and encouraged her father in all the right spots, leaving her silence unnoticed.

When the servants cleared the table and the hounds rushed in for crumbs, Jutta excused herself. She exited into the hallway, stepped by memory through the disorienting darkness, and entered the overcrowded gallery with shadows fanning out from the pair of hearths over the new crates and bundles.

Jutta made her way toward her tower door, full of perplexion. *Some of my books contain references to dragons, but I thought they were no more accurate than my father's stories from peasants about lead-heavy beings interrupting sleep.*

Her shins bashed into a crate, and Jutta winced and grunted, sliding her feet forward one at a time to avoid unseen edges.

Are you there?

Entranced, she turned around, stepping through the mess of goods toward the trunk. Shadows played over the remaining parchment, unsealed.

As soon as she touched the wooden box, a peaceful communion began stretching into long moments, and the tiny life within pulled at her, as did the quieter forms to the right.

His brother and sister, she thought. *From the same clutch.* They did not interact with her but made her aware of them.

Someone grabbed her arm, stunning her back to the present. The humming of the spinning wheel across the way jarred her as she looked around. *How long have I stood here? Has no one thought to shake me?*

Brightness drove shadows toward the center of the gallery. The fires had been built up in hearths. Jutta turned toward the touch. She detected sandalwood and cedar and astringent spices. It was Bořivoj, tenderness softening his angular features.

"You were caught in its snare. The servants tried to free your attention. You didn't respond to their voices or touch. Only I managed it."

I hadn't wanted to be freed. I didn't know I was ensnared, she thought.

Her face must have betrayed her thoughts because her intended traced his finger down her cheek. "That won't happen again. I'll replace the seal tonight. When we have a few moments of quiet, I'll tell you more. Now, you were heading upstairs. You had taken your leave."

He was close enough that his eyes weren't just indistinct patches of color; at this proximity, she noticed the flecks of gray in his irises and the striations of violet fanning around his pupils. However, his smile held too many teeth, and though it reached his eyes, she didn't trust it.

Handsome but off-putting for no good reason, he stirred feelings of curiosity and lust and fear within her. With a stiff tongue and depleted words, Jutta nodded before taking a step backward and bumping her heel into another wooden box.

"Goodnight, my dear," he said, a rumble in his chest stirring mixed feelings in her.

My body responds one way but my faculties another, she thought before reacting to his words. *I'm not his dear. Yet.*

Jutta, still wordless, nodded, then darted across the layers of uneven, mismatched rugs until her slipper met the brick floor leading to her library.

His eyes burned against her back as she left.

Where the brick gave way to wood, a final wall sconce burned. She was responsible for any flames within her sanctum, so Jutta retrieved a candle and lit it from the sconce, its wax soon spilling over her grasp.

Jutta ascended the last landing into her tower and lit a candelabrum and the fireplace, careful to avoid errant sparks. Then she began her search for books on dragons. Her past organizing served her well, and soon, she'd located several books and was re-reading their passages on great dragons.

They seem to be poetic allusions to greater ills plaguing a group of people rather than actual creatures, she thought. A disappointing volume like the one before it—and the one before that.

Rapping at her window startled her. Jutta couldn't make out much. White streaks of moonlight stretched over the triangular pane along with golden blotches from the candelabrum. She shifted her candles, thinking the sound must have been from an owl or a particularly large moth.

Certain owls migrated around this time of year and birds sometimes flew into glass, though she couldn't recall an owl doing so. *That must be it*, she thought. *A moth or an owl.*

But the rapping came again, more insistent this time. Jutta stepped to the window and saw Bořivoj. He waggled his fingers in greeting, and a devious grin overtook his face. She unlatched the window and swung it open, inward.

"It was a lovely night for a stroll, and I saw your light on."

"You must have scaled the wall or floated. How did you…?" She sat down in her horsehair chair with the table and its pile of books between them.

"I climbed it," he said, shrugging. Then, seemingly unable to resist, he stepped forward and showed her his hands.

They looked unremarkable. Her eyes flitted back up to his, and the confusion on her face must have shown, for she now realized her mistake in opening the window, in sitting behind the table where she was now stuck.

Though I doubt a window could stop him.

Her heart pounded in her ears as he reached forward. She felt frozen, but then his palm covered her hand. It was warm and sticky. She pulled away, hiding her hand in her dress pocket.

"My father wouldn't approve of you being here unchaperoned. Nor would the rest of the household. We might be country folk, but we do adhere to certain niceties."

"I'm sure you do. That's why I came up this way. To preserve your reputation and all."

She didn't offer him absolution. She offered him nothing. She lifted the book she'd been reading as at least a sort of barrier between them.

His brows scrunched together, eyes darkening. "I didn't mean to frighten you." He pulled a handkerchief from his pocket and wiped his palm. "It was presumptuous of me to show up here. And my hands aren't always so sticky. It's a skill I've developed after consuming salamanders."

"Monster magic is forbidden," she blurted out, placing the book on the table with a thud to add finality.

"By whom? By people and traditions that want to keep us scrabbling under their boots."

He has a point, she thought, but she wasn't ready to voice it.

Bořivoj was undeterred by her silence—encouraged, even. "We worship four spirits, one for each nation. Each important one, that is. We enact plays at different points of the year, but what does this accomplish?"

He stepped closer, and her panic surged.

"There are more than four spirits, and the four that are worshiped are just ghosts anyway. There are so many out there, and some are much stronger."

"You've summoned your share, eh?"

He didn't affirm this. Instead, he pushed closer, leaning over the table. "I knew as soon as I heard about you and your collection that you would be perfect for me."

He just wants power, and he thinks the spirits and my books are power.

"The eggs hold untold might. Of all the forms of creature magic, these and sea serpents are the untapped forms."

"You're going to eat the eggs? To gain their powers?"

The realization made her ill: this was no duck egg unfertilized, wasted if uneaten. These fertilized eggs were self-aware and intelligent, though their legends spoke of thralldom for the people near them.

"I will consume two, and you will get one. With our knowledge and raw power, no one will be able to stop us. We will remake the world however we please," he said, caressing her arm. "Archaic traditions will be the first to go."

Jutta swallowed, her spirit wavering as much as the candlelight against the open window. The wind growled and the shutter banged, drawing her attention.

Bořivoj stepped closer, moving to shut it. *He probably means to keep the glass from breaking.* That also meant she would be further trapped with him.

Heart slamming and hands shaking, Jutta rose from her horsehair chair, pushing away the lightweight table.

Turning back toward her once the hook was latched, a shadow passed over Bořivoj's face. "I've pushed too fast in my eagerness and overstayed my welcome. Maybe I misjudged you." His tone dropped as he uttered the last sentence, chilling her.

Father misjudged you, too. Jutta's breath quickened as she searched his face. *How much does Father know? Any of this?*

"Good night, Lovely Lady Jutta. May the night's peace and the morning's light bring you clarity."

With that, her suitor unlatched the window again and climbed out into the light of the moons.

As soon as she latched it behind him, she grabbed her candelabrum and rushed downstairs into the brick hallway leading toward the bedrooms. When she rapped on her father's door, the reply was a muffled grunt. It was dark under his door, so he had probably been sleeping.

Jutta knocked again. There would only be so much time to talk to her father before Bořivoj made it back inside and interrupted her. He might have ways of knowing about her conversation. She wasn't sure what his abilities were. Having the grip of a salamander, he might also have their power to breathe fire. Perhaps he'd gained other monsters' powers, like the lindworm's lightning or the grindylow's persuasion.

Horymír stumbled to the doorway, his nightcap askew. "What is it? What's wrong?"

"I have to talk to you about Bořivoj. He's not what you think he is. I can't marry him."

"Oh, Daughter. I've entertained your nonsense for many a year. You turned down Gesdow. You turned down others. There were some I didn't even mention, knowing full well you'd find them dull or ugly.

"But the truth is you have to get married. Bořivoj is going places. He will be a powerful man, a good match. We've long been relegated to the countryside, and it's helped us grow our wealth but not our importance. This match will be what's best for you, for me, for the people who rely on us for protection. Go to bed. Things will seem better in the morning."

With that, her father shut the door and shuffled off.

Jutta turned toward the main gallery, where the torches had long since burnt out, and the light of her candelabrum fanned over the mortar lines. With a deep breath, she opened the arched doorway. Taking deliberate steps around boxes and bundles, Jutta walked as straight as she could to the crate with the magenta seals.

Bořivoj said he would replace these tonight, she thought. *He's probably on his way back right now, waiting for a moment when the guards won't notice him clinging to the walls.*

Jutta placed the candelabrum on a trunk behind her labeled silk, undyed. Careful of the parchment spells, Jutta pried away the magenta wax, which took on a bloody hue in the light. She swung the lid open to see the charmed silk, itself embroidered with spells, and the three large spheres.

Jutta touched the pink sphere.

You're back, he said.

"I am. I have to hurry, though. The man who has you, he doesn't intend to ever let you go. He intends to kill you and take your power."

I understand. His mind feels wrong and bad. He doesn't like us even though we've not even been born yet.

Jutta steeled herself before putting the next sentence into words. "I can't take all three of you, but I can try to rescue one."

I want to be protected, but my sister is the strongest of us. He must not get her. Take the brown egg.

So, Jutta shut the lid with a quiet clunk, a result of failed gentleness with the cumbersome weight of the egg and the candelabrum, and fled from the gallery back to her library.

She pulled blankets out of a wicker basket and wrapped the egg inside it. Already the egg felt chillier than it had inside the trunk laden with spells. With the egg snug and sound, Jutta donned a cloak and grabbed her most useful treasures, stuffing them into her deep pockets: a key, a small mirror, her most-used grimoire, her ornate athame in its leather sheath, and her small purse.

Looking around this room of wooden comfort, a wave of sorrow hit her—this was goodbye. Then she told herself, no time for self-pity. Jutta clutched the cold iron of the fire poker and spread out the logs on the grate, leaving smoldering logs to snap orange sparks.

With that, she blew out the candelabrum, its flowers of smoke curling toward the dark ceiling in the faint moonlight. She whispered words of concealment against Bořivoj, hoping this would be enough to save her precious books. The spell would make the grimoires worthless to him, gibberish.

As if she'd been punched in the gut, Jutta doubled over, breathless from the spell. After a moment, she caught her breath and began her escape again.

Jutta surrounded herself in shadows, clinging to the darkness and taking the servant hallways. As her heart slammed in her chest, she took these less familiar steps to hopefully avoid Bořivoj.

Swinging open the side door toward the smokehouse and the forge, Jutta watched for movement since that would be all she could make out. Mud clung to her shoes, and with each step, the leather squelched.

She had it in her once again for another spell, so she breathed out words to make her body and her noises less noticeable. The gentle sounds of the river made her impatient. She shut the door with one hand and balanced the wicker basket with the other.

Once the guard had made his way round this side of the wall, she rushed toward a locked door by the river. Jutta glanced around. She couldn't be sure there was no one there. It was dark, and there seemed to be no variation or movement, so she turned the key in the latch and opened it, half expecting Bořivoj to be waiting for her on the other side.

Glancing over her shoulder every few moments, Jutta stepped through, shut the door again, and relocked it. Bořivoj's vessel was anchored in a dammed-off area, with lights bobbing up and down and drunken singing carrying on the air. Its guards carried on, unnoticing.

Jutta padded to a small rowboat and lowered her wicker basket with the egg. The boat jostled as she stepped one mud-slick foot in. A post nearby proved excellent for steadying herself, then she sat and untied the boat.

Two oars leaned against the seat. She pulled one up and used it to shove the boat away from the dock—not something she had much experience in. She sat, a useless mast in the wind, carried only by the fast-moving current, and she wished for more distance between herself and that power-hungry man.

As if on cue, an inhuman roar came up from the manse. A glow flared from the wicker basket, and panic seized Jutta. She opened the lid and touched the round egg.

You are not like the man, the voice from the egg said.

"No, I'm not. I couldn't save you all, but I'll do my best to keep you from harm."

It is you who will need saving, it said.

Before Jutta lost herself, she wondered, *Was this a mistake? Should I have listened to Bořivoj?*

ABOUT THE AUTHOR

Melissa Rose Rogers writes speculative stories and is inspired by mythologies from all over the world. She currently lives in Denver, CO, where she experiments on her husband and daughters with recipes she finds online. She loves board games, memes, and long walks in the dry, thin air. Her fiction appears in Bear Creek Gazette, Tales from the Moonlit Path, 96th of October, Harvey Duckman Presents, Bewildering Stories, and various anthologies.

You can find out more about her at melissaroserogers.wordpress.com

A Load of Balls

Ross Young

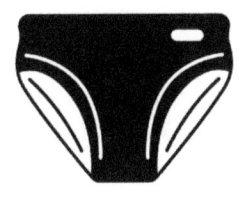

*H*ere's the short and sweet version: I'm dead, but I'm still hanging around the living like some kind of bad smell. "But why?" I hear you ask. I'm still here because my body is still up and walking around, I'm just not in it.

Imagine taking your clothes to a charity shop and then spending your days following the person wearing them around. It's pretty much the same thing. Only without the charity shop. Or the clothes. Christ this is hard to explain. Something is wearing my body like a tired second-hand meat suit, and they're not taking good care of it. I call them Chad.

As a lodger, Chad is a piece of shit. He doesn't know how anything works, and he won't listen to instructions. Watching him trying to dress is the most painful part of my day, every single pissing day. The weird bit is he's got a real thing for buttons. It's as if he hates zips and sweatshirts. Also, he wants to eat brains and can't really speak. I'm not sure if my body is decomposing really slowly or if it's just falling apart due to lack of care, but it's not looking good. I'm a zombie, watching from the outside.

Don't worry, there's bound to be something positive in all of this, right? Well, when you find it out, be sure to tell me. Oh wait, you can't, because most people can see me.

It's worse, though, worse than you imagine. Remember the charity shop? Well, imagine if the person wearing your old clothes looks better than you in them. Not that Chad looks better than me – he doesn't, I think, but he is likeable.

So that's where we are. I'm a spectre lingering around my possessed corpse just trying to get by, and this is a story about my balls.

Now, Chad has no interest in my balls, and to be honest, now that I'm dead, nor have I. Except, well, shit happened.

Quarter past three on a Tuesday afternoon is one of those times when the world rumbles along, doing what it's supposed to. Exciting stuff does not happen on a Tuesday mid-afternoon. We were in the office, and I was watching Chad spill Cheerios all down our one clean shirt while scrolling through my phone. My one outlet to the outside world. I can't call anybody, though, because they can't hear me, and interacting is hard. Typing takes so much effort that by the time I've written half a response to some click-baiting internet troll, I've run out of steam.

Don't believe me? Try it. If it takes you half an hour to write the first sentence in what is to be a lengthy diatribe on the media's response to sports washing compared to its response to arms sales (they're disproportionate, if you're wondering), you'll run out of steam too. No, I stick to the handy little button with a heart on it. You can call me a lurker, if you like. It's pretty much bang on the money.

A knock came on the door, and we went through our little charade.

"Chad, there's someone at the door."

"Ur."

"No, Chad, you have to open the door. I, like the last several hundred times, am still unable to open it."

"Ur?"

"Because you're in my body."

"Ur..."

"No, it is not a shared vessel. That would suggest that I can get back in, and I can't, because you're a shitty squatter that has barricaded all the doors and windows."

"Ur."

"No. Just open the damn door."

The knock came again. No louder than before.

"Ur."

"Chad, if you don't open the door, I'm not going to help you with anything for the next week."

"Ur?"

"Like everything. Like getting dressed, like ordering food, like reading, like working the television, like… like everything a normal functioning adult in their own body can do."

"Ur!"

"Thank you."

Chad stood up, put a hand in the cereal bowl, and knocked it all over himself. No good crying over spilt milk? How about weeping over the fact that it takes almost an hour to get Chad to load the washing machine? Last time, he slammed his hand in the door so many times that I had to spend the next hour getting him to bandage it up, but that's another painfully dull story for another time.

He lurched towards the door and pulled it open to reveal a woman. She was younger than me but old enough that it wasn't weird that I found her attractive. She was also heavily pregnant, and my keen investigative powers told me she was upset. It was probably because she was crying.

"Ur?" Chad asked.

"Oh, hi. I… This is hard to say. Something really weird is happening, and my friend, well not really my friend, more of a friend of a friend, said that the hairdresser used to be some kind of witch, and so I booked in for a—"

"Ur."

"Right. You've heard this all before. So, um, can I come in?"

"Ur," Chad said, then he stumbled back to the desk and tried to take a seat. It took a while. Look, I bought the chair when I was in control of the body. It's not like I considered 'What if my body is taken over by a lurching zombie and needs to look vaguely competent in front of potential clients?' when I was picking cheap office furniture off the internet. Don't act like that's a normal thing to think about.

"So, how does this work?"

"Yeah, Chad, tell the nice pregnant crying lady how all this works," I said.

One thing Chad can do, and the thing that most makes me believe that he's some kind of demonic entity, is glare. If looks could kill… well, I can't get any deader, so Chad can suck it up.

"Ur," he said with a wave to the stand of leaflets positioned by the desk.

It had taken weeks to painstakingly write the things, but they were pretty comprehensive. Most importantly, they made it really clear that Chad cannot talk, but we can listen.

She turned one over in her hands for a moment, like she was new to the concept of the written word. A moment later, she wrinkled her nose up, threw a couple of glances in Chad's direction, looked around our admittedly pokey and filthy office, and read the pamphlet.

"Well, beggars can't be choosers, I suppose. I think my baby might be a demon," she said as she slipped the leaflet into a huge handbag. It was the kind of scuffed leather hold-everything handbag that definitely had the things you never expected anyone to carry inside it. Spork? Got it. Sewing kit? Yup. Triple-A battery, phone chargers, a battered copy of 50 Shades and a Dan Brown novel? Check.

"Ur?" Chad said.

Oh, right. The demon baby thing.

She stroked her belly, the t-shirt type dress she wore pulled taut over it, and let out a sigh as she looked away from Chad. She was actually looking straight at me, but I'm pretty sure she didn't know that and was going for something more wistful than the whole 'I see dead people' thing.

Then came the story.

"Let me explain…"

As explanations went, it was a meandering story that wove from the emotional highs of new love to the crashing crescendo of realisation. In my opinion, the majority of relationships follow the same trajectory, like being shot up into the air on a rocket and then jumping out to plummet to your inevitable doom. Sure, sometimes you get a parachute, sometimes the rocket falters before it gets too high, and once in a blue moon, you get into orbit, trapped circling around the rest of humanity, unable to communicate how it really works to anyone else.

This being the world I inhabit, though, there were a few unusual aspects.

"…and then he burst into flames, waved goodbye, and stepped through the transdimensional wormhole, I suppose, and was gone forever."

"Ur?" Chad said.

"What? How do you think it happened, Chad, you zombie moron? When a woman loves a man… you know? The birds and the bees? Remember the videos you weren't supposed to see me watching? Not that there's much thrill when you're made of ectoplasm, and that's not some weird innuendo. She had sex with the guy she met on the boat. It's not that complicated."

"Ur."

"Oh, right. Well, it could be an abyss creature," I said to Chad. "Or some kind of wizard who realised he was going to live a hell of a lot longer than her, so decided to bail early. Or it could just be a douchebag who was good at practical special effects and really didn't want to get tied down."

"Ur," Chad said, moving his head up and down too far. Like there was a hinge at the back of what had been my neck. I winced. It would probably hurt.

I stepped around the desk to hover over Chad's shoulder. "Turn the tablet on."

"Ur."

"Please?" I asked, because sometimes, it does pay to be polite.

Chad gave out a snort and fumbled with the tablet computer on the desk. It had a circle of milk on it from where the bowl had been sitting on top of it. There's no point in trying to prevent Chad from breaking stuff. I used to try, but it's like fighting internet trolls – he takes too much pleasure in my frustration and isn't bothered about the actual problem.

Eventually, the screen blinked on, and he pushed it across the table. Our guest stepped forward to get a better view of it, and I tapped on the screen. The milk wasn't helping, but I managed to scrawl on the drawing app.

"Due date?"

"Um, is this some kind of telepathy?"

"Ur," Chad said.

"Incredible."

Sure, love, he's a telepathic moron. If Chad was telepathic, we'd all just hear a constant 'Urrr.' Wait, maybe he's telephonic. That might be that 'hum' thing that people talk about. Maybe it's not electricity and wifi signals at all?

"I'm at thirty-two weeks."

Ouch. So if that thing inside her is about to burst out like some kind of xenomorph, she's going to have to sit and wait a little longer—

"I'm keeping the baby, obviously. I just want to know what I can do to prepare, reverse a curse, maybe stop the antichrist…"

The great thing about being invisible – and there aren't as many as you think, unless you're a pervert, and I'm not… often – is that they don't know when you're laughing. This was not the antichrist. How did I know? Well, she'd been able to walk in here. Someone carrying the antichrist would have been surrounded by demons and probably some creepy nuns or something, because, you know, creepy nuns. I wrote as much on the tablet.

Okay, I wrote, "Not 666."

"Oh, thank God."

"Ur," Chad said, and I had to agree. Nobody in this room needed to thank any kind of divine entity for our situation.

"So what do we do?"

I had to admit, it was a very good question. Sure, I could reach out to a few contacts, but short of—

"Ur," Chad said. He was looking at me.

"Take a look? What?"

"Ur."

"Do you think I'm a sodding gynaecologist? Sure, I'll just go set up the stirrups and—"

"Ur!"

"Oh. Ew. I'm not just going to shove my head up—"

"Ur…"

"Oh. Yeah, that makes more sense. You think I can do that? So, what, just shove my face into her stomach, no, I mean, womb? That seems really intrusive. Actually, intrusive seems like an understatement."

Chad slammed his – my – head against the table, and he did it a lot harder than necessary.

Our guest flinched but bit back anything bigger than that. At this point, I was sure the only reason she hadn't sprinted out of here was because running down three flights of stairs when you're in your third trimester is probably pretty tough.

I'm not really into the whole spiritualism thing, which I realise might sound ridiculous given that I'm… well, my preferred term is spectre, but people dealing with the paranormal can be really rude about this stuff. I don't want to get into the whole political correctness thing, but let's just say you living types can be complete arseholes. Anyway, let's just say I can sense otherworldly stuff when I'm close to it.

There had been an inkling of something when this woman had walked in, but that's not unusual. The majority of people give off something, and some people have more of it than others. It would have been weirder if there had been nothing at all. The thing is, I've never encountered something growing inside someone else, like a malignant otherworldly tumour.

I've seen textbooks, and I've known the opposite sex, but nothing can quite do justice to shoving your spectral being through a woman's placenta. Wait, I'm not clear on ownership rights. Is it a woman's placenta, or is it the foetus' placenta? It's probably not important. It definitely isn't right now. What I saw was… not helpful. It was really dark. The thing people don't consider when you see those photos and scans and stuff is that there's not actually any light involved. So I basically shoved my ectoplasmic face into a woman's womb and saw nothing of interest.

Feelings, though. Oh boy were there feelings, and no, not weird, creepy ones. Just bad ones. Really bad. Oh, well excuse me for not being able to translate the uncomfortable sensation that feels like having the back of your skull hacked at with a small garden trowel, like someone's trying to plant bulbs in your grey matter… Huh, maybe I can explain it. The garden trowel thing, and whatever it were trying to plant, wasn't friendly. There's a plant, the Amorphophallus titanum. No, it isn't a transforming metal penis, it's the corpse flower. It rarely flowers, but when it does, it gives out the sickly sweet stench of rotting flesh. I imagine that was what it was trying to plant – metaphorically, of course.

There was something about this unborn child that had more than the faint whiff of a bad 'un. Oh sure, nobody wants to admit it, but we all know that sometimes you can just sense something a little off-kilter, a kind of sinking feeling, that one kid that nobody really wants to be left alone with, who you just know is the reason the neighbourhood pets have been vanishing. You have a memory of it now, a time when you could just sense, 'This one is a bad 'un'. Now take that feeling and multiply it a few times. No, not ten times. It's an unborn child, not pissing Caligula.

"Ur?" Chad said, breaking me out of my contemplation.

"It's a bad 'un," I said to Chad. "But I can't tell if it's genetic or something else."

"Ur."

"Genetic is when... Forget it, Chad. I'm just saying we need to meet the father."

Chad's mouth opened and closed a few times, and drool started to run down his chin. I like to pretend I can interpret what Chad means when he's making vocalisations – vocalisations sounds a lot better than going 'ur' or making zombie noises, and I'm sticking with it – and sometimes I can, but a lot of the time I'm just projecting my own thoughts onto... well, onto my body, which is what the living do all day every day. We're basically just thoughts, electrical impulses that make a meat machine move. We're nothing more than a series of differences in polarity. You're one electron from a completely different decision at any given time... maybe. Of course, that school of thought has to make you wonder, 'How do I exist, then?' Not you, I mean me when I say 'I'. Forget it.

I moved back to the tablet and managed to scrawl, 'Meet Dad?'

The question, or possibly the uneasy sensation that came with a spectre shoving its head literally inside her, seemed to make our guest uneasy.

"I guess I should've expected that. I mean, will it do any good, though? Aren't you supposed to tell me I'm crazy or something?"

"Tell her she's not crazy, Chad," I said.

He blinked, one eye a little faster than the other, which shouldn't bother me much, but it really does. Then he stood up. For a moment, the light coming in from the window behind him made it look like me again, a dashing, handsome—

"Ur," he said, shattering the illusion. Then he unleashed a belch that turned my stomach, and I'm pretty sure I don't even have a stomach.

Our guest, or our new client, ignored Chad's behaviour, and it made me like her a little more. This woman was a fighter. She'd walked into my office well aware that we deal with what is technically called 'weird shit' and told us that she thought she might be pregnant with the devil's child and that it didn't matter because she was keeping the baby regardless, but it might be nice if it wasn't the antichrist. Pretty ballsy.

"I guess I still have his number and where he worked, but... he vanished into a different dimension."

"Sure he did," I said, giving Chad a nod to hand over a pen and paper.

Chad, however, remains a sodding zombie, so he didn't take my cue, didn't proffer up writing paraphernalia, and didn't acknowledge the fact that I had very much doubted the reality of the man who was lost to the abyss. So, I guess me saying that was pretty much just for you. You're welcome.

* * *

In predictable but disappointing news, Captain Knock 'em Up and Run didn't work in a bar. Bars are more fun. I can't drink, but I can make Chad drink for me, and I get a little buzz from it. We share sensations, which is nice for nice things and terrible for pain. I say share, but it seems that I get pretty much all of it when it comes to pain, but other stuff, things that I might actually take some small pleasure in, they're all Chad's. He's a bastard.

"Chad, Chadmeister, The Chadtopus Rex, ain't no-one badder than my main man Chadder! How you doing, bro?"

Ah, shit. I forgot about this. Meet Scrote. Yes, that is what we call him, and no, that's not his real name. Scrote is what everyone calls him, and while it is short for Scrotum, I'm confident that even his parents weren't cruel enough to name their kid 'ball bag'. Scrote is… well, his nickname suits him.

"Ur," Chad said, giving a kind of salute with two fingers off his brow. It made me scowl because it was kind of cool, and he played it off really smooth. He does this, smooth and confident for brief moments in time, and then he'll stub my two toes four times in a row before working out he's not lifting his leg high enough to climb a set of stairs. I fucking hate him.

"Hi, Scrote," I said, because Scrote can see dead people. In my little niche of society, there's a number of people who can see me. The general populace… well, do you see dead people?

"Oh, you're here too," Scrote said.

I said there were people who could see me. I didn't say they liked me.

"I messaged you. You're here to meet me, not Chad."

"Hm, pretty sure ghosts—"

"Spectres."

"Right. Pretty sure the dead can't own phones, so I came here responding to Chad's messages."

"Fine. Thanks for dressing appropriately," I said with a glance down at Scrote's, um, well, scrotal zone. He was wearing a less than fetching pair of swimming trunks, also known as 'budgie smugglers'. Scrote was hirsute, short of stature, with a pot belly that spilled over the waistband of most items of clothing. I can't imagine anywhere less preferable to bump into him than the local public pool. "You can keep your towel on in this section, you know."

"Oh, I know," Scrote said with a toothy grin.

I turned towards a counter where people were able to collect towels and purchase or rent various other necessary aquatic paraphernalia. "That's our fella," I said, pointing out our in-person sperm donor. I've got pretty used to not needing to be subtle around people. The folks who can see me... well, most of them think there's something wrong with them, so they keep their mouths shut. Sensible, really. The only time I need to be careful is when someone's around who knows about... stuff. You know, people like Scrote, or non-human folk, some mediums – yeah, some are real – witches, wizards... and that's when the guy at the end of the counter with the ornate tattoos, overly coiffured beard, and roguish good looks stared right at me.

"Bollocks. Looks like you might not be needed after all," I said to Scrote, who scowled back at me.

Scrote picked up a towel from a nearby bench and turned to leave, then stopped himself. Grunting as he wrapped the towel around himself, he looked up at me. "I get paid either way, right? So, I might as well stick around. This could be interesting."

"Ur," Chad said as he dropped his own towel, revealing a pair of swimming shorts and my body, which hadn't improved since I was in possession of it. Not that I was a slouch. I mean, I was average. Just a guy, you know?

The pool boy flashed that almost crooked smile at Chad. I don't think he was flirting with the lodger in my body, but it would've been an easy mistake to make.

"Urr," Chad said, and for once, I didn't pretend I knew what he was saying.

We approached the counter, Chad on one side of me, lurching like he might be seasick, and Scrote on the other side, looking like he was definitely on some kind of register.

"Are you..." and I paused here, because some names need a pause. Some names are the kind of thing that people write in romance novels with half-naked, brooding men on the covers. There are names that belong to characters in films and don't belong in your everyday council-funded sports centre in Yorkshire. This kind of place needs a Dave, Chris, Dan, Phil, Tom, or Simon and some old bloke wielding a mop named Clive. Some names are only meant for people desperately trying to break into the film industry or crafted by strippers and wannabe gigolos, and if there was ever an example I could give you, it was, "…Coulter Lonestar?"

"You must've misunderstood something, fella. You're not allowed in this section unless you're dressed for swimming," he said as he grabbed a used towel off the counter and tossed it over his head. It landed in a large hamper behind him, and if I hadn't known better, I'd have sworn it folded itself in mid-air.

"That's not a real name, is it?" I said.

"What do you want?" he asked, staring at me.

Scrote let out a cough. Confrontation isn't the kind of thing he enjoys. You don't end up being called Scrote because you're big on sticking up for yourself.

"I'm here because you've been using magic tricks to disappear on women like some kind of—"

"Magic tricks? Listen, Casper—"

"His name's not—" Scrote tried to interrupt.

I didn't need Scrote, especially in his current state, sticking up for me.

"He means like Casper the Friendly Ghost. It's a very weak insult. Maybe a two out of five at best. Disappointing, to be honest."

The polo shirt-wearing pool boy didn't like being interrupted, but I wasn't too bothered about making him angry. I'm already dead, so there's not a lot he can do to me, and Chad… well, Chad has an innate ability, which might be magical, or it could be something inherent within… Ah, forget it. Chad just doesn't give a shit. He's got a very 'not my circus, not my monkeys' attitude to violence, except it's 'not my body, not my excruciating pain'. It would have been refreshing if it wasn't my body and my pain.

"Not that it's any of your business, but I'm not running out on women all over the place," the man said. "Now, I'm at work, so if you want to talk to me, let's do it some other time before I report you all for… something."

"Ur?" Chad said. He was looking around for the towel he'd dropped as if someone had whipped it away from his waist when he wasn't paying attention.

A Load of Balls

As a spectre, I can pull some pretty spectacular faces. I've practised in front of a mirror. Try a smile. Make it wider, wider, wiiideeeerrr, and you'll reach a limit. Not me. I can keep going. Get the idea? Well, my eye rolls are impressive too.

The rockstar sperm donor placed his hands on the countertop between a torso mannequin showing off another pair of budgie smugglers and a counter rack of swimming armbands. The standard issue polyester polo shirt was too tight, and there was a needless amount of definition being shown through what should have been the least attractive of uniforms.

"What's it got to do with a sodding ghost, a goblin, and a… whatever this guy is? Is he dead?"

"Ur," Chad said, snapping his head up and fixing Polo Shirt with a glare. I don't remember ever being that menacing when I was in the old meat suit.

"That hurt his feelings. Mine too. It's complicated. Listen, there's something you need to know."

Scrote let out a cough. "How does he know I'm a goblin?"

I turned my scowl on the little man and forgot to reduce the intensity. "He's a wizard, you bellend. Also, you look like a goblin, Scrote. All you need is a cudgel in your hands and we're straight into Tolkien territory."

Polo Shirt glanced towards the pool area. There was a corridor between the pools and us, and in between, there were those strange foot-washing areas, lands of bacteria-ridden mystery. Something about them made me uncomfortable, even more now that I was in ethereal form. Confident nobody was coming, he turned back to us.

"Look. I don't know what this is about, but unless you want me to start unleashing some high-ether in here, you need to leave."

I rose up. Spectres can do that – we're all for show. Hovering above Scrote and Chad, the lights flickered, and I focused so that the goggles, swim hats, and earplugs on the shelves behind Polo Shirt started to shake and fall from their perches. A frost spread along the tiled floor and moved down the corridor towards the foot pools. "You shall—"

"That's quite impressive," Scrote said.

Chad looked over his shoulder in my direction and gave a shrug. "Ur?"

"Yeah. I mean, as far as being all ghostly goes, he's not bad. Didn't know he had it in him," Scrote continued before turning to me. "Have you been practising?"

"Shut up, Scrote. I'm being intimidating here."

The wizard, Coulter Lonestar, looked up at me and sighed. "If you freeze the water, people will start freaking out, and this isn't a good place for the mortally disadvantaged. Ever wonder why public swimming pools aren't known as magic havens?"

"Why don't you stop me, magic man?"

"I don't need to. This much chlorinated water, hundreds of kids coming in and out of here all the time, laughter, fun and games, the awkward act of shedding all your clothes to go in there. This place is a whispered prayer away from being holy ground."

I hesitated. He had a point. There was a reason the dead like dark and seedy places, and then there was the water. We don't like water.

"All of that's true," I said, "but a wizard should've been able to just click his fingers and get rid of us."

"Fine," he said. "I'm a crap wizard, okay? Happy now? I was cursed by a witch, and now whenever I have, um, sexy time, I get teleported away."

I dropped the act. The armbands immediately stopped being buffeted around, which was less scary than the quivering and rattling I'd been going for, and the lights came back on. "That sounds pretty implausible. Wouldn't that mean you could just be a horrible shit and sleep with as many women as you like with no consequences?"

"I get teleported butt-naked into a cell at the local police station."

"Ah."

"Oh."

"Ur."

"Yeah. So someone's upset at me. It'll be Yvonne, right? She was really nice as well. I don't do it on purpose, and every now and then, I hope it's worn off or something. It isn't like I'm sleeping with loads of women and using this curse as a way to escape. Though I'm sure that's what you all thought."

"Yeah, well," I said. "Men are pigs."

"Sure. Well, can you tell her I'm sorry and—"

"She's pregnant with some kind of demonic entity."

What? You wanted me to sugar-coat the situation? The guy is either a prick who uses his powers to scare the shit out of women he's just had sex with, or he's a prick who upset someone enough to get cursed with a spell that enabled him to do it.

He started crying.

I lowered myself between Scrote and Chad and looked from one to the other. Scrote gave a shrug and pulled that face, the 'I don't know what I'm supposed to do either' face. Chad was too busy watching an old lady approach while trying to grab a towel. Who'd have thought he'd be so body-conscious? It's not even his body.

"Excuse me," the old woman said in a voice that screamed 'I've been coming here for years'. "Why are you men all crowding out here together? You're making the aqua cycle class quite uncomfortable."

"It's okay, Joyce, we're just trying to sort out some swimming lessons. This gentleman here needs a little support."

"Pfft, men today," she said with a shake of her head before turning and splashing back through the foot pool.

"Uh… are you okay?" I asked once she was out of view and I'd managed to get beyond the idea of someone believing people would perv on a class of pensioners doing aqua cycle classes.

"She can't be pregnant. The curse made me impotent," the wizard said, in between the kind of shuddering, heaving breaths that come with too much fluid. He was a mess.

I placed a hand on the counter and tapped my fingers against it, not that it made a noise. Ghost problems. "This curse," I said. "What exactly are the parameters?"

"Your knackers are knackered, completely cream-crackered, and when you shoot your lot, you'll be sent to another spot. As long as you claim your magic, all will be tragic, you sodding tosser… I'm not sure if the last bit was part of the curse."

"I don't think it was. As long as you claim… was it *you're* or *your* magic?"

He wiped his face with a used towel from behind the counter, which was really gross. "What do you think it means?"

I looked at Scrote, who shrugged, because he's about as much use as a chocolate teapot. Then, turning to Chad, I realised my advisory team were less than elite.

"It could mean that if you stop being a wizard, all will go back to normal."

"That's a big ask—"

I raised an eyebrow, by which I mean my face contorted to the point where one eyebrow was several inches above the other. "You realise a woman is pregnant with your child."

"Hang on, though. How do you know it's mine?"

People are infuriating.

"Ur," Chad said, grabbing a pair of goggles out of a box that had 'Lost and Found' scrawled on it in marker. He held them up, pulled them like an elastic band, and fired them at Polo Shirt. I think he did it for emphasis, and it was kind of frightening – in a really impotent, lacklustre way.

"He's right," I said. "What exactly do you imagine the odds are that she slept with another man who just happened to have cursed… spunk?"

"Yeah, you're right. I'm gonna be a dad."

"If you give up magic—"

"Who gives a shit about magic? I'm gonna be a dad!"

It turned out Polo Shirt was happy to beg forgiveness, and he was just happy in general. I've never met someone who cared so little about being magic.

So, back to my balls. Once upon a time, those things mattered to me. It's rare that my 'life' catches up to me, but this was one of those times.

The cursed balls thing was weird. Yvonne and Coulter were going to be fine. Giving up magic isn't all that hard, especially not when you've got someone like Scrote hanging around. He had certain unique – and disturbing – abilities that help with situations like this.

The curse itself, and who it had been cast by, was a mystery. Coulter claimed it was a woman he'd had a one-night stand with who didn't take it well. He couldn't give us any more information, or he didn't want to.

If it was the latter, I can't say I blame him. Telling tales on the kind of person who would curse you to teleport into a police station butt-naked and cause you to produce evil sperm was probably a dangerous idea.

It tickled something elusive at the back of my mind. That kind of curse didn't come out of a book; it came from natural innate power. And then there was the cockney twang. It's not often you get rhyming slang in a curse.

This case left me with something else to ponder. A memory had slipped back. I'd been young, short on cash, and had seen an easy opportunity. One that was going to be tricky to undo.

We were standing outside Westfield & Gates fertility clinic, a place I had visited once before. The rain was falling at 'deluge' levels, making it difficult to see. Fun fact, if it wasn't for air resistance, rain would fall all at once, and it would kill us. I often think about things that would kill 'us'… or maybe more Chad. If he dies, do I die? Does this torment end? God I hope so.

I was hovering to Chad's right, trying not to lose my temper as he flapped at the right mitten that had fallen off his hand. Yes, I make him wear mittens. At some point, pride needs to be abandoned for practicality, ergo mittens, the kind that have a piece of string running through the sleeves and over your shoulders so you can't drop one by accident.

"Okay, Chad. We're going to go in there and ask for my sperm back."

"Ur."

"Yeah. Maybe they'll recognise me… us… you know."

"Ur?"

"No. Not a bank like that. Can't imagine many people deposit stuff and expect to pick it up further along the line. Then again, maybe they do. I don't know."

"Ur."

"Interest? How would that even work?"

"Ur."

"Yes, it's awkward, but is it more awkward than discovering that my sperm is plagued with whatever you are? Or worse, that someone chose me as a donor and now has some kind of half-demon child, and not in a fun, 'turns out they're a good guy' way?"

"Ur?"

"It's a trope. Let's just go and ask for my sperm back, okay?"

"Ur."

"Yeah, I'm tired of saying sperm too."

ABOUT THE AUTHOR

Ross Young lives in France with his wife, daughter, and a walking carpet that insists it has canine DNA. He was born in Newcastle Upon Tyne in a hospital that has since been knocked down.

He is the author of multiple books in the Gloomwood series. They're all set in the Grim Reaper's personal slice of the afterlife, they're offbeat and silly and they are available now, go get them...please?

His writing has been described as; ridiculous, funny, weird, and macabre. Despite his appearance and demeanour, he does not write from experience, as he's not dead. He also draws silly comics featuring Beelzebub and the Grim Reaper.

You can find him on multiple social media sites posting the same stuff he posts on all the other sites (seriously, just pick one he's usually ryoungsulk or rossyoungsulk.)

You can also read his ongoing horror-comedy fiction series, Necromance in the Air on substack (rossyoungsulk.substack.com) for free, or visit his website for more oddities (rossyoung.ink).

Add to Cart

Halo Scot

Bo Wilder is an ugly fuck.

Everyone tells him so, and he has a bad habit of believing what everyone tells him.

They don't say this in words, of course, but their looks of disgust are his native tongue. He's fluent in exile, a born-and-bred outcast, always a pity invite, a sloppy second, a failed loser one step above wank sock.

Some would say he's paranoid: ex-lovers, failed therapists, third cousins twice removed.

Bo has told them all to fuck off.

He sits on his moldy wood countertop, picking his toenails with a needle. He's waiting. Impatient. He needs something to channel his nerves. So he picks deeper. Harder. Till blood reddens his toes, a slow trickle like a dick-pierced hymen. He's bored. Not for long. He has a job. He hates his job. But it's better than nothing. Nothing has always gotten Bo in trouble before.

His phone chimes near his left ass cheek, beside his unwashed, three-day-old briefs. He checks the notification. A client. A new shopper. He's needed at the store.

A smile mutilates Bo's face. He tosses the needle in the trash and dresses in his wrinkled uniform: a grimy navy shirt, stained khaki shorts, and Birkenstock sandals. It's supposed to make him relatable. Approachable. But it makes him neither, and Bo doesn't give a shit. His job is a means to an end—others' ends, not his.

Bo smooths the banana-yellow logo on his shirt: a crown in a cart that rests above his company's name, CrownCart. Trite, yet simple. On the back is their tagline: Because we treat you like royalty.

It's a shitty name. A shitty tag. The tacky, cheapjack, middle-school-home-ec class of grocery delivery services is a polished turd masquerading as fool's gold. They're only in business because their prices are rock bottom, same as their staff.

Bo sighs. This isn't the life he wants. He doesn't belong here, but belonging isn't the sole reason to stay. Besides, too much freedom is a dangerous thing, so he chains himself to their fucking app.

It chimes again.

He's late.

Bo shuffles out his door and toward his rusted, twenty-five-year-old sedan. Forest green paint curls from the hood. His tires are bald and half-flat. He opens the door. It doesn't lock anymore, but no one in their right mind would steal the car, same as Bo wasn't in his right mind when he bought it. Then again, he's rarely in his right mind, if there is such a thing.

Sinking into his car, he slams the door and winces. He dug too deep beneath his toenails, and his feet are as swollen as unmilked teats, bulging in his sandals like over-proofed dough.

The app chimes again.

Fucking nouveau riche twats. Always thinking they're better than everyone else, entitled to impossible words like "instant" and "elite." The woman who's bombarding his phone—Valedy Burminhower—sends Bo a message.

Hello, Bo. I've been waiting three hours for a shopper to be assigned, and I have a party in ninety minutes, so I would appreciate your alacrity.

Bo doesn't know what alacrity means. It wouldn't matter if he did; he won't obey first-class words on a third-rate salary.

He drives to the nearest grocery store while his app keeps chiming. Val—he suspects someone with a lofty seven-syllable name would hate to be reduced to just Val—continues to add and replace items in her cart.

This used to amuse him. Entertain him. Would engage his putrid, rotten mind during severe bouts of loneliness. It doesn't amuse, entertain, or engage him anymore. All Bo has left is annoyance. He grips his steering wheel tighter. The faux leopard cover twists between his fingers. He could mute Val, but he'd rather do that in person.

By the time Bo reaches the store, Val's list is fifty items long. He wants to scream, but there are people around, and he only likes others' screams, not his own. Instead, he exits his sedan and leans against the closed door. His reflection warps in the car window.

Then again, it's warped in real life, too. His features are bumpy, his lips thin and pale. An upturned, snot-encrusted nose sprouts from his face. His eyes are small and watery like two mushy slugs, his irises a tawny gray. He has a full head of straw-colored curls, unkempt and disheveled in a way that others find appealing. Bo knows better, though. They're lying to him. All of them. He's ugly, has always been ugly, because beauty cages you.

Bo refuses to be caged.

The app chimes. Another message from seven-syllable Val.

Please ensure you contact me before any substitutes are made. The previous shopper swapped sweet potatoes with yams, and I am sure we both agree that is an egregious replacement.

Bo rolls his eyes. He doubts they would agree on anything, much less root vegetables. Yet he appreciates this message, as opposed to the previous one. It's an insight into her psyche. Groceries are a door to the soul, a list that shows secrets, needs, wants, struggles, how someone yearns to change, what someone craves to grow. The fact Val places such an emphasis on sweet potatoes versus yams is telling. Most people wouldn't know the difference, but she does. He'll need to handle her with care. Any slip-ups could land him behind bars. Been there, done that, wouldn't recommend.

The store's automatic doors swish open. Bo doesn't remember walking across the parking lot. He doesn't remember a lot of things. Or rather, he chooses not to remember. It's safer this way. Too many memories to fit in one skull.

He grabs a cart, then walks down each aisle, piling the basket with Val's items. There's a note below each. He ignores these. Instead, he tosses in cheddar cheese, tortilla chips, and lumpy guacamole. They don't have Val's preferred brands; he doesn't update her. No one will care. She won't make her party.

Through the store's speakers, a tinny voice squeaks: You're busy, stressed. Work is a pain, and your kids refuse to behave. Bills multiply each month, and your spouse threatens divorce. After school, sports, lessons, and homework, who has time to run errands anymore? No one, that's who! Let us make your life easy. CrownCart is here to help. Our shoppers will tackle your honey-do list so you can focus on what matters. At only $13.99 a month, live in luxury for an affordable price. Choose CrownCart, because we treat you like royalty. Then, in a rushed, frantic whisper: *Tips and service charges not included. Store options may vary. CrownCart is not responsible for...*

Bo tunes out. He hates this ad. He cringes each time it sounds, and it sounds a dozen times daily.

Val sends him another message, something about a shellfish allergy. She's lying; she ordered crab rangoons last week. But she wants to seem interesting, mysterious, with a tragic backstory, and this is the best she can conjure from her boring, sheltered life: an inconsistent aversion to shellfish. Bo sends a thumbs-up. In his experience, this emoji confuses people the most. Half think it's rude; half think it's practical. Val falls into the former category.

Sure enough, she sends a follow-up message. Bo doesn't read this one. He finds the last five foods in her fifty-item hell-list: garlic, sour cream, broccoli, turnips, and carrots.

He gazes at the carrots, fond, nostalgic. They were his first tool, sharpened beautifully. You aren't legit till you kill someone with a carrot. But he can't use them again. No repeats, no patterns. That's why he changes his name weekly, why he moves states monthly. Soon, in fact, he's moving out of Maine. He'd thought it'd be harder, a struggle to juggle lives, yet it was child's play.

It's simple to hide in a world where everyone wants to be seen. Their spotlights cast huge shadows, and Bo skips between them with ease.

Bo checks out. The app tells Val her shopping is done. She sends him three more messages, asking if he got this, if he swapped that, why the price is higher than she expected. He sends another thumbs-up. She adds something else to her cart. Then another item. Then another. *Add to cart, add to cart, add to cart.* Bo chuckles and lets the items hang there, forgotten, as Val will be.

A Load of Balls

He takes his time loading the flimsy paper bags into his trunk. His shitty car groans beneath the extra weight. It's a fingernail above the humid asphalt. Bo wipes his forehead. Sweat slicks his hand, then the bags, and paper rips beneath his clumsy fingers.

A dozen eggs crash to the ground. Amber yolks stream across the pavement, running beneath Bo's swollen feet. If he were one to care, he would care here, but he hasn't cared about much for a while. He chuckles again, scoops the cracked shells and runny eggs into a Tupperware, then shoves the container near the bottom of the grocery heap.

As Bo finishes stocking his trunk, he wonders if he's done enough this time. See, he's a creative person, a talent no one sees—as he prefers. If anyone knew the sheer extent of his artistic genius, he couldn't live a real, raw, honest life.

He's a humble soul, a modest savant who wants to better society. Everyone should thank him. They won't, he knows they won't, but the thought that they would if they knew how devoted he is to this planet, to its people, buoys him. His sandals squelch through the eggs' slimy remains as he slides into the driver's seat and turns the key.

The engine won't start.

It often doesn't, but today, Bo has no patience for inconvenience. A hypocritical trait, as is his elitism.

Val sends him yet another message: *Are you here yet?*

Clearly not, Bo thinks but does not type. He tries the ignition again. This time, his relic of a car burps and gurgles to life. A ghost of a life. He'd be lucky to milk another hundred miles out of it, but that's all he'd need.

Bo drives to Val's address. It's not far. Two minutes for a healthy car; his makes it in seven. When he turns onto the fresh-paved driveway, Val is already waiting for him on her front stoop.

Bo has anticipated this. He smiles at her. His tawny eyes twinkle. He's sweated so much that his flaxen hair has darkened to brown. Val doesn't smile back. To be fair, she doesn't look like she can physically smile. Her chestnut hair twists in a tight, high bun, secured by a neon green scrunchie, stretching her waxy skin across chiseled features.

That's the new fad, Bo recalls. To pin your forehead skin back till your eyelids gap from strain. Rib extensions are also fashionable, to look emaciated, and Val boasts a full set. He's heard it's painful. They crack open your rib cage and fuse metal to your sternum. It costs more than a new car, though Val has one of these, too, a shiny red coupe with custom paint and semi-legal headlights.

Val clears her throat. She's also had work done there; branded chevrons on her scrawny neck burn in the sweltering sun. Bo feels sorry for her. He allows himself one second of pity, no more. One second to watch as her lotion-greasy hands pat down her gingham skirt. One second to sigh as she sucks in her stomach beneath a designer silk blouse. One second to wish she hadn't caked on eyeshadow, lipstick, and blush so heavy it looks like a toddler fell into their parent's vanity drawer.

Val wants to feel beautiful. No, not beautiful. She wants to belong. That's all beauty standards are, after all—not an objective measure, but a subjective pressure. Bo smiles. He thinks he is clever. No one else thinks he is clever, but no one else knows his real name anymore, either. A fleeting thought stalls him: *I would treat her right.* And he would. He would love her, care for her, always tell her she is more than enough.

But she would never love him. He sees that now as she stares at him with bristling disappointment. Though her eyes do wander over his twisted features and sweaty hair with reluctant interest. Others have called him attractive at times—not handsome, not quite, but magnetic in his own way. He doesn't believe them, of course. It's easier to be self-loathing than deluded with self-loving.

Val makes a twitchy motion with her wrist and nods inside. "The party is in an hour," she says, and she's perfected the near-impossible skill of sounding blunt yet not rude. "Please leave the bags in the foyer."

She dips inside her house—a pale yellow bungalow the same shade as CrownCart's logo. Bo takes this as a sign. His purpose is obvious. He can't stop now, not after all these years. With a ragged breath, he brings the bags inside.

Then closes her door behind him.

Val doesn't notice. She doesn't notice much in her ignorance cocoon. No, that's unfair. Val isn't ignorant. She's worse. She's disinterested. Apathetic. She chooses to ignore. Still, Bo pities her. She wants to be loved—that much is crystal—and she's willing to mangle herself to earn its façade. Her calf muscles have been suctioned so much that only a fourth remains, barely enough to hold her upright. Hypodermic plastic has been fused to her pelvis to make her hips jut, and the skin over her shoulder blades stretches so taut it rips. Blood wets her blouse, blooms of red flowers. Val doesn't notice this, either, same as she doesn't register the pain.

Bo could release her. Help her escape. She doesn't need to die like the others.

But then the Orb would come for him, and despite all his relentless internal monologuing, Bo cares about himself more than anyone else.

"Useless, absolutely useless," Val murmurs to herself as she removes the Tupperware of smashed eggs from a paper bag. She is still unaware of Bo, as most are. That was why the Orb had chosen him. "You'd think they'd hire someone competent."

Bo snorts. "You'd think."

Val notices him now. She whirls around, a creak of metal and plastic and warped, sharpened skeleton, a marionette crushed beneath acidic insecurity. Her eyes would have widened if she could still make expressions, but as she cannot, her eyelids merely flutter.

Bo notices her irises are blanched blue, like a glacier's frosted skin. It's not an important detail, but it's one he collects, just as he collected details from all those who came before her. Details are treasures to him, reminders they were real, that he is real, too.

"Leave," Val rasps. The air conditioner whines behind her, lodged in her crooked kitchen window. It's not the ideal place for a cooling system, but now is not the time to suggest an alternative.

Bo recites CrownCart's marketing spiel, testing tiny footsteps to close the distance: "Apologies, ma'am, I only wish to ensure your complete and total satisfaction with CrownCart's delivery service today. We endeavor to—"

"I'll rate you on the app. Leave. *Now.*" Val trembles, terrified. She grabs a steak knife and waves it at Bo. But she's had her arm muscles suctioned, too, so the knife dips within seconds, the threat limp, deflated—same as herself.

Bo is right before her now. He holds her hands, gently, and extricates the knife from her fingers, the phone from her pocket. Both clatter to the ground behind him. Smug, chest puffed like a pastry, he envisions what the newspapers will say: *A grocery-delivering serial killer terrorizes suburbia. CrownCart conspiracy case reopened after latest unsolved homicide.*

Because they are always unsolved. The Orb guarantees that. After it approached Bo long ago, when he still called prison home, it'd promised it'd erase everything, that he'd be a ghost, a phantom, unseen and unknown. Now, a decade later, Bo has no reason to doubt that promise.

"Don't," Val croaks. "I'll… I'll scream. The neighbors will hear. My husband will be home soon."

Bo holds her hands firmer, though still gently. "You can't scream after last week's voice-alteration surgery. Your neighbors don't care. Your husband is on a business trip." Calm, he corrects each of her lies with the patience of a preschool teacher. Val's skin chills in his palms, clammy as maggots.

"Why?" she asks, drained of fight faster than a cyst. "Why do this? Why… me?"

Bo nods toward the sun outside, the Orb that tells him everything. "This is its choice, not mine."

Val gapes at him as if he's crazy. He's not. It would be easier if he were. Many think he is. The press calls him a lunatic. A maniac. Demented and deranged. They don't know his name, of course, or his looks, but they know of *him*, and Bo thinks this is wonderful, a true gift, to be known by fear instead of identity. Most people become famous for beauty, intelligence, talent, skill, but Bo transcends them all. He is famous for anonymity.

"You're insane," Val whispers, her voice unable to sound.

Bo becomes annoyed. He has already defended himself in his head, and he hates repeating himself aloud. So he just says, "No," then lunges for Val.

This is his favorite part. The Orb gives him a name, then Bo's creativity crosses it off. He has shopped for Val several times before, so he knows her vulnerabilities. Some people may find it difficult to deduce this from a grocery app, but Bo has never been some people.

Purchases reveal problems. From her hydrocortisone cream order, he knows Val has a rash behind her ears. From her bulk-bought pumpkin seed oil gels, he knows she has an overactive bladder. From her obsession with chamomile tea and lavender candles, he knows she struggles with anxiety. Bo relates, and he also takes advantage. It's a skill he's refined for many years: wield his weaknesses as strengths. For what use is a weakness if it can't also be a weapon?

Bo chuckles to himself. Because Val is nearby, he accidentally chuckles at her, too. He's waxed poetic, the silly man, and has again become too clever. The sun flares through Val's air conditioner-clogged window, and Bo takes that as the sign it is. He's stalled long enough. The Orb demands promptness, if not perfection, and it has already waited through several mental soliloquies.

Bo straightens his shoulders, grips Val's throat, and squeezes. Her lips flap like dead fish. Her eyes bulge. Her capillaries burst. Her skin turns grape-purple. She dies in seconds. Too fast, yes, but his hands are his last weapon. For weeks, he has laced her cream with arsenic, coated her gels with cyanide, and spiked her tea with lectins.

Best of all, no one can blame him. Arsenic occurs naturally in swordfish and tuna, both among Val's favorites. Cherry pits and apple seeds contain cyanide. Raw kidney beans and peanuts contain lectins. Everyone knows Val was—Bo cherishes the past tense—obsessed with belonging, and her neighbors are health freaks. She wanted to be like them. They would have noticed her nausea, vomiting, and indigestion, thinking it was from copying their diets. A heart attack—the final cause of death—will seem likely to them. She was weak. Frail. Unable to stomach society's chains.

Bo frowns at Valedy's gape-mouthed, death-bitten body. He's disappointed in himself. The Orb is disappointed in him, too. It drifts behind a cloud. Val's death was anticlimactic. She deserved better, so Bo will give her his best. The autopsy won't reveal his interference if she fell during cardiac arrest, if she hit her head and shoulders and spine…

Yes, Bo thinks, *that will do fine*.

Bo lifts Val's limp, drooping body. He plants a kiss on her sweat-silky brow. She weighs next to nothing, and this is a shame. He has never understood the desire to fade. Again, he vows, *I would treat her right*. He would cook for her and clean for her and show her every minute of every day how beautiful she is. She doesn't need surgery. Doesn't need procedures. She is perfect as she is, even dead, and if she had listened to the Orb as he did, she would still be alive.

But she didn't listen to the Orb. Didn't listen to him. And now, she's dead. As the Orb demanded. That's how it chooses, the great star in the sky. It speaks only to him, only in signs, a sluggish Morse code he extrapolates from the flickering of clouds. Sometimes, it spells nothing. Sometimes, a name. Or close to it.

The Orb has given Bo the power to interpret, and he is the only one who can understand its cosmic tongue. Then, when he receives a name, he studies the person and offers them options, opportunities. *Come with me*, he scrawls on scraps of crinkled paper. He lists his current address, one that changes faster than fads. *Leave all this behind.*

They never do. Even when he pledges money, security, safety, eternity, they all say no. So he invokes the Orb, warns them of its temper, and they laugh. *They laugh.* If they could hear, if they could listen, they'd understand he could help them, save them, before the Orb possesses him.

It never works.

They all die like fruit flies.

Bo wants everyone to love themselves for who they are. Is that too much to ask? Apparently so. He kisses Val again, on the lips this time. Death tints them violet, a striking hue against her blood-drained skin.

He sighs. So pristine. So perfect. Especially like this. Her air conditioner wheezes and then dies with her, a captain going down with their ship. That's okay, though. Bo doesn't mind. Val's dead flesh cools him from the roasting summer heat.

But he can't stay like this forever.

The Orb is already giving him a new name. The message is faint—a slow, meandering blink as feathery clouds veil its shine—but the letters are there. *B-R-I...*

Bo knows who the Orb means, even if other letters muddy the Morse code. Only the B, R, and I are important. They stand for Brianna Fitzpatrick, a bank teller two towns over who banned Bo from her branch after he asked to borrow her tampon—for a nosebleed, of course, and he didn't mind it used. Rude to deny him, even if she didn't know or trust him.

The Orb trusts him, so everyone else should, too.

Bo gazes at Val. He holds her tighter. Brands her self-doubt-mangled features to memory. The Orb chose her because she hadn't let him drink her smoothie. Bo had wanted to be merciful, but the Orb is ruthless. It protects him when he so rarely protects himself.

The sun blinks again, I-R-B this time, and Bo knows he must move fast to appease it. If he falls out of favor with the Orb, if he doesn't obey, if he refuses to listen, he will be the next name carved in the sky.

Bo dips his lips to Val's again. He can't help himself. This is rare for him. Usually, he is composed, calm, collected, controlled. Not today, not today. He kisses her, licks her, savors the way her temperature continues to drop. She's wonderful like this, silent and pliable, his own little doll to cherish, worship,

A Load of Balls

break.

With a stiff breath, he lifts her higher, then smashes her head against her countertop. The granite cuts into her skull and reveals stark white bone. Her flesh curls like apple skin from the glugging wound, her blood slow and viscous as death drowns her fast. Next, her shoulders. A bruising, crushing wound. Last, her spine. A teeth-grinding scrape down the counter's corner to the floor.

He stares at her roughened skeleton, laden with ill-fitting meat. Proud, yet disappointed. He would have had so much more fun if the Orb had let her live.

No.

Enough.

It's foolish to doubt the Orb.

Val had needed to die, so she had. That's all there is to it.

Bo kneels beside her. His saliva is on her face, his fingerprints all over her body, her house. But that's okay. He was sloppy this time, but she was sloppy, too. The Orb will forgive him; it won't forgive her.

Bo knocks her bleach from the top cabinet. It floods her body, the kitchen, the floor. She was clumsy, so clumsy, from all her procedures, so she had a heart attack and then fell, taking the bleach with her. Sad, so sad. That's what the reports will say. They won't suspect Bo because he is no one, nothing, gone.

The CrownCart app chimes on his phone.

He's assigned a new shopper.

Brianna Fitzpatrick.

Bri doesn't remember Bo, but Bo remembers Bri.

She messages him instantly.

Bo, I have the stomach flu and would be grateful for your expeditiousness.

Another fancy word. Another fancy woman.

Bo smiles. He shouldn't. He should change his name and move before targeting her. Police love a pattern, so Bo thrives in chaos. He's been Frank, Tony, Jeremy, and Matt, but he hopes to be Bo for a little longer. Perhaps he could make an exception this once.

The Orb flashes. It approves.

Bo will stay Bo for one day more.

His app chimes again. Bri updates her list.

Bread, cinnamon, rice, bananas.
Add to cart, add to cart, add to cart, add to cart.
Bo grins.

ABOUT THE AUTHOR

Halo Scot is a dark fiction author of book monsters, many of which bite. Reviews and press are available on http://HaloScot.com. Halo has been featured in Publishers Weekly and BookLife. Also, as a founding member of http://QueerIndie.com, Scot has appeared at Brooklyn Book Festival and Pop Pride Week, an event hosted by ReedPop, BookCon, and New York Comic Con.

Halo pretends to be cool, dark, and mysterious, when in reality, Scot is a clumsy and awkward creature who eats shadows and harbors a severe distrust of ladybugs. Prone to chaos, this nightmare-dwelling beast aims to achieve galactic domination through a void-screaming expertise, dormant telekinesis, and aggressive cackling. To summon this obscure and skittish writer, one must align the following items in a circle as an offering: three shots of whiskey, two bowls of jelly beans, something shiny or lit on fire, and a printed photo of Nicolas Cage as a duck.

Hex, Lies, and Blue Balls

Chris Hooley

As I pulled out of Sandra, Tina, Indy… to be honest, I can't remember her name, she's one of the newbies, I felt it.

I felt the change in my balls, and in that moment, I knew I was fucked, but I also knew that it was all because of her.

The one I had ghosted. The one with the black cat. The one with the angel number tattoo. The one who had whispered her curse in Latin.

As I backed out of the cleaning cupboard, a strange sense of finality settled in the pit of my stomach, and as I zipped up my fly, I heard a shuffle.

Then Mr Jacobs walked by and momentarily took my mind off the ping in my ball sack. It snapped me back to work.

He was looking for something again. Like clockwork, he roamed the halls trying to get his kicks, so I known my shift was almost done.

The women won't clean his room on their own after the incident with Ashley, but if he found out that the real action happens in the cleaning cupboard, that would put a damper on future shifts, so sending him in the opposite direction was always my plan of action.

I held the door shut so that Sandra, Tina or Indy knew the coast wasn't clear and nodded at Jack-off Jacobs.

'You seen that blonde with the big hips, boy?'

He always called me boy, but he's my steady supply of Viagra, so I'd let this slide. I don't always need the purple pulse racer, but Mavis has a gash deeper and dryer than most deserts, so that little pill helps stiffen the wood when she's the only one on nights. It's like my old mum used to say, sometimes you've gotta work with what you got.

'She went that way.' I'd pointed.

'Well, if you see her, tell her daddy's down for dessert in his room.' He'd thrusted his hips and groaned. His teeth slipped out a little with the thrusting motion, but he didn't care.

The only thing they care about is sex, but I'd wondered if they ever think about the end... I sure had been lately. There's something about the grave staring them in the face, whispering them in, that makes them want to fuck like a rabbit.

Trust me when I say you never forget the first time you witness a grown man fondling his dead mouse dick as a team of nurses tries to clean the shit from his trousers.

'If I see her, I will let her know, Mr J... I'm sure she'll come running,' I said as I'd mopped up the piss trail that had trickled down his trouser leg on his tireless hunt for a hole to burrow his mouse in.

He'd grabbed his cock, muttered something that resembled a growl, and shuffled off into the main room to join flatulent Florence, bottom-loose Beryl, dandruff Derek and arsehole Angela.

Florence has dementia, but she's also blind as a bat and deaf as a dog with no ears, so I'd made a mental note to check in on her before the end of my shift to make sure he wasn't fondling her fun bags like last time.

To say her son wasn't happy would be an understatement, but they simply brush a little nipple fiddle under the carpet for sixty a week, along with any chance of compensation.

From what I remember, that was when the notification pinged in my pocket.

Balls blue yet? Shit bag!

Shortly after that, I left Florence to fend off old man Jacobs by herself.

Sandra, Tina or Indy walked out of the cleaning room and straightened her skirt.

'Well… that was… fun. Same time next week, big boy?' said Sandra, Tina or Indy.

I stared at the message.

Balls blue yet? Shit bag!

Number withheld.

I couldn't remember giving her my number, but I'd known it was her. The one who'd sucked it like she was trying to draw blood.

'Hello…?' said Sandra, Tina or Indy.

I snapped back into the care home.

'Yeah, babe, definitely. Loved it. Watch your step now. Old Man Jack-off has left a piss trail again.'

Sandra, Tina or Indy blew me a kiss, sidestepped the wet patch on the floor and headed back towards the second floor.

That was when the pulsating started as I watched her butt jiggle from side to side, her long legs providing the pedestal of desire with a little extra sauce.

She had been different to the other nurses, tighter and on the right side of thirty, but I hadn't enjoyed it as much as I should've. Maybe it was the sensation of knowing that Old Man Jack-off had been roaming the halls and could've burst in and shoved a finger, or worse, up my arse at any moment, or many it was some strange feeling that I had somehow known that my whole life was about to change when I shot my load. Either way, it had dampened the mood.

When I think it through now, I could swear that as I'd pulled her hair to arch her back and force her further down my shaft, I'd felt a slight twinge. At the time, I'd put it down to her being freshly shaved or one of those acrylic nails they all have these days, but I know better now. It was the start of the quite literal blue balls.

Before all that, though, I'd had to contend with a flat tyre.

Casey Johnson was a bitch, and she intended on staying one until her very last breath. She liked to take the valve caps off staff members' cars if they'd pissed her off any, and sometimes even if they hadn't.

Turns out she'd wanted coffee on the morning in question and not the regular tea she had every other bastard day, so I had been victim number three by the time my shift punched out.

Finding a pump was harder than actually getting to pump in that place, so after a couple of wasted hours asking around, I gave up and opted for the bus, which was just a short evening stroll away.

It started spitting with rain the moment I left the home's long-arse driveway, which was shit because coats were only necessary when you lost the use of your limp-dick car. And believe it or not, finding out that your car is useless doesn't automatically make a coat appear, which, if you ask me, is one of life's failings.

The wind had been picking up, and it had a bitterness to it that made it feel colder than it was. No amount of shoving my hands deeper into my pockets helped, either.

Even though the tyre wasn't her fault, part of my mind went to her. I had fucked and fled, and now she was fucking with me. She and her weird-arse roommates were collaborating to make my life miserable. The three witches out beyond the heath plotting my downfall. Is this a pair of blue balls I see before me? Will all the water in the great Neptune's ocean wash them clean? I needed to get to her and find out, and that meant a long arse bus ride with the arsehole leakage of society.

* * *

The bus had pulled up, soaking my shoes and the bottom of my trousers in the process as it settled into the puddle that had formed at the mouth of the grid, just in front of the bus stop.

As I'd climbed onto the bus, the driver looked at me like I was one of his distant relatives who had just been released from prison for committing some unspeakable crime, probably against children, and who he'd been forced to collect.

The look of disgust quickly shifted to one of confusion as he angled his head and looked down at my trousers. I thought he was going to comment on the state of them, as if he hadn't noticed the storm pelting the bus's windows. But then I realised he was staring at my crotch.

"Your phone's going off, lad," he said as I stepped up to the plastic window that cocooned him in behind the steering wheel.

I looked down. A bright, pulsating light shone through my trousers, its rhythmic glow protruding slightly to the left.

I put my hands over the light and hurried to sit down.

"...hang on a moment, son. You've got to pay if you want to ride this train," said the driver from behind his Perspex prison, his voice cracking like it was one more cigarette away from being burnt out forever.

I pulled a dishevelled note from my drenched wallet and slapped it down on the plastic tray in front of him. A little splatter of water sprayed the Perspex and trickled down into the tray.

"Keep the change," I said with a forced smile.

Your balls are glowing – just pay the man, get the ticket and sit down.

The driver tutted, took the note, and punched the machine with his porky, bitten-down-to-the-wick sausage fingers. The machine chugged, clicked and then pinged before it spat out a ticket that would make a normal piece of paper feel bloated in comparison.

"This isn't a restaurant, mate. Take your change and sit your arse down. Oh, and switch that phone off. Don't want that blue light flashing in me mirrors, do I?" said the driver after counting my change back to me in tens.

I looked down at my crotch, and sure enough, it was flashing like a beacon on a dark stormy night, ready to guide the lost ship of souls home to safety.

I didn't argue with him – to be honest, I wanted to punch a hole through the Perspex and drag his chunky arse off the seat and beat him until a few teeth dropped out, but I knew it was the fact that I was angry at the blue balls' rhythmic flashing and not his jowly double chin strap, so I cracked my knuckles, closed my eyes, took a deep breath and stuffed the change into my pocket.

A teenager was blaring out some angry gangsta shit from a speaker the size of his head. I hadn't noticed it before as I was too lost in my own thoughts to care, but now it irradiated my very existence.

"Turn it off," I said as I walked towards a spare seat at the back of the bus. The bus was full of people mindlessly going about their lives. Every one of them engulfed in a screen of some sort. Every one of them distracted in their own little bubble. My balls were fucking blue and pulsating, omitting light bright enough to find a nun's arsehole. and nobody other than porky-drives-a-lot had noticed.

"What?" grunted the teenager, who, on closer inspection, was probably early to mid-twenties and way too old to be sharing his horrible taste in sounds. His limp dick tie hung loosely around his neck, and he looked like he'd borrowed a dead man's second favourite suit. That musty metallic smell that lingers on clothing right before the moths swoop in evaded my nose and sparked a rage in me that was difficult to suppress.

"Turn. It. Off." Through gritted teeth this time. My knuckles ached, and I felt the burn of excitement run over the back of my neck.

He shifted in his seat. The person beside him shifted too but didn't look away from their phone. The headphones firmly jammed into their ears meant that they could pretend to be blissfully unaware of the awkwardness of the moment.

"Fuck yo—"

I didn't let him finish his sentence, slapping him hard across the face with the back of my hand. The sound of my knuckles cracking against his cheekbone made the rage go limp, and my dick stiffed a little.

His eyes went wide and his mouth opened, so I stuck my finger inside his mouth and hooked it into his cheek like trying to retrieve a hook from inside the mouth of a baby koi carp.

I pulled him off his chair and brought his ear right up to my mouth, letting the heat of my breath work its way into his ear before repeating the words, slower and less acidic than before.

"Turn. It. Off."

* * *

"What are you looking at, Sadie dearest?"

Sadie shifted on her cushion, looked back at Rachel and then tried to subtly put her body between the globe and her sister.

"Nothing. Just practising a focus spell."

Rachel walked towards Sadie and sat down next to her, pushing her weight against her to move her slightly away from the glowing orb that had been placed in the middle of the circle.

"Nothing, really? Who is that? Let me see."

Rachel peered into the orb and then looked back at Sadie the way an angry parent might look at a child who had just found a turd in one of their shoes.

"Sadie Winterspell, please tell me you haven't used the exploding genitalia spell on this young man."

Sadie looked immediately sheepish. It seemed as though she was trying to reply but had suddenly forgotten how to use basic words.

"But Rach, he said he loved me… then he…"

Rachel stood up and planted her hands firmly on her hips.

"I don't care what he said, Sadie! That's a forbidden spell for a reason! Women like us have been hung and burnt alive for even whispering about that spell. Do you realise how much heat a spell like that can generate?"

Sadie stood up. She tried to make herself bigger as Rachel had at least a foot on her, but even standing on her tiptoes didn't make her feel confident. She wasn't confident; she was angry. She wanted to wag her finger and remove the pin from her hair to show she meant business, but crossing her arms was all that she could muster the courage to do.

"I'm sick of men whispering I love you to me only to leave after they get what they want," said Sadie with only a hint of justification in her tone.

Rachel was wandering around, but Sadie's words seemed to act like a rod in her spine. She snapped into a towering stance and slowly walked towards Sadie. She stopped a little too close and then bent down to look her in the eyes. Sadie felt Rachel's warm breath on her nose, and it made her feel like a child facing a grandparent's wrath for the first time.

"Getting literally fucked over by some arsehole isn't a legitimate reason to put the rest of us in danger, Sadie. Just keep your legs closed in the future. Learn your lesson, eat some ice cream and move on like the rest of us."

Sadie felt like she was about to cry or cast a spell strong enough to make Rachel shit her pants for the next week when their front door opened.

"What's up, bitches!" said Maya as she shimmied into the room with two bags in each hand and a phone balanced under her chin.

Neither of the two women wanted to break the silence as they both thought the other was morally obliged to explain themselves.

Maya put her bags down on the table, took a quick selfie in front of the bags, took several more at difficult angles, scrolled through them all and found the one she liked, selected it, typed #FeelingCuteHaul and #SugarDaddyTreats, then posted the same picture on all of her socials.

Upload. Share. Repeat.

Only then did she sense the tension in the room.

"Wow, ok. Is it an argument about whose turn it is to clean the cat tray? Because if it is, I did it last time."

Rachel crossed her arms, gave Sadie her best I'm-four-years-your-senior-stare, letting her left eyebrow travel as high up her forehead as it would dare to go, and held her position.

Sadie mirrored Rachel's stance, only with a little less eyebrow and a tad more pleading eye movement.

After a few seconds of tension, Rachel snapped, throwing her arms up in the air as she broke her stance.

"Sadie! Sadie's gone and put an exploding genitalia spell on some guy!"

Maya's mouth opened slowly like an owl yawning for the first time and being scared but slightly curious at the same time. Her eyes widened as though she had suddenly seen the tip of a nuclear bomb explode in the distance before she fixed them on Sadie.

"O. M. G! You go, queen! Oooh. Oooh, let me guess… Was it that arsehole you let nut in you and then he just ghosted you, or the dad bod one who stuck his finger in your arse without asking?"

"Maya!" shouted Rachel. "This isn't some kind of fucking joke! This is serious. If the ministry finds out about this, we'll lose our home. We'll have to move. And that's if we're lucky. If the general fucking magick-killing public find out… well, Jesus Christ, I don't know what they'll do, but fire, drowning and lynching would be a pretty good starter for ten."

Sadie wanted to stop the thoughts, so she blurted out, "It was the one who nutted in me, even though I asked him to only do it if he loved me. He told me he loved me… the spell… it just came out…" She broke off as the tears came.

Maya waved a dismissive hand towards Rachel, walked over to Sadie, and gave her a hug. She whispered, "Good for you, girl," in her ear and kissed her sister on the cheek.

Rachel watched her sisters as they embraced. It was a sweet and tender moment of affection between two loved ones, and as she saw Maya cradling Sadie, Rachel knew she needed to protect them.

The realisation dawned that she wasn't angry with Sadie, really. She was angry with the world. She was angry about the prospect of being dragged into a world of blame, injustice, and ignorance. She didn't want a world where people would see her sister as an evil predator instead of the victim she was. A victim of the patriarchal system of feminist oppression and sexualisation.

A smile, the type of smile that can only accompany an idea, grew on her face. Rachel had a plan.

She walked over to Maya and Sadie, who were still holding one another with their eyes closed, and wrapped her own arms around them both and gave them a tender squeeze. Both women, feeling the presence of another, opened their eyes and smiled at Rachel like two perfect china dolls, grinning in the midst of an afternoon of playtime.

Rachel placed her head on their foreheads, joining the three of them together.

"What's done is done. If his dick is going to explode, then we'd better make damn sure that it explodes when and where we want it to… hadn't we, girls?"

Maya wiped a fresh, single tear away from Sadie's cheek, then pulled her little sister into her chest and shouted, "Yes, Rachel! Oh man, it's going to be so fucking gross… but so fucking cool to see his Johnson pop off… Oh man, and when the smell of fried man-meat smacks the back of your throat!"

And for the first time in her life, she cackled. A deep, guttural cackle fuelled by all those wronged women who had suffered at the hands of men before her.

* * *

Everyone's staring, but I couldn't give a fuck.

The kid deserved it. Blaring that shit out for everyone to hear. Instead of staring, they should be thanking me.

I'm the saviour that this world has rejected. The type to stand up and say no to the bullshit. The type to stand firm whenever the occasion calls for it. The type to break a bitch rather than act like one.

The flashing lights pulse through my jeans and distract my thoughts. Block out the stares.

The old woman who smells like bleach casts a side-eye every few seconds. She wants to see it, and I want to show it to her. Make her day. Show her the goods. See if those dry walls can find a little moisture for the beacon of light.

Somewhere between fifty and sixty would be a polite guess. Old enough to be going through the later stages of the menopause, but young enough to still appreciate a good seeing to. A shag from a stranger must be just that little bit more exhilarating, knowing that it could be your last chance to ride the vain pole.

I give her a wink and clutch at the long, flowing hair draped over her shoulder. Catching a few strands, giving her a firm tug. She smiles, and I know she wants it. The blue beacon of light illuminates the dark hole hidden between her legs.

Before we get carried away, this one has tits like two balloons that have had the air punched out of them. They flop down and rest on her chest.

She's probably someone's mum or grandma. She's got that smell. That comforting pang.

It's not too hard to imagine that she was once the light of that dad's eye. The thing that put a spark in his rod. The arse that helped him get up (quite literally) in the morning. But now? Now, she would barely generate a spark with that figure.

All the meat from her arse has melted away, probably through years of being manhandled and railroaded. She's got that look of sexual deprivation in her eyes, and her lips are desperate to be caught in between somebody's teeth.

Without a doubt, those love handles have been worn down by a man who didn't need to consent to give his wife what he wanted.

When you really think about it, we're from a long line of women like her.

Our fathers, grandfathers, fuck, even our great grandfathers, put it away whenever they wanted. Owners of the little meat cave of wonders can pull back and push between the curtains whenever they want.

Shit, you might even be the result of a not-so-consensual session. You might even carry his name on your back like a badge of his fuckery. Share his urges. But you can't handle them like a man, so you take your little pills or drink your little drink or pick up a sponge and clean the dishes like the good little light beer bitch that you are.

Our Father, who art in heaven, hallowed be thy name; thy kind cum; thy will not be done; on earth as it is in hell. Our Fathers, Father is so fucking disappointed in you. He gave you the world, and you snapped on a pair of marigolds.

***

Jingle. Jingle. Jingle.

"Look alive, ladies, he's here," said Rachel with the calmness and composure of a well-fed cat.

"Oh shit, really? How do you know? Are you still looking at the orb?" said Sadie from another room.

"No, dear. That's what the *Ring* doorbell is for. Humans have taken a few tips from us whether or not they choose to acknowledge them as magick… Well… they're just… What are you two doing in there, anyway?"

Sadie appeared in the doorway mere seconds later dressed in her underwear, her hair curled and her makeup flawless.

Maya slid into the picture beside her sister and held her arms out, accentuating Sadie's figure with her gesture.

"Ta-da! Isn't she a stunner?" said Maya. She grabbed Sadie by the hips and pulled her in close. "If we weren't sisters! God, he's gonna be all…" she added as she started dry-humping Sadie's leg.

"Girls! Girls! What the fuck? Why does she look like that?!" said Rachel, who had lost her cool and was now more like a spitting ally cat than a calm and well-composed one.

"Because… well, we're going to want to pacify him long enough for his dick to explode when and where we want it to, and if he thinks he's got a chance of getting laid, then he'll stick around," said Maya with a smile.

"And what makes you think that he's going to want to fuck whilst his balls are beacons of blue flashing light?" said Rachel as she threw her hands in the air and grabbed her dressing gown from the back of the door before tossing it to Sadie.

Maya caught the gown and threw it back.

"Sadie and I were just talking about this. We'll tell him it's a curse that can only be broken by slipping back into Sadie's glory hole."

Rachel caught the gown and threw it back towards Sadie.

"And what if he gets the bright idea of raping her as a result? Then we've got an even more aggressive male on our hands. We need to keep this contained. If anyone sees or hears him, we're all done for."

"Rachel, please…" said Sadie. "I can do this. I know it'll work. I'll keep him quiet. You two just stay out of sight until he explodes." She slipped the gown over her shoulders and pulled the rope around her waist with an air of confidence and excitement.

She took Rachel's phone from the table and held it up to her sister's face, unlocked the phone and opened the app. Then she slid her finger across the screen and spoke.

"Hello, big boy, I've been waiting for you to come back to me," she whispered in her best sex worker voice.

The look of surprise on the man's face was clear for all the sisters to see. He hadn't been expecting that kind of greeting, and for a split second, he didn't know how to respond. Then he was himself again.

"Big boy? Never mind big boy! You dirty fucking witch! My balls are fucking blue here. Let me in, or I'll see to it that you're on a spit roast by the time the sun rises!"

"Is that a promise?" said Sadie, without even thinking.

Her sisters looked at her, one with a smile and the other with a sense of disbelief and concern.

Sadie pushed a button on her phone, and the door downstairs buzzed and then clicked. They could all hear it from where they stood. Three sisters frozen in time. Waiting for the footfalls of the beast with a glowing pair of plums to come into their lives.

"*Umbra noctus obumbrat lux, tenebrae regnant sine fine,*" chanted Rachel, and with that, the apartment's light faded into darkness.

* * *

As I walked up the steps, I thought about the last time I'd been in this shit-hole of a building. I could vaguely remember how her pussy had felt as she rode it – the thought brought a twinge back. It was either excitement or adrenaline – or both.

She'd been decent.

I closed my eyes as my foot hit the first step, and there she was again…

Slowly grinding down into me, spilling out her curse whilst holding me down, her fingernails digging into my chest as she tried to steady her rhythm.

"Hey, hey, babe. What are you saying?"

"Relax. And enjoy yourself. It's just Latin for 'I want you to cum inside me'."

"Wait. Do you really want that?"

"I do, if you want to," she whispered in my ear as she nibbled on my earlobe. "But if you do, the next time you shoot your shot, if it's not in me, your balls will turn blue, ok, hun? Now shut up and pull my hair, my housemates will be home soon…"

I gripped her hair and tugged her into kissing me. She tasted of cherry vanilla ice cream, and it brought an added stiffness to her ride.

"…and don't do it yet. I'm not close enough," she said as she lifted her weight up and quickened her pace.

I opened my eyes. That was then, and this is now, I told myself. Now, I'm going to bounce her little blonde head around the room until she sings like a little Latin tune hummingbird, singing for its life in the mouth of a lion.

One last song before the jaws clench and the bones snap.

The look of fear in the man-child's eyes on the bus floods back and sends the blood rushing through my body and down to my fists. It was so easy to get him to fold.

People don't like confrontation these days.

I clench my fists and feel their weight. It feels good to squeeze them into balls and then relax and release as I move further up the stairs.

I feel strong.

Bold.

Then the hall light flickers, holds for a second and then dies. I catch a blue pulsing light streaming from my crotch.

Rage fills my chest, and the pace of the glowing light in my trousers starts to quicken in the darkness of the hall. Instinct tells me that I need to run and get to the dumb blonde quicker than I'd originally wanted. Some worrying guttural feeling, deep in my balls, told me that I needed to make her sing quicker than I'd wanted. I didn't have time to fuck around and enjoy the show.

As I reached the doorway of her poxy apartment, it felt like crossing a threshold I could never return from. I saw her cat in the doorway. It hissed and spat at my boots, so I stamped down hard on its neck, forcing it into the bottom of the door frame.

It squealed, hissed and clawed at my trouser legs, but if it was breaking skin, I couldn't feel it. Its tiny claws grew weaker by the second.

I could feel its little neck tightening but buckling under the weight of my foot. Its spinal column ready to snap. Its harsh, wild screeching went from a raging shower of pain to something barely above an audible whisper.

"Nighty, night, puss."

I hadn't planned on saying it. The thought hadn't come, it just slipped out as the smile grew across my face.

Slowly, I adjusted my stance, took hold of the door handle and forced all the strength in my body down onto its neck, and my smile grew wider as a sudden rush of warmth gathered at the bottom of my leg.

Blood?

Vomit?

Who cares?

Nobody likes cats anyway.

I raised my foot off its neck and smashed it into the door just below the handle. The first kick made it swell in the frame, but it stood firm.

The second… well, that made its mark, and the door opened with a sigh, reminding me of the sound my grandmother used to make after she finally decided to get up after sitting on her fat arse for too many hours.

* * *

"Salem sounds like he's in pain. We have to help him!" said Maya, moving towards the front door.

Rachel shifted nervously. She grabbed her sister by the arm and pulled Maya away from the door.

"He's lived this long and not lost any lives. He can lose one. You, on the other hand, if he stamps you out? You ain't coming back! Stay here!" she demanded in a whisper.

Rachel pulled out her wand and stuck it under her sister's nose.

"Let him in. When he's in here and safely on the other side of that door, I'll deal with him."

Maya's eyes widened, and she withdrew into herself.

"You can't use that, Rachel. What will the ministry say?"

"To hell with the ministry. I'm not about to let some low-life tear into my sisters! Where did you meet this guy anyway?!" she said as she shot a look at Sadie.

Sadie lay on the bed with her robe open, positioned so that her underwear was visible.

"Tinder. We got talking, and after a few weeks, he said he loved me, so I let him come over. The full moon was out, and I was just… you know. In need of some affection." She looked down at the bedsheet, hoping it would take away her embarrassment. Hoping that she could simply stare and somehow fade into an endless pit of satin and silk.

Rachel rolled her eyes and pointed her wand in Sadie's direction before waving it around in a pointy, jabbing, irradiated way.

"No. More. Dating apps. You hear—"

BANG

CRACK

* * *

"Come out, come out wherever you are. I smell a little blonde piggy who has some explaining to do," said the voice in the dark.

The musky smell of alcohol and excess testosterone invaded their senses, but none of the sisters moved.

Then Sadie's voice broke the silence as she spoke out into the darkness.

"I'm in here."

Now that he was inside the apartment, she felt safer for some reason. Even though she was semi-naked, she felt a great deal of comfort knowing that her sisters were only a few meters away.

Out of sight in the bathroom, but not out of mind – and definitely within reach if something went wrong.

She saw the blue light flashing like a strobe light. He didn't have long left before his balls exploded, and if she could get his heart rate up, that would speed up the process.

It was her time to smile.

Rage or lust?

It was a simple decision.

"I told you not to do it in anyone else, didn't I? You worthless idiot. What is it with men? You said you loved me, but you lied, and now your dick... well, your balls, actually, but your dick will definitely be collateral damage, are about thirty seconds away from exploding all over my bedroom floor... and you've got no one to blame but yourself! You shouldn't have nutted in me if you knew you weren't planning on being truthful."

"You stupid blonde..." He made a lunge towards the bed, but a brilliant bright light stopped him dead.

"*Gracius vinculum, aer altum tenet*," Rachel intoned.

He instantaneously felt lighter on his feet, and he could suddenly see the top of a wardrobe. A few teddy bears stared back at him with vacant expressions, their beady little black eyes smiling at his predicament.

Sadie lay in a protective heap on the bed, and although he wanted to see her, his head was frozen in place, only allowing him to see her legs. He felt a quickening, dull pace deep in his groin. He tried to scream, tried to pull himself loose, but nothing budged.

Rachel moved out from the shadows, her wand pointed directly at him, and Maya looked rather sheepish behind her.

"What now?" whispered Maya from behind her sister.

"Now? We watch his balls explode. Set up an alternating bucket system underneath him to catch the blood. Clean the ball debris from the room. Wait for him to drain out into the buckets whilst pouring it all down the sink with a healthy helping of bleach. Then we fill the bathtub with bleach, drop his body into it, wait for the flesh and organs to melt away, and bury the bones in the forest on the outskirts of town," said Rachel in a matter-of-fact manner.

He tripled his efforts to move, but it made no difference.

"Shit... that's a bit..." said Sadie as she stumbled off the bed and looked up at the man she'd once thought would be the love of her life. Her husband, maybe. Now, he was just a massive problem that was literally a ticking time bomb of regret.

"A bit what?" barked Rachel. "A bit fucking grim? A bit unnerving? Well, maybe you'll think twice about the consequences before you hop onto the next erection that offers you the illusion of love."

"Rach, that's a bit harsh, she only wanted—"

Maya didn't finish her sentence as, at that moment, there was a loud bang, followed by a shower of flesh and blood splattering across their faces.

The shock from the explosion shook Rachel, but she managed to recover her spell quickly and hold him in place.

Sadie screamed.

Maya started to heave and splutter at the thought of testicle juice landing on her face. She finally vomited when she thought she felt a pubic hair sliding down her throat.

Rachel simply held her wand firmly in place and calmly addressed the room. Blood painted her face, and bits of hairy flesh covered her shoulders.

"Can somebody please… pretty please with sugar on top… the best please you've ever heard… just get a bastard bucket? I reckon we've got about five more minutes of spell time left before the ministry gets an unauthorised spell alert. And I'd really like to wash this waste of magick's ball meat off my face before they arrive."

ABOUT THE AUTHOR

Chris Hooley lives in a house with his two children and fanciful partner Paige.

He can be found on the internet by typing in The Writing Community Chat Show into the search engine. There you'll see him talking to much better writers about the craft of writing.

Chris also features as one of the three authors who worked together on The Inevitability of Evil, the other two are featured in this edition of Malarkey's ImaginOmnibus.

He is the author of Death, Just Grin and Bear It (novel), The Covid Criminals (short stories collection) and in this particular collection Hex, Lies and Blue Balls. His ultimate goal, in writing, is to have someone physically react to the words on the page… vomiting… fainting… just anything other than falling to sleep will do.

Acknowledgements

The creation of Malarkey's ImaginOmnibus is always a rewarding and enlightening experience, but it doesn't happen in isolation. The authors who have been involved in every edition, including this one, have contributed more than stories. They've offered ideas, invested time, enthusiasm, and encouragement to both me, and our fellow authors. So, a huge thanks to each and every one of them for their stories, and their contributions towards a friendly and engaging environment where all our authors can share their thoughts, and get encouragement, for their future endeavours.

I must also thank Anthony Wright, for his excellent editing which is appreciated by all of us.

Malarkey's, and the Malarkites, is something different, and I hope it will continue to bring authors together in the future.

MORE MALARKEY'S!

You can find Malarkey's ImaginOminibus Volumes 1, 2 & 3 at all good online ebook retailers, and in paperback form to order online.

**MALARKEY'S IMAGINOMNIBUS 1 -
THEY WALK AMONG US**

**MALARKEY'S IMAGINOMNIBUS 2 -
FADE TO NOIR**

**MALARKEY'S IMAGINOMNIBUS 3 -
HUBBLE BUBBLE**

FIND OUT MORE AT THESULK.COM